D0482469

NINE DAYS TO MUKALLA

ALSO BY FREDERIC PROKOSCH

Novels

STORM AND ECHO

THE IDOLS OF THE CAVE

AGE OF THUNDER

THE CONSPIRATORS

THE SKIES OF EUROPE

NIGHT OF THE POOR

THE SEVEN WHO FLED

THE ASIATICS

Poetry

CHOSEN POEMS

DEATH AT SEA

THE CARNIVAL

THE ASSASSINS

FREDERIC PROKOSCH

Nine Days
to Mukalla

A NOVEL

1953

THE VIKING PRESS · NEW YORK

In memory of

George Santayana

Library of Congress Catalog Card Number: 52-14033

PRINTED IN THE U. S. A. BY THE COLONIAL PRESS INC.

Contents

BOOK ONE

The Islands

1

Far below lay the Indian Ocean, unfurling its million waves. Slowly they crept toward the invisible shores of Oman. From up in the sky they seemed hardly to be moving at all; they stole over the sea with a lazy, damascened precision, like a great white web drawn over a sheet of blue glass. Here and there, in that transparency, the shape of a fish stirred and vanished—a giant ray, possibly, or a shark on his way to cooler waters. To the north lay a group of islands, dark and puckered, like a row of crocodiles; to the south lay a flock of narrow, copper-green boats, pearl-fishers perhaps, poised on the glass like mosquitoes.

The sun still hung high over the distant ridges by Ras Fartak, which were just beginning to unroll on the edge of the horizon—a chain of wine-red mountains, fortress-like and forbidding, guarding the huge desolation of the Rub' al Khali. The plane trembled, slowed obliquely. The line of the shore drew nearer. The volcanic isles gradually took on shape and nuance; the foam cast by the cliffs shone white and ruffled, like a collar of lace. Qamr Bay opened out into the dead flat sands to the north; Saikut lay coiled in the niche between two conical summits straight to the west. To the south there was nothing but the vast arena of the sea, with the fiery tints of the evening crawling stealthily closer. And now two more islands rose out of the water, one of them sandy-hued, barren and smooth as an egg; the other shaped like a violin, clouded with stray puffs of greenery, a white-walled village flashing in the nook of a harbor like a row of dice.

The plane sank slowly; an imperceptible tremor shook the

3

wings. The motor roared, coughed, sputtered. Sparks shot forth in a sudden flurry. A plume of russet smoke sprang forth, spread casually toward Africa. The silver wings sloped uneasily as they moved toward the long red beaches. Neither the gulls nor the fish, not even the distant aisle of fishing boats, had time to wonder at the enormous bird that sank on the sand, heat-stunned, like Icarus.

2

Idris shot through the shallow water with his fishing spear. Spring was turning into summer; the bay was warm, silky, indolent. Even down in the grottoes the sea was warm as a paw. A rush of delight shot through him. He dove deep under the rocks. Claws of coral shone through the ripples, tinged with fine little halos of opal and rose. Beneath the corals floated long green tresses of seaweed; threads of a bright prismatic amber and blue played on their petals. He hurled his spear savagely. A flurry of fish scattered like lightning, their scales flashing through the water like a cloud of gold-dust.

He turned over and floated lazily in the smooth bright water. The sky was cloudless overhead. Nothing disturbed this hot serenity. On the edge of the beach, in the shade of a rock, his friend Ahmed was opening a shellfish, scraping the meat from the shell with his ivory knife. Idris let himself be carried in the arms of the long sleek waves, up and down, up and down, till the slap of the foam took hold of him suddenly.

He plunged through the surf and went running across the sand, spear thrust forward as though he were waging a solitary attack on the cliffs.

"Idris!"

He glanced behind. Ahmed was waving his arms violently. "Idris! Look!"

The plane swept slowly out of the sky, trailing a garland of smoke. Gently it sank toward the cape at the eastern end of the island. It shuddered, rose slightly, dipped again, grazing the cliffs. Then it swam low over the beach and went skidding across the sand, spraying a geyser of bright red dust be-

hind it. It lurched, reared slightly, and came to a sudden halt.
Idris could hear the neighing of the motor—sick and angry,
like the cough of a pregnant *naga*. He waved to Ahmed, and
the two young Arabs ran swiftly through the rocks, threading
their way in and out, ducking and darting and peeping, keeping well out of sight of the great noisy bird.

They knelt behind a fan-shaped precipice which overlooked
the cape. The plane snorted furiously. Four figures leaped
through the clouds of smoke, and five seconds later, as the roar
of the motor died in a stifled gasp, a giant flame shot out of
the snout and swallowed the wings like a great red tongue.

✿

The four survivors had gathered in a little cave at the farther end of the beach, below the cliffs. The plane was a smoldering ruin: crests of flame dancing nervously over a black,
steaming skeleton. Ahmed and Idris tiptoed closer and
crouched among the boulders. They craned their necks and
peered through a crevice. The young man with the yellow
hair drew off his jacket and flung it on the sand, then cupped
his hands and called loudly, first to the west and then to the
east. Then he ran to the water's edge, dipped his arms in the
bay, and started splashing his face and shoulders with water.
The older man, bald and spectacled, dressed in black like a
sand-beetle, was slowly unfolding a large pink map. The white-
haired lady took off her enormous green hat, spread her shawl,
sat down, and started fanning herself gently. The black-haired
girl in the sky-blue dress knelt close beside her, quite motionless, gazing across the beach with a delicate, troubled surprise.

Ahmed tugged at his *futah* and leaped over the rocks.

The man in black rose and beckoned violently with both
hands, crying, *"Harra!"*

Idris followed his friend; they strolled up to the cave and
bowed decorously.

"*Marhaba!*" said Ahmed gravely, crossing his hands on his chest.

The man in black peered through his glasses. "Do you live here?" he said in a quavering voice, using Ahmed's own language but with a high, pedantic accent.

"Not quite," said Ahmed. "We have come on a boat. Tomorrow we leave for Sabaya."

"Where are we, exactly?" said the little man, fingering his spectacles with agitation.

Ahmed looked puzzled. "You are on a beach, honored sir!"

"No, no!" cried the man in black. "You misunderstand. What is the name of this island?"

Ahmed brightened. "Darib!"

"Are we far from Aden?"

"Oh, quite far, sir!"

"And Mukalla?"

"Far also. A little less far than Aden, however." Ahmed glanced thoughtfully toward the west. "One day to Sabaya by ship. And there we wait three days. Another day to Ash Shihr. Three more days of waiting. Another day to Mukalla. And that is all." He counted on his fingers. "Nine days, sir. If we are lucky."

The white-haired lady spoke softly. "Please! You must try and help us."

Ahmed gazed at her with sudden interest. She too knew their tongue but she spoke it crisply and naturally. She was English; Ahmed could see it in her stiff, comfortless costume. And she knew the East; he could hear it in her cold, authoritative tones.

"I speak English, madame," he said proudly. "Idris also speaks English. Speak to the madame, Idris!"

"Welcome to Darib, honored madame," said Idris, lowering his eyelashes.

"You must go for help," said the old lady, speaking tensely and firmly. "Two men have been killed. Is there a village on the island?"

Ahmed shrugged. "Just an ignorant little village, dear madame!"

"Go. Tell them to send some men," said the white-haired lady. Her eyes met Ahmed's; they were surprisingly bold and piercing.

Ahmed hesitated. There was something impressive and gallant about this English lady who had dropped from the sky. Would it really be wise to run to the village? What would the *nacouda* say? Would the *sayyid* make trouble? Might it be better first to speak to old Akbar, perhaps?

The yellow-haired man stepped into the shade of the cavern. His face was still dripping. He was beautiful as a god, it seemed to Ahmed—broad and tall, curly-headed, with the cool gray eyes of the North.

Ahmed gazed pensively at the four *faranchis*. He had seen men from the West before, in Mukalla and Aden—brisk, masterful officials and their great noisy wives. These were different: helpless creatures in exotic garments, absurd and pitiful in this spear of land dividing the desert from the sea—a clumsy virgin in azure, a young athlete with yellow hair, a feverish gentleman who looked like a sorcerer, a withered spinster in dotted poplin.

The athlete beckoned. Ahmed and Idris followed him back to the beach. Small blue flames were still licking at the shattered fuselage. They peered through the wreckage; Idris tore at the tangled metal with his fishing spear. The pilot's body lay twisted over the wheel, black as pitch. Beneath him, scarcely recognizable as a human body, lay the crumpled shape of another man.

Ahmed nodded, struck with awe. "It is the will of Allah," he whispered.

The fishermen were landing on the farther edge of the beach. Three men stepped out of a *houri* and came running across the sand, gesticulating feverishly.

"Salah! Salah!" called Ahmed.

A one-armed man waved his crimson futah, and now from the direction of the village a group of men came riding on horseback, white-turbaned men on coal-black mares, scattering veils of sand over the boulders.

They came to a halt beside the plane. The nacouda dismounted—a suave, aquiline personage with a sharp black beard. There was an air of insinuation, distrust. The pale-haired man bowed grimly; the nacouda bowed, expressionless. He glared at the wreck with velvety eyes and stroked his beard sedately.

Slowly Ahmed led them back through the dying light to the little cave.

✿

Two hours later the necessary bargaining had been completed. The four faranchis were to leave in secrecy that night on the *Guleïfa*. A suitable sum—thirty-three thalers—was paid to the nacouda for his hospitality, as well as for his subtlety in evading the laws of the local sayyid. Baths were prepared in his guest-house; beds were spread for the evening nap. Appropriate purchases were made by Ahmed—rice and dates, three goatskins of water. At eleven o'clock Idris brought an enormous bowl of kous-kous to the cottage, and an hour later Salah, the one-armed man from Bengazi, parted the curtains and whispered, "The boat is waiting, Your Excellences."

3

The little village lay fast asleep. It was way after midnight, but the moon hadn't risen, and the night hung black as an umbrella. In the harbor the tackle of native craft creaked rhythmically. The water gleamed under the jade-green pier.

Salah slid off his loincloth and waved it into the night. Three minutes later a dinghy came gliding through the darkness. They all stepped in, Ahmed and Idris following, and soon they caught sight of the *Guleïfa* swaying beyond the rocks. Worms of phosphorescence played in the tar-black water. Jackals were yelping in the distance, and now at last the moon was rising—a thin white splinter sailing on the dark horizon.

It was a neat little *dhow*, high-pooped and long-prowed, with a crew of seven, including two Negro boys from Massawa. They set sail. The snowy triangle of the lateen sail unfolded silently with a kind of surreptitious majesty. Suddenly the moonlight grew clear and hung focused on the trembling canvas. They slid smoothly out of the harbor, past two light-buoys which rocked heavily, moaning and clanking away at their chains, casting a glow from their restless beacons.

The wind dropped as they entered the open sea. The island vanished in the blackness, the beacon light dimmed and died. The sea lay strangely still; a trail of foam flashed in the empty vastness. The tall Egyptian at the helm started to sing in a low, grief-stricken tone. The yard groaned against the mast, the water soughed under the stern. They crept on slowly for half an hour; then Akbar, the captain, decided to take no chances in these shoal-infested shallows. They dropped anchor, and the two black boys hung the lantern at the masthead; the tiny light hung trembling in the still black water. Two young sailors brought out a drum and a viol, and the Negro boys started to dance, writhing like saplings in the wind. Miss Todd lay wrapped in her shawl; at her feet sat Miss Howard, listening dreamily to the music. Dr. Moss crouched by the railing, scanning the sea through his glasses. A strange sensation, not so much of peace as of immobility, passed through the young American. The sea, the music, the dancing Negroes, the fragrance of salt and spices: they might have been crossing the Gulf of Aden five hundred years ago.

✧

Ahmed sat beside David, resting his chin on his knee.

"Are these friends of yours, Ahmed?"

"Friends and acquaintances," said Ahmed carefully.

"What are their names, Ahmed?"

"That is Akbar over there, sir. With the broken nose." Akbar looked like a pontifical old brigand with his brown, battered profile and wispy, henna-stained beard. "Akbar has sailed for fifty years. He has killed many men. No man is braver or more vengeful or more cunning than Akbar. And that, on the left, is Hassan." Hassan was plucking away at his viol. He was a magnificently built young Arab, with loose black hair floating about his shoulders. "Hassan comes from Medina. He is silent and full of piety. No man is more simple or innocent than Hassan. And that, on the right, is Idris." Idris was a slim catlike fellow with a black, adventurous gaze; a curved dagger in a silver scabbard was tucked in his cotton girdle. "Idris comes from Mukalla. He is more supple than a gazelle. When no women are about we all make love to Idris."

He gazed speculatively at David. "And now," he said, "tell me, sir. Are you all one family? All four of you?"

"Oh, no." David smiled. "We first met three days ago. In Bombay."

"You come from India? All four of you?"

"Miss Todd comes from Calcutta. She has lived in India many years. Now she is going home to England."

"And the little virgin?"

"She is English too. Her father has died; she is going back to London."

"Poor little lady! And the elderly sir?"

"He is a scholar, I believe. He has been traveling through Persia. He is on his way to Cairo."

"He is English too? Like you?"

"No, no," said David. "We are both Americans."

"Americans!" said Ahmed, taken aback. "Americans are wicked men, sir. Forgive me! But Akbar says you have no god, no spirituality." He leaned closer, running his hands over his dirty old tennis shoes. "There. Listen!" The Egyptian kept on chanting. "It is a *qasida,* honorable sir. Very devout and lovely. Do you have qasidas in America?"

"Yes," said David, feeling mellow. "Fine qasidas. Just as here."

"Sad ones too? Brave and saintly ones?"

David nodded discreetly.

"Oh, recite an American qasida, honorable sir!" cried Ahmed.

David hesitated; he racked his brains. Finally he thought of some lines from *Hiawatha.*

Ahmed listened politely, liquid-eyed, disillusioned.

"A very interesting little qasida," he said doubtfully.

The moon was high. They caught sight of a tiny sail rising from the edge of the sea. It caught the light of the moon like a flake of ivory. The men bent forward, taut, suspicious. Ahmed's breath came faster. The air was filled with the rich, clandestine flavor of the Arab world.

A great wave reached out of the dark and scattered the spray on David's cheek. A voice called. He turned quickly. But no one was stirring—nothing but the hiss of the water, the faint creak of the mast; sea and sky, arrowing sails set against the conglomeration of stars. Ahmed sat crouched, peering tensely into the night.

David felt all around him the tension of an alien mind on an alien sea. Something in this lost secret world of taut white sails skimming the night gave him an inkling of some vaster struggle, some antique horror prowling across the face of the world.

✿

The breeze was light, but toward dawn warm puffs began to trouble the air. Soon a harsh, panting sound came wandering up from the south—the *khamsin* crawling forth from the desert lands beyond Assab. It swung down quite suddenly, hot as an oven in the first gust, whistling fiercely and treacherously through the rigging. The sea grew rough in five minutes. The wind was dead against them.

And then at sunrise the air was utterly still again. There was something fabulous in this gray-gold stillness which seemed to rise from the birth of the world. The stars were gone; the sunlight sharpened. The stillness grew metallic as the sun rose higher. Hassan and Idris dove overboard to draw out the anchor. The men pulled on the sweep to the sound of the Egyptian's chant. One hour later the heat grew stinging, suffocating. The gulf was a pallid sirupy green. Finally at noon the sea changed color; it turned abruptly into an echoing blue. The wind came at them, the sails came to life in a flash, and the *Guleïfa* slid lightly over the white-scaled water.

A sullen coast rose in the north—volcanic knolls dark as onyx, and at their feet a wavering strip of dunes. Bleak, lifeless, forbidding—a land still haunted, David imagined, by ancient armies passing through the leafless Arabian loneliness.

Ahmed came up and sat beside him. "You look sad, sir. Are you sad?"

David smiled. "Not really, Ahmed."

Ahmed touched him delicately on the wrist. "Don't feel sad! I will protect you, honorable sir."

David felt a gust of instinctive affection toward Ahmed. There was something gentle yet tenacious about him, restrained yet caressing. He gave an impression of inner strength, even a certain ruthlessness; but in his eyes there was a watchful, solicitous sweetness.

"Look at the waves, sir!" Ahmed pointed. Small white crests leaped from the water. "There are spirits dancing about in those little waves."

"Bad spirits, do you think, Ahmed?"

"Bad and good. More bad than good!"

"Spirits of men?"

"Oh, of everything!" Ahmed spread out his thick brown fingers. "Spirits of kings and of horses, of sunken ships and Abyssinians, of big and bloodthirsty fish. They keep dancing on top of the waves. Now you cannot quite see them. But on a summer's night you can see them; they keep dancing like witches the whole night long!"

He leaned closer and whispered, "The gentleman in black, sir—is he a witch?"

David glanced at him playfully. "Does he look like a witch to you, Ahmed?"

"No, no," said Ahmed, apologetic. "It is only that he looks so much like a turtle, honorable sir."

Two hours later the wind died again. The sea grew viscous, the sails hung slack. They were completely becalmed. The heat echoed over the gulf like a drum; the very air was bursting with sweat. A violent thirst seized them all. One of the sailors rose dizzily and poured some water out of the tin. Sweat flowed in rivulets down his nut-brown belly.

David tossed a loose white *jerd* over his head, lay back, and closed his eyes.

4

It was night when David woke up. Ahmed was shaking him by the armpits. It had grown eerily cold; a dull hiss filled the air. And then, as he sat there rubbing his eyes, he saw the Big Bear crawling behind a cloud. A gusty wind was arising. A feverish power was being loosed—a hot angry wind prowling across the sea from Ethiopia.

The night grew still darker. The breeze was turning into a gale. David felt himself lashed in the face by a cloud of spray. The sailors were shouting and gesticulating orders across the deck. They were no longer able to control the canvas and were getting ready to lower the mainsail.

Overhead the black whirling clouds raced through the night. The *Guleïfa* rushed wildly into the darkness. The wind howled. No one spoke; everyone listened intently, feeling in his own wind-stung body the agonizing strain on the slender masts. Flashes of foam went rocketing by, almost level with the lee rail. A flurry of large white flakes flew over the deck. David felt his blood leap with a kind of fearful delight as he heard the wild wind singing, and through the wind now and again the shout of a giant wave. The lantern was blown out; the stars hung eclipsed; there was only a huge black void filled with the sob of the seas and the sting of the gale. A shrill blaze, cold as an arc-light, whitened the scene for three seconds; a zigzag of lightning went shuddering over the south. The wet ship was aglitter in the sudden brilliance. Her one set sail was throbbing, silhouetted against the tattered immensity. The sea lay shining in all its disheveled fury.

Now the wind grew still stronger. The seas raced by, still

more menacing. Clouds rose out of the west, swiftly broadening and deepening. The breaking sea came galloping toward them like a herd; the squalls screamed savagely as they overtook the ship. She ran on wildly, grunting with pain, her ropes dripping, her spars all streaming. A swampy odor was in the wind, a whiff from the bowels of the sea. The wind seemed suddenly to lessen, but the heavy seas kept breaking over them—no use trying to steer past them in this lunatic darkness. David strained his ears and listened; a new note, like a siren, crept through the clash of the storm. He caught sight for a moment of the other three passengers, huddled in a windblown cluster beside Ahmed. But then the darkness grew inky. Only the crests of the nearby waves, white as flames, were still visible. It seemed that the mast might be smashed, the ship struck down in the hollows. At one moment there was a sickening shudder, and a shriek rose from Akbar, whose profile loomed over David, vast and calamitous as a Hebrew prophet's. The *Guleïfa* moaned and shivered as though she were being hurled on a bank. David caught sight of Idris frantically unleashing the houri. But then the whole sea gave forth an enormous sigh, the whole fury expired in a mammoth gurgle. Strips of a miserable slate-gray crept forth in the sky. The ship whined in a trance of panic and exhaustion.

"We must make for the bay," squealed Akbar, pointing. And soon they were heading northeast, carefully aiming to round the cape. The gale had finally forsaken them, but now they found themselves in a new dilemma: the threat of seeing the breakers loom suddenly before them, when it would be too late to put about. They headed for the shore, shattered by the wind, fleeing the sea, frightened of the reefs, staring into the darkness, listening tensely for the roll of the breakers.

Hassan cried hoarsely, "Listen!"

The wind still shrieked in the distance, but beyond the sound of the wind rose a hovering roar—the call of the breakers. It grew stealthily louder, like approaching hoofs. The sound deepened to starboard. The sea was breaking only a few cable-lengths away. Hassan peered into the night, his right arm upraised. But still they couldn't quite detect the tell-tale line of white foam.

Hassan swung his arm and cried. The *Guleïfa* shot forward. Two seconds later the water grew silent and calm. The growl of the breakers now came clearly on the beam. They had entered the peaceful waters of the bay. A strange happiness enclosed them, a feeling of hard-won security. One by one the stars crept out from the clouds.

✿

Salah brought them a bowl of salted fish and a platter of *dourah* cakes. The great cliffs towered above them, strangely peaceful and luminous. The men spoke of their luck. "Luck is an odd thing," said Salah, "isn't it? Bad luck always ends by bringing good luck, if you just wait patiently."

"If one is clever," said Idris.

"If one is fearless," said Hassan.

"If Allah wills it," growled Akbar, shaking his long blue finger.

Idris started to sing. He began very softly, his girlish voice caressing the air like silk. Then his voice grew vibrant, touched with an echo of heroism. He sang of struggle and violence, of love and catastrophe. One by one the young Arabs lay down and fell asleep. David watched them sleeping—the dreamless slumber of sailors whose ship is riding well and safely between her anchors. He found himself filled with a delicious glow of well-being; an awareness of freshened senses, of old habits being stripped from his skin like a tunic.

He knelt beside the black-eyed girl, who lay shivering under Salah's *djellaba*.

"Are you well, Miss Howard?"

She nodded, forcing a little smile.

"Were you frightened?"

"Well, a little."

Her teeth were chattering with exhaustion. She looked quite pale, quite pitiful. He felt a twinge of pity touched with a furtive irritation.

"Where do you live, Miss Howard?"

"Hamilton Terrace, St. John's Wood." Her voice hung pleading, bizarre in the desert silence. "Miss Howard." She sighed. "It sounds so strange to be called Miss Howard!"

"Shall I call you Sylvia?"

"Please call me Sylvia!"

"What will you do when you get to London, Sylvia?"

"Play the piano," she said softly. "Play tennis. Go for walks. Tell me, Mr. Maxwell, will I ever get back to London?"

"You'll get there," said David gently.

"It's dreadfully far," said Sylvia.

"Do you long to get back?"

"Well—perhaps. I suppose so." She turned to him with a tiny glitter. "And you, Mr. Maxwell. Where do you live?"

"Nowhere, I'm afraid."

"Don't you have a home?"

"Not any longer."

"Not even a family?"

"No. No family."

"And where will you go, then?"

"Wherever I'm told. Anywhere from Reykjavik to Tasmania!"

"But someday won't you want to—"

"Yes?"

"Won't you marry, Mr. Maxwell?"

"Perhaps. Who knows?"

Sylvia cast a quick sidelong glance at him. "Tell me, Mr. Maxwell. Where *are* we?"

"In a place called the Hadhramaut. Nothing to worry about!"

"And what will happen to us now?"

"We'll be heading for Mukalla. In Mukalla we'll take a boat to Aden."

"I see." She grew thoughtful. "Do you think, Mr. Maxwell—"

"Yes? What?"

She glanced evasively at Miss Todd. "Oh, nothing!"

There was a shy, troubled pause.

"Good night, Sylvia. Sleep well!"

"Good night, Mr. Maxwell!"

She closed her eyes and fell asleep instantly.

David watched her sleeping. Her breath came more slowly.
Her quaint homely face fell into smooth, anonymous lines.
She ceased being Sylvia; she ceased being English. She melted
into the universality of her young, yearning body. Her hand
trembled; an eyelid fluttered. She was trapped in a dream.
And David, sitting there in the darkness, felt her dream reach
out and touch him. It pleaded with him, fled from him, co-
quetted with him, spied on him. He leaned over and gazed
at her face; now it looked almost beautiful, steeped in the
poetry of slumber. He lowered his head, kissed her lightly on
the forehead. She didn't stir; but suddenly he sensed that she
wasn't asleep, that she wasn't dreaming.

He rose noiselessly and tiptoed across the sand toward the
base of the cliff.

5

Far away, at dawn, a white triangle moved closer—an Arabian *sambouk,* afloat on the sea like a cabbage butterfly. A tiny black man hung on the lookout in the rigging. Akbar waved; the man waved back apathetically.

"A friend from Sabaya," whispered Idris.

All morning they kept maneuvering among the rocks of the archipelago, sailing within sight of the other ship—what the Arabs called "sailing *sangar.*" Finally both ships entered an inlet, and the sails were hauled down. The men poled their boats up a winding canal.

Miss Todd lay back, feeling the glow of the sun bake her body. Veins of warmth trickled through her, tender as wine. The familiar ache in the pit of her chest had subsided; the twinge of neuralgia was gone. The panic and misery of the day before had melted into a suave, lucid peacefulness. There was something a bit uncanny in this subtle recovery. The reckless spaciousness of Arabia was beginning to rock her in its arms. She felt curiously receptive—a warm unease, a troubled sympathy. One tiny gesture, she felt, one momentary glimpse of real happiness, and everything would fall into place.

The canal broadened slowly. On one of the shores rose an aisle of plum-blue hillocks. On the other spread the snow-white dunes with their silvery grasses. A small oasis appeared— crumbling walls, quite deserted. The boats came to a halt, first the stranger and then the *Guleïfa.* The men disembarked. Miss Todd was lifted into the houri.

They strolled through the blinding sand toward the tiny

palm grove. The heat was pirouetting across the sand, but under the leaves it was cool and shady. Ahmed scuffled among the ruins for bits of camel-thorn and driftwood. Salah brought up the goatskins of water and started boiling their tea. Miss Todd felt her strength returning in gradual, fragrant draughts. She looked around, suddenly caught in a rush of wonder. Two of the men were digging busily in the sand down by the ruined walls. The little professor from Boston was chatting amiably with Mr. Maxwell. Idris was climbing a tree. Sylvia was combing her hair. Everything looked weirdly natural, inevitable all of a sudden, as though all that had happened and still might happen were blessed by some casual, omniscient logic. They were sitting under a *qaradh* tree, whose coral-shaped boughs gave out a faint scent of aloe.

Salah poured her a cup of tea. "Recite us a poem, please, madame!"

"A poem?" said Miss Todd, delighted. "What kind of poem, Salah?"

"A happy poem! About a feast, perhaps," begged Salah.

"Or the brevity of life," said Akbar, frowning.

"Or gardens." Hassan hummed. "Full of fruit . . ."

Miss Todd smiled helplessly. "I wish I could," she pleaded.

She glanced up at the twisted branches; an echo shaped itself in her mind:

> Here at the fountain's sliding foot
> Or at some fruit-tree's mossy root,
> Casting the body's vest aside,
> My soul into the boughs does glide . . .

A group of Arabs was passing along the opposite shore—skinny men with quilted packs, swathed in shawls and turbans, walnut faces shining among the swirls of yellow and red. One waved and cried, *"Salaam aleikum!"* They vanished beyond the dunes.

"Where are we, by the way?" said Miss Todd, tapping Ahmed on the shoulder.

Ahmed hesitated. "Taima," he said carelessly.

Miss Todd grew thoughtful. "How long do we stay in Taima?"

"We leave tomorrow," said Akbar sternly.

Miss Todd nodded. "I see."

But she did not see; she scarcely listened. Her senses were marvelously alert; never had the sky looked so blue to her, the light so blinding, the sea so vivid. But the course of human incident was hidden from understanding. Why precisely were they here, on this particular little island? It took an effort of the intelligence to fathom the reasons. Where were they going? What were they waiting for? What were they whispering about? What were they scheming? Something a trifle unsavory, it occurred to her, was in the air.

She opened her leather bag, looking for a tin of magnesia tablets. She glanced inside: folds of money, a necklace, photographs, hairpins and needles, a spool of thread, pills, sunglasses, an unmailed letter. And the jewel-case, of course. She snapped it open: a brooch, a bracelet, a string of pearls. Was this her past? Her link with the world? This tongue of leather, brimming with stale and futile embellishments?

She leaned back and watched the boughs of the qaradh tree above her, rigid and glossy in the azure air.

✿

At dusk the *Guleïfa* was poled back to the sea. The sister ship from Sabaya had left two hours earlier. They anchored behind a sandy cape which spread from a cave-dented promontory. The black apprentice boys dove in and groped in the grottoes for shellfish while Salah built a fire in the *moufa*, a vase-shaped oven left by the local fishermen. The men began to chant—three of them singing in unison, and then, from the other side of the beach, three others singing in reply. The naked boys crept out, their hands dripping with mussels. Salah was bustling and clattering away among his pans. They started eating as the daylight died, and a purring silence fell over them. The waters were noiseless, broken occasionally by a rip-

ple of pursuit—a shark, conceivably, chasing a school of mackerel. Night fell. The tide rose. Idris whispered to Akbar and
then got up and bound a handful of tow to the end of a pole.
He lit a match. The flame jumped, hurling its light over the
shallows. The men waited sullenly, peering out at the sea.
The torch-head flickered and hissed as it fell at the edge of
the water. Two shots were fired in the distance; Hassan called
into the night. A voice replied, low and raucous. *"Min!"*
shouted Akbar. Five minutes later two small houris came gliding toward the beach, and a group of men jumped out some
fifty yards from where he sat. They stood motionless near
the water, half hidden by the brushwood.

"Min! Min!" called Akbar, which meant, "Who goes there?"

"Friends from Mukalla," cried the strangers. There were
four of them. Their shadows crept closer, moving like tomcats
through the darkness. One of them stepped up boldly and drew
a paper out of his futah. Akbar stooped, lit a match, and
peered at the paper scrupulously.

There was a pause, a flicker of uncertainty. One of the new-
comers gesticulated. Salah's voice grew threatening.

"Be quiet," said Akbar crossly. He bowed, somewhat ironically, and motioned to the men to sit down.

"There were two cases, not three," Salah kept growling.

"Three! Three!" snapped the newcomer, shaking his fist.

"Two," said Akbar, impassive.

"Ah, well." The stranger sighed, suddenly yielding.

Akbar drew out a little green bag from his djellaba. The
men started counting the coins by matchlight. Finally they
rose and said, "So it is."

"So it is," said Akbar.

"Farewell, then!"

"Peace be with you."

"You too!"

"Into eternity . . ."

The men leaped back into their houris and vanished into
the night.

6

The next day was cooler, ruffled by a faint wind from the east. Miss Todd woke up at daybreak, feeling fresh and invigorated. The rest were still sleeping. She straightened her shawl and got up, sniffing the cool, tart spice in the air, the lingering smell of decaying shellfish. She strolled past the beach to the edge of the promontory.

Down beyond the fringe of the cliffs the island spread into desert, but a desert which once, centuries ago, must have been fertile, and eons before that, presumably, had lain buried in the sea. Fossils lay scattered about: veins of coral, fine as lace; ancient shellfish transformed into feathers of stone. There was an aroma of timelessness, a stillness richer than mere solitude. Tiny ponds shone in the sunrise, filled with rust-colored water. Not a bird was stirring, not even an insect.

Suddenly she felt, without warning, a bit unwell—a fit of nausea welling up from an unknown source. It passed, leaving behind only a dull, bleak weariness.

She walked on. The ground was rising. The sand darkened to a dappled slate color. There was something ugly, amorphous, about these bulging ripples rising out of the desert; they suggested an unimaginable past, the ravenous idiocy of the dinosaurs. She turned and started back. Suddenly the ground gave under her feet. She lost her balance and fell headlong on the hard, rolling gravel. She lay still for a minute, wondering what had happened. The smell of the earth, vaguely sulphurous, enclosed her like a vapor. She brushed the dust from her dress and looked around. Had someone called? Was someone watching? No. Nothing but emptiness.

A grim, mineral vacancy. She rose clumsily, clutching at the wisps of dry grass, and hurried back to the yellow beach.

✧

Salah was boiling his pot of rice when she returned. She mentioned nothing of her little excursion. Two of the men began their morning qasida, spreading their arms grandiloquently. Idris brought out his pipe, which he called a *mizmar* —a fragile instrument, semi-transparent, made of an eagle's feathers. Hassan started to sing. His muscles shone like an athlete's, bright with the effort of song. Idris was wearing his skullcap, which was embroidered with tinsel and sequins. His cheeks ballooned as he piped away cheerfully. But Hassan's face as he sang was distorted with anguish; his great chest heaved with the weight of the qasida.

"Is this a love song?" said Miss Todd, leaning closer toward Ahmed.

"No, no," said Ahmed disparagingly. "It is only a light, wispy song from Ispahan. The songs from Egypt are sad. And the songs from Java are even sadder. These Persian songs are nothing at all—just little snippets about birds and flowers."

A green snake crept out of Ahmed's shirt as he listened to the mizmar.

"Good heavens," cried Miss Todd. "Ahmed! A snake!"

"It is my *personal* snake," said Ahmed soothingly.

"Is it poisonous?"

"Of course it's poisonous," boasted Ahmed.

"Won't it bite you?"

"It has bitten me three times," said Ahmed proudly. "The first time I was *very* sick—so sick that I almost died. The second time I was *quite* sick. I lay in bed for two days. The third time I was a *little* upset for an hour or two. And now, of course, I am not afraid."

"How odd," murmured Miss Todd. "I should think you'd dislike the animal."

Ahmed grinned. "We are great friends! We have forgiven

each other. Iuslim, look at me!" The snake peered at Ahmed with a blurred, drooping look. Ahmed plucked it out of his lap and kissed it affectionately on the snout.

✿

That afternoon a large sailing boat passed the island. The two Somalis rolled their eyes and sniffed the air, stirred by some fleeting intuition.

Toward sunset they noticed two men in a fishing boat rounding the cape.

Akbar sent Hassan to climb the cliff and scan the shore on the other side. It was dusk when Hassan returned, creeping swiftly over the sand. His brown body moved like a lizard, almost invisible against the coppery beach. He explained. The sister ship had apparently been seized and now was anchored beyond the cape two miles away, three cable-lengths from the marauding vessel. Akbar and Salah made their plans, gesticulating fiercely. Night shot down; they all slipped back into their little houris and went skimming over the calm black water. The *Guleïfa* was only a blot, a hint of deeper shadow, until her masts rose sharply against the stars, the lateen yard triced close. Three silent figures stood on the deck as Miss Todd peered wearily from the houri; she was lifted out, the pirogues were raised, the glint of danger shone in the darkness. They trimmed the sails and carefully hauled out the length of the cables. They heard two shots fired in the distance—from the edge of the cliff, it appeared. They raised the anchor swiftly. A ripple flew over the moonlit sea; a land breeze was rising. "Allah be praised," growled Ahmed. The sails were freed and billowed out, and the boat flowed silently from her anchorage. The distant land faded. The ocean began to surge.

A rash and reckless thing to do, groaned Ahmed—setting off in the darkness, with the reefs abounding! But the land breeze kept bearing them along in fine trim; luck was with them, and they sped through the pungency of the night.

Miss Todd was sitting by Dr. Moss. "Look," she whispered. "How happy they are!"

"They are savages, after all, Miss Todd," moaned Dr. Moss. The wind began to growl. They were heading directly for Arabia. Toward midnight a great luxury liner crossed their bow. Every detail was clear and festive—the first-class passengers in their evening dress were strolling along the decks and stretched on their chairs. The strains of the dance-music spread over the waves, light as insects.

Dr. Moss glanced at his watch. He turned to Miss Todd rather petulantly. "Do you have the time, Miss Todd, by any chance?"

Miss Todd smiled quizzically. "Does time exist here?"

"Precisely as everywhere else," snapped Dr. Moss. "Time is ubiquitous, I'm afraid."

Miss Todd peered toward Arabia. "I dare say. I dare say." She added gently, "I can hardly believe it, though. It must be a different kind of time, don't you think?"

The liner faded into the night. The *Guleïfa* was alone again.

✿

A bit later, an hour after midnight it might have been, Miss Todd woke up again. The water hissed under the stern, the rigging squealed softly. The African boys lay naked beside her, curled up like wolfhounds. She detected the musk of their salty bodies—male and pungent, like raw hickory. Ahmed and Idris were sleeping too, side by side. Their motionless djellabas looked like sculptured folds of marble. At the tiller sat old Akbar, his vulture face drenched in moonlight, looking like some terrible old patriarch steering his lonely vessel through the gulf.

Her forehead burned. She opened her bag and reached for the aspirin. The ship gave a jolt; the little jewel-case went spilling across the deck. She crawled forward on her knees, snatching clumsily at the scattered ornaments.

Old Akbar sat without moving, eyes closed like a blind man's. Idris stirred softly, tightening his fist in his sleep.

Miss Todd sat quite still, breathless with incredulity. Could this be real? Was she really here? She felt she was shawled in some antique secrecy, like an unborn child, crouching in this hot, expectant, impenetrable gloom.

She lay down again. Now she saw only the sea and the stars. The wake pointed east, white and clear as a chain of beads.

7

Dr. Moss woke up at sunrise, feeling weak and rheumatic. There was an ominous sense of oncoming heat. The sun was a dead vermilion as it oozed from the sea, and the sea itself was calm, smooth as a sheet of lead, stirred here and there by a sudden ripple—a school of minnows, a drifting cat's paw. The sails hung limp from the yard, the loosened sheet flapped listlessly. The rays grew fiery, the sea grew dazzling. The heat shot down like a shower of embers.

Then everything changed. The east wind approached, and the sea was transformed into a glorious, foam-dappled blue. The sails billowed, and the boat cut swiftly through the leap of the waves.

They passed a group of tall rocks—crags of bronze striped with maroon, with a tuft of snow-white beach at the base. Two skinny boys were fishing in a small black boat, the only sign of life in all this sun-stunned serenity. The far-off islands floated like fans over the water. On they sailed. The wind subsided. The *Guleïfa* grew languid. Something in this reef-infested region suddenly startled Dr. Moss, some air of singular remoteness, something more than geographically distant—a prehistorical stillness. History had passed this region by, where masses of sea-fowl shrieked over the rocks, which rose like domes in the rosy light—some conelike, some thimble-shaped, some blunt and jagged. The clangor of sea-birds filled the air, but it seemed to Dr. Moss not quite real, not wholly audible; it seemed to hover just beyond the range of the ear.

Clouds passed. The tints in the archipelago shifted from

blue to a sickly lavender. But the water itself hung clear as glass in the eerie calm. He could see the shrubs of coral passing under the boat, precise and opulent. These were colors, this was a brilliance, he had never seen before. The whole scene suddenly commanded him: Look! This is light, this is color! This is the reality of air and water, this is the texture of the visible world! Look again, look quickly, before it's too late!

A thrill of expectancy passed through him. His uneasiness vanished. He borrowed a tattered jerd from Idris and wound it turbanwise around his forehead.

✿

They worked their way carefully through the treachery of the archipelago and presently rounded a spur-shaped peninsula.

"No. Not here!" called Akbar.

The gloomy Egyptian steered the *Guleïfa* toward a barren island, which quivered in the heat waves like a great bronze helmet.

They passed a group of sambouks, the little sailboats of the pearl-divers. Dr. Moss felt troubled. On every side the young divers, brown and naked as Adam, stood enthusiastically waving their futahs at them. Two little *zarougs* slid past —light, arrowing vessels, free of ballast. Inside them sat a group of Arabs, holding their guns. They passed the *Guleïfa*, eying it truculently.

"From Mocha," said Akbar with a dejected air.

The subtle-eyed Idris came up and squatted by Dr. Moss. "Are you thirsty, honorable sir?" He held out a cup of water.

"Thank you," said Dr. Moss, drawing back an inch or two.

Idris's sloe eyes passed casually over the doctor's person. His voice was decorous, impersonal. "How many years do you have, sir?"

Dr. Moss hesitated. "What would you guess?"

"Ah!" Idris grinned. "Thirty years, honorable sir."

"I am forty-four," said the doctor crisply.

Idris smiled gallantly. "Still very young! Young enough to make love, Your Excellency." He leaned closer, confidentially. "The elderly madame—is she your mother?"

The doctor blushed. "Not at all. I scarcely know her, as it happens."

"The two young ones—do you know *them?*"

"Hardly at all," snapped Dr. Moss.

Idris looked at him shrewdly. "You are alone? No friends at all?"

"I have acquaintances," said Dr. Moss.

"Whom you love?"

"Whom I respect."

"But whom do you love?"

Dr. Moss glared at the Arab. Idris's face shone with sweat. His eyes dug like spurs into the doctor's consciousness.

"I have my work," said the doctor, scowling. "I have no time for the usual nonsense."

"Work?" purred Idris.

"I study the past. I am an archaeologist," said the doctor sternly.

Idris looked puzzled. "When we come to Kumra," he whispered, "I will find you a lovely girl. Or a hairless boy, if you prefer. I am too old for you, I suppose?"

Dr. Moss got up and walked rapidly across the deck. His black, wrinkled coat flapped behind him in the rising wind.

✿

A heavy swell came up from the gulf. The monsoon was blowing, and a powerful current bore the *Guleïfa* westward. They spent all afternoon tacking in the rough angry waters. Countless isles hovered like beetles on the darkening horizon. The wind grew stronger; the men started to lower the mainsail. Hassan squealed. The half-lowered sail suddenly slid and trailed in the water as he slipped and fell on his knees. It scooped up a wave and then, with a violent twist, smashed the lateen yard. The ship rolled and tossed. Akbar groaned, flinging his arms.

There was nothing to do but run before the wind and hope for the best.

The boat trembled as she sped into the uneasy twilight. The men were alert with a tension half joyous, half fearful. The water throbbed under them like a giant motor. Stars twinkled, the moon crept out. They slid through the arms of the night. Plumes of foam leaped through the air like flying fish. The *Guleïfa* flew along on firm swift wings, and Dr. Moss began to feel a new agitation in his blood—the thrill of the rising sea, tremendous and delicate.

With the night came a heightened air of suspense. The fear of the hidden rocks began to creep over them. An hour passed. Hassan was keeping a close lookout at the masthead; he was watching for the dangerous line of the reef. The tension grew curiously gripping. *"Aya!"* cried Hassan. A basalt cliff rose above them. It looked like an ancient threat, sending back the muffled sound of their voices. The *Guleïfa* rushed past, quick and light as a gull. There was a hint of enormous depth and intensity in the echoing waters.

"Do you see anything, Hassan?"

"No. Nothing at all."

They were drifting with the currents. The swell increased and passed darkly over the far-off reefs without breaking.

"Hassan! Any sign of the reefs?"

"Not yet, Akbar."

Now it seemed they must drift helplessly over one hidden reef after another until they finally met the one shallow enough to destroy them. Salah and Idris were leaning over the water with boat-hooks, waiting for the vessel to strike a rock. Time passed. They drifted on. Now the tide was running against the wind, stirring up a choppy, irritable sea. Once there was a jar in the boat, a quick sharp shudder, and somewhere the sound of a brittle vibration. They got ready to jump into the houris. But nothing happened. "All is well," sang

Akbar. They floated on. The minutes passed in a black suspense. Now and then Dr. Moss imagined he could see a clump of coral protruding, writhing among the waves like a giant hydra.

Suddenly they caught sight of the snow-white breakers rolling in the distance. The Egyptian was at the helm. Hassan cried, "Quick! Quick!" A wave broke directly under the stern. The Egyptian swung the helm sharply over. The ship lurched. The reef was fifty-odd yards away. Hassan's eyes were burning as he lay in the bow, staring at the sea. The rest of the men were watching him feverishly.

Then he cried, *"Djoch! Djoch!"*

The helm was pulled over, and the sheet grew taut instantly. The *Guleïfa* sped into an opening between two arcs of foam and entered the mild, protected waters. The men sank back with relief. Hassan's teeth shone in a giant smile.

"Well done!" cried old Akbar.

Three minutes later the crisis was forgotten. The men chatted lightheartedly as they dropped the anchor off the beach.

"This is the place," said Akbar solemnly. He pointed. "There lies Sabaya!"

✿

The moon dimmed. All was still. The water lay glossy as tar. The Arabs were curling up in their djellabas, ready for sleep.

"Good night," cried young Idris, spreading his jerd for Dr. Moss. "And may Allah bless you in your sleep, honorable sir!"

Dr. Moss felt remarkably well. A sentiment of kinship welled up in him, a wave of esprit de corps, almost exuberance, such as he had never experienced. He got up noiselessly and strolled down the beach, scenting the fragrance of the night, feeling the cool soft sand give under his feet. He stripped off his tie and tucked it in his pocket; then he knelt and pulled off his shoes and socks. The sand oozed through his toes. A twinge of pleasure shot through him. He leaped in the air, swinging his arms.

Something stung at his heel. He squealed with pain and sank to the ground. A splinter of flint had pierced his skin; he could see a dark bead of blood.

He limped back to the crumbling fire, feeling lonely, dispirited.

But as he lay near the fire, watching the embers die away and the sleeping bodies fade into the reef-stilled darkness, a new sensation came over him. The strange tension in his body gave way to a feeling of numbness. He felt as though he were being rubbed with camphor: his skin gently evaporating, his outer self drifting into the night.

His heart froze. Something stirred by the water's edge: a shaggy, half-human silhouette, like a gorilla's. It crouched on the glossy sand, jaw thrust forward, eyes burning. The whole body was poised in a kind of horrible expectancy. The doctor's eyes began to water; a twinge of hysteria dug at his spine. But, as he stared, the shape dissolved. It faded like steam into the darkness.

All was still. The embers died. There was nothing but sand, sky, and water.

8

The lateen yard was repaired the following morning, and they sailed through the mist down the jagged coast toward Sabaya. They slid through a narrow isthmus between two towering islands. Great rocks caught the waves like a giant's fists; the spume unfurled, the stone was alive with a coruscating silver. The mist thinned, the veil parted, and then quite suddenly, like some illumination from the pit of the world, an explosion of sunlight flooded the coast. The rocks grew marbled. A torrent of colors flowed over the sea. Dr. Moss caught his breath, stunned by all this magnificence. Then the light grew hard, and the splendor died into bleakness.

At noon they passed a group of pearl-divers' boats. Ahmed explained. These vessels would anchor off the pearl banks for months at a time, fed by diminutive supply ships from the mainland. In the heat of summer, when the sharks had drifted to deeper waters, the men could dive naked with safety, armed with knives for loosening the shells and round containers to carry them up. Each of the divers had a stone-weighted rope tied to his toe: this would help draw him down, and when he tugged at the end after a minute or so would rapidly draw him up again.

The shells were opened on deck; a nauseating stench spread from the boats. One shell in a hundred, said Ahmed, bore a tiny white pearl.

✿

Sabaya loomed at the end of a long still bay. They stole up and dropped the anchor in an uneasy swell. Forty yards of

35

cable were laid out before the anchor touched bottom. The heat was appalling.

Akbar whistled. "A bad town!"

He sent the houri with Hassan and Ahmed to buy food and consult with the local authorities. They waited two hours; no sign of the houri. Dusk fell, and Dr. Moss sat on deck, nursing his foot. Here and there a yellow light was beginning to twinkle, furtive, inimical among the iron-gray walls. A distant drum was beating. Some sort of feast, possibly? The anniversary of a local saint? The town spilled its odor across the bay— an odor of ailing humanity, breathed out of hot, crowded cellars.

Salah served dinner. A boiled fish was set before Dr. Moss, pink as a lobster, with eyes protruding like china beads.

"I caught it myself, Your Excellence!" said Idris, sidling up with a fig in his mouth.

Dr. Moss caught the scent of the Arab's body, fresh with the salt of the sea.

"Do you eat fish in America?" inquired Idris.

Dr. Moss nodded. "Occasionally."

"You eat pork?" said Idris, suspicious.

"Not very often," said the doctor curtly.

"Dates and honey, perhaps?"

"Just a bit. Now and then."

"Almond tarts? Maize biscuits?"

"From time to time." The doctor sighed.

Idris ran his fingers across his nipples. "What do you feed your camels in America? *Natsh* leaves and wisps of *lasaf?*"

"I dare say," said the doctor, drawing a bone from his mouth.

Idris looked piqued. He cocked his head toward the early stars. "You are making fun of me." He pouted. "You are treating me like a woman!"

He rose and walked sulkily off into the darkness.

✿

Ahmed and Hassan returned in the morning and rowed the party ashore. Sabaya lay blazing in the ruddy light, the red cliffs behind it and the tapering little forts, white as tusks against the harrowing blue. The harbor was alive with wooden houris and sambouks. Bales of sugar, rice, sesame lay piled on the shore. The boats and bales, even the fishing nets, had an old Phoenician look about them, cast at random along the crescent of sand.

Dr. Moss stepped ashore and entered the beehive of Sabaya. Everything radiated a kind of seething fertility. The gourds and limes shone like illuminated bulbs. The copper pans and platters vibrated with light, like cymbals. The smells sharpened into a gradual symphony of spices—the smells of camels, dates, donkeys, human flesh, and perfume, and the leathery scent of excrement down in the shadows. There was an air of luminous proliferation, as though in the very aridity of the land the sun had created its own abandon. Arches and latticework cast shadows sharp and delicate as an etching. The facial shadows were so black that Idris's eyes lay hidden in a mask, and his mouth and nostrils seemed painted with kohl.

They walked past the mosque and came to an open field where a great black stone lay on the edge of the wadi. Idris, who had been in Sabaya before, explained that the stone was sacred, venerated by the natives. It looked like a meteorite which must have fallen centuries ago, for it was pock-marked by the sands and polished by an infinite number of human hands. Life even here, it seemed to say, bears a human patina.

Dr. Moss caught sight of an inscription near the base of the rock. It was worn smooth by the years, just barely decipherable. He took out his notebook and scrupulously copied the words. They spoke of an invasion by the Ethiopians, who had sacked the town and killed the king, and then ten years later had been driven back into the sea. In the very slant of the lettering, the sinuous pattern of curves and dashes, still lingered the glint of ancient hatreds.

Idris was sitting beside him with dusty eyelashes.

"The Ethiopians have an evil, many-faced god," he said bitterly.

"Every god appears wicked to other people," observed the doctor.

"You too have a god?"

"All men have a god, Idris."

"A clever god?" said Idris, squinting.

"Our God is gentle and forgiving," said Dr. Moss somewhat thinly.

"A god must be hard and cruel, I think," cried Idris in his limpid way.

The doctor narrowed his eyes. "Our God is—Love."

"Love!" Idris's eyes flashed indignantly. "Love is not a thing for religion, sir!"

"Not sexual love," hinted the doctor. "Love for mankind, my boy."

"I have loved men sometimes," confessed Idris, blushing faintly and spreading his fingers. "But it is a weakness, honorable sir!"

He crouched by the rock, closed his eyes, and told the doctor about Mohammed: how he was painlessly borne by his mother Amina, already neatly circumcised, with little rings of kohl painted around his eyes. . . .

"He was a great man. A *holy* man," breathed Idris, torn by emotion.

Pearls of sweat were rolling over the doctor's eyes. The scene grew blurred. He leaned back, faint and breathless with the heat. His foot was throbbing; a twinge of fever rose in his temples. He drew out his handkerchief and spread it across his skull. Then he drew off his sun-glasses, wiped them carefully, and put them on again. As he brushed his cheeks he felt the coarseness of beard against his palm. There was something sickening in the sandy texture, as though the skin were turning into a hide. And suddenly everything within him seemed on the point of disintegrating. The mosque, the marketplace, the meteorite, the Ethiopian invasion, the birth of Mohammed—a vicious, demoniac quality permeated them all. His sun-glasses fell from his nose and slid to the sand. For the first time in his life he experienced doubt on the scale of terror.

He glanced at Idris, who was staring at him with speculative eyes.

"Come," he gasped, and clutched at the rock, which burned his palm like coal. Idris helped him to his feet, and they walked in silence back to the harbor.

9

Above the harbor lay a grove of tamarisks, where some beduin had pitched their tents. The young ones were drawing water out of a well while the elders sat in the shade for a pull at their hookahs. A goat was grazing nearby, her udders huge and laden, ears dangling with silver talismans; she had the look of an aging odalisque.

Here the crew of the *Guleïfa* settled down for the evening. Salah was getting ready to cook a feast; Hassan had shot a gazelle up in the hills.

Ahmed cast his djellaba on the ground, and Sylvia sat down beside Miss Todd. Dusk was settling; a pastoral calm floated by. A bell was tinkling on the nannygoat, and the air was full of a heathery scent. Sylvia closed her eyes. It might have been an evening in Devonshire, almost.

"All this, my dear"—Miss Todd sighed—"will seem very unreal to you back in England."

Sylvia watched Idris holding a tiny mirror and carefully painting his eyes, flicking his long blue fingers like a ballerina. Hassan was squatting beside the fire, biting his nails. Ahmed leaned over intently, plucking lice from the seams of a blanket. The water was bubbling lazily in the pot.

One of the nomads came up and started to sing. Everyone listened, breathless. Idris held his fingers poised in the air; Hassan sucked at his thumb. The old man's voice was blurred and eerie, vaguely like an oboe. The song drifted into the boughs, joining the great blue spaciousness.

The old bedu turned and gazed at Sylvia with withered eyes. His face was pitted and wrinkled, so yellow it seemed he must be dead. Even the whites of his eyes and his teeth were a saffron yellow. The hair on his chest waved softly, like thistledown. He was ugly and hard as flint. But a magical youthfulness still clung to him. He looked at Sylvia with a cold deep glare, pitiless as a cobra's, seeing everything, feeling nothing—at least nothing for which there was a word.

"Sing, Idris!" cried Hassan.

Idris started to sing. The bedu's song had been of the land, of the deserts crossed by the caravans. It had told, explained Miss Todd, of the evanescence of things, of the pangs of love, of the merciless slaughter of rival tribes. But Idris's song was of the sea, of its loneliness and yearnings. It told of blossoming flowers and the stirring of distant boughs, of silence and starlight, of remote, unappeasable gods.

Wonderful scents were rising from Salah's gazelle. Mr. Maxwell and Dr. Moss had joined Miss Todd under the tamarisk. They spoke in low, casual voices. It was like a holiday picnic. Sylvia lapsed into a momentary daydream. The scene grew transformed; Miss Todd loomed like some antique queen over the tattered landscape, weaving the air of vagrancy into a stern, controllable pattern. Dr. Moss crouched mysteriously over his notes, like an alchemist, scrawling busily with his pencil. Mr. Maxwell, still wet from his swim, was drawing patterns in the dust with a broken twig; he looked like some Scandinavian voyager, sketching a crude, primitive map.

✿

The old bedu returned, bearing a bowl of coffee mixed with ginger. He bowed to Miss Todd with extreme ornateness and gave a flowery little speech. Miss Todd bowed in return, rather stiffly.

"What did he say, Miss Todd?" said Sylvia.

"Oh, the usual kind of thing. That he is the descendant of the saint Sa'id bin Isa Amudi, who is buried near Hajarain, and to whose grave the pilgrims pay a visit for a four-day feast in the month of Rajab, and so on." Miss Todd seemed out of sorts, thought Sylvia. Her face was flushed; was she feeling ill?

The day was narrowing into a bank of sulphurous blue, and on the other side of the hill it was already turning to a bat-wing gray. Hassan kept tossing thorny twigs on the blaze. The gazelle turned slowly on the spit, a sizzling bronze. Salah was pouring a sauce over the rice.

Sylvia felt drowsy, strangely lulled. All this soft, calm activity; all this patient, wordless preoccupation—it made her feel that she had been here for years instead of hours. It was a feeling of huge, unbreakable peace, so intense that all thought of the outer world grew unconvincing. Waves of warm, heavy indifference lapped at her consciousness. She closed her eyes and whispered desperately, "I am Sylvia Howard." She added tensely, "I have come from Bombay. I am on my way to London." But the words remained meaningless. Sylvia Howard . . . Bombay . . . London . . . They floated away like gusts of smoke. *"I am here!"* she whispered. *"I am in Arabia!"* The words crackled and broke, like flying embers.

Miss Todd's voice entered her consciousness. "There, my dear. Wake up. You must eat."

Salah came and set his gazelle in front of them. It was stuffed with dates and honey, wreathed in garlands of steam. The roasted skin, crisp and burnished, cast a delicious fragrance into the firelit air. Sylvia took a bite. The meat was tender but vaguely disgusting—like stale mackerel, a little. But the Arabs belched greedily; their eyes grew glassy. Their lips shone with grease, and they sank back happily on the warm blue dust.

The moon rose presently. The Arabs lay scattered among the trees, still and drowsy. There was a cry from the distant rocks.

"Listen," hissed Idris. "A hyena!"

"Are there hyenas here?" said Sylvia anxiously.

"This is a *ghost* hyena," said Idris, with mysterious eyes.

Sylvia grew pensive. "I see. Are there many ghosts in Arabia?"

"Certainly," said Idris cuttingly. "Why shouldn't there be?"

"I just wondered," said Sylvia.

"Have you never seen an Arabian ghost, mademoiselle?"

"Not yet, I'm afraid." Sylvia sighed.

Idris flicked a mosquito from his eyelashes. "Someday I'll show you a ghost." His gaze grew playful, indulgent. "What kind of ghost would you like to see?"

"Oh, just a harmless little ghost," pleaded Sylvia.

"A rabbit ghost, perhaps? Or a moon ghost?"

"What is a moon ghost, Idris?"

"Ah! Let me tell you. There are sun ghosts and star ghosts and moon ghosts," explained Idris, crooking his forefinger didactically. "And sea ghosts and wind ghosts. Also mountain ghosts and sand ghosts. Mountain ghosts are evil and bloodthirsty. Sand ghosts are lonely and sad. Wind ghosts are playful, naughty. Sea ghosts are nervous, irritable. Sun ghosts are very rare; they appear only to the dying. Moon phantoms are sweet and gentle. Sometimes they sing, like Persian nightingales. Some night, mademoiselle, we will look for a moon ghost!"

✿

Sylvia was troubled by dreams in the middle of the night. The feast lay heavy within her; strange visions frolicked across her brain. She found herself floating in a canoe on a palm-edged canal, moving slowly toward a passage between two cliffs. A procession of white-robed men stood along the shore, watching her intently. The wind caught her clothes and carried them off; she suddenly realized that she was naked. A stab of horror shot through her. The air was filled with a hum of voices. A long black arm reached out of the sky—the sleeve like a minister's, the hand like a gorilla's.

She forced herself awake with sudden desperation. Everything looked still and dead around her. She rose and tiptoed past the sleeping Arabs down to the beach.

The moon shone on the ruddy sand, the waves were white and pearly.

She forced herself, in this strange new fear, to think of England.

But England seemed infinitely remote, quaint and brittle as a painted fan. She closed her eyes as she sat on the sand and tried to conjure up the landscapes of Devon—the rolling moors, the parks with their streams and the red deer grazing, the badminton court behind the willows, the scones and strawberries served for tea, the click of the croquet ball on Miss Weatherill's mallet. Girls passed over the lawn in their pale blue dresses; elderly aunts with enormous hats sat stiff under their parasols. . . . It was a vignette from a long-lost album, musty and obsolete. She thought of India—the boat-strewn Ganges, the floating corpses, the crouching *saddhus*. These seemed real enough to her; but they loomed in a world of trivialities, a succession of tinkling little ceremonies.

She opened her eyes and stared at the gulf. The moon, sickle-thin, hung like an emblem over the harbor.

A man was squatting on the beach some fifty yards away. He crouched by the edge of the water, washing his arms and legs with sand, then his ears and face and mouth with salt water. He was black and shiny, muscular as a serpent. He rose slowly and stood facing her for a moment, his face upraised, his arms outspread. His white futah lay on the ground beside him. He wore nothing at all, and as he stood there silhouetted against the gleam of the rippled sea he looked to Sylvia like something ancient and terrifying—like Man emerging from the primordial emptiness, with the indescribable majesty of manhood about him.

He flung the sand from his arms and legs with a single powerful gesture. Then he bowed toward the east, where the first hint of light was already lurking, and stole silently back through the trees and vanished from sight.

10

The sailors sat in a ring around the fire, passing the hashish pipe. The moon was low. The night belonged to the Arabs.

Akbar's eyes were glittering. "What do you see in the stars, Idris?"'

Idris grinned. "Danger! Bloodshed!"

Salah chortled. "Idris is hiding something. Tell us the truth now, Idris."

"I see two men on a camel," chanted Idris. "Carrying baskets of incense down toward the harbor."

"Beduin or Unbelievers?"

"Pale men with golden hair. They are bearing shields marked with a cross."

"No, no, Idris. Control your fancy. What do you see?" said Akbar, scowling.

Idris gazed thoughtfully at the Big Dipper. "Nothing," he said in a strange thin voice.

A listless silence fell over the men. Old Akbar began to hiccup.

Hassan whispered, "Idris!"

"I feel a sadness in my blood," said Idris, petulant.

"Come," said Hassan. "Let's go." He seized Idris's hand.

The two young men rose and wandered through the heat down to the shore. They cast their robes on the sand and stepped into the shallow water. Idris felt the wind rippling across his body as he waded along the edge of the sea. A great emptiness gnawed at his heart. The world of the flesh ceased to matter.

Hassan took him by the forefinger and drew him into the

water. They lay floating, arm in arm, gazing up at the stars.

"What is the matter, Idris?"

Idris said nothing.

"Idris! Tell me! Did you see something evil in the stars?"

Still Idris said nothing.

Hassan sneered. "Are you afraid, Idris?"

"These are evil waters, Hassan!"

"You are afraid," growled Hassan contemptuously and tugged at Idris's arm, drawing him deeper into the water. Idris twisted and squealed; a handful of water shot into his windpipe. He gurgled, gripping Hassan fiercely by the throat. There was a quick little struggle. Hassan swung with his fist; Idris bit him savagely in the forearm. Hassan lifted him out of the water and hurled him through the air. Idris fell and struck his temple against a rock.

For a moment he lay senseless, half floating in the tide.

Hassan rushed up to him. "Idris! Are you dead?"

Idris saw the world moving through ring after ring of darkness, then entering a sphere of blinding light, zigzagged with veins of fiery red. He opened his eyes and began to cough.

Hassan was murmuring, "Forgive me, Idris." He clasped Idris in his arms and carried him tenderly up onto the sand. There he laid him down gently, stroking his forehead. "Are you well now, Idris?"

"Yes," said Idris hoarsely, and a clutching happiness seized him as he saw Hassan's head above his own, the luminous, stupid eyes filled with tears.

"Idris, forgive me!"

"I forgive you, Hassan."

✿

Idris woke up an hour later. The fire among the tamarisks had crumbled. All the men were asleep; only Hassan, beside him, was still awake, tugging persistently at Idris's arms. "Wake up, Idris!"

"What has happened?"

"Nothing has happened. It is late!"

A powerful silence filled the night, stripping it of human content. Even the sound of the little waves had a flat, lifeless tone. Idris felt a twinge of pain in the side of his head.

"Remember your promise," murmured Hassan.

"What promise?"

"The bracelet!"

Idris shook his head wearily.

"Abdullillah says it is worth—"

"Abdullillah is a viper."

"A thousand rupees!"

"Abdullillah is a toad."

There was a moment's silence.

"It was a promise," growled Hassan.

"No. Not now. Please, Hassan."

"Look. They're sleeping!"

"Oh, Hassan."

"You're a coward! A *kumarra*—"

"Be careful, Hassan."

"You're a woman. With a woman's timidity!"

Idris listened to the sound of the waves. His heart rapped unevenly. He glanced at Hassan, whose hair clung, wild and curly, to his forehead, like a bullock's. Idris felt himself seized by something beyond his control. He rose and crept across the beach without a word, watching his shadow as it kept dodging beyond the reach of the crisp white moonlight. He climbed over the rocks and stood for a moment under the tamarisks. He had cut his toe on a shell; the blood oozed forth, warm and painless. Even the pain in his temple had died away. His body felt numb, caught in a surge of inescapable terror. An eerie lightness carried him on. He felt himself moving among the sleepers, noiseless as a cat, light as a phantom. The excitement gripped him by the throat. He saw the girl asleep in the snow-white djellaba, and beside her the old woman, long and dark as a fallen branch. Her bag lay beside her, the buckle gleaming. The two men lay to the left of them, half lost in shadow. Idris crawled on all fours, feeling the soft

warm dust under his palms. He drew close to the sleepers; a
thread of nausea passed through him—not guilt, not fear,
merely a sickening sense of compulsion. A slant of moonlight
hung over the blond man's face; it looked beautiful, heroic,
inscrutable to Idris. Something stirred behind a tree trunk.
An animal wailed in the distance—the ghost hyena, could it
be? Idris paused, fixing his eyes on the circle of slumbering
Arabs.

He crept closer. Now he was crouching beside the bald little man in black, the one whom Hassan suspected of being an
ogre. Idris was sweating with suspense. A ring of dryness tin-
gled in his gullet. His body felt stiff as a grasshopper's. He
wormed his way past the little man, clinging to the patches of
shadow. Now he was kneeling two feet from the old woman's
head. He hesitated; a bitter taste, like dirty brass, clung to
the roof of his mouth. His fist tightened. Was she stirring?
Or was it the bald little man? His lips were moving. Was he
awake? No. He was snoring peacefully. Idris reached down
gingerly; his fingers crawled over the dust until they were
three inches from the shining buckle.

But then something happened to Idris. He sat paralyzed.
His hand was frozen. One tiny gesture and the precious jewels would be his. But he could not do it. His heart was seething
like a beehive. He waited helplessly, hoping that the bracelet
might leap out of the bag into his palm.

But nothing happened. It was no use. The elderly sir had
bewitched him. Or perhaps some benevolent sprite was pro-
tecting the elderly madame.

He crept back into the shadow of the trees and lay on the
ground, panting violently. The leaves overhead, scarcely
stirring, were silhouetted against the sky, which hung un-
naturally radiant, intense. He sensed a new hostility in the
gaze of the stars. One leaf was shaped like a glove. Another
looked like a crab—or perhaps it was several leaves. The foliage was infested with a kind of crawling malignance. He
could hear the waves licking away at the beach below him.

He rose and hurried back to the shore.

Hassan was lying on the sand. He smiled at Idris. "Did you do it?"

Idris blushed. "The elderly sir was awake."

"Did he see you?"

"Yes!"

Hassan's teeth flashed angrily. "Did you speak to him, Idris?"

"No."

"Did you touch him?"

"No!"

"Why not?"

"He is ugly, Hassan. I am frightened of him!"

Hassan seized the boy's wrist. "He will pay you, Idris! Go and try. Ask for three American dollars. Then we divide it." Hassan kept staring tensely into Idris's eyes.

"Not now," pleaded Idris. "Tomorrow! I promise!"

Hassan's eyes were bright with hashish. His chest heaved with excitement. He brushed Idris's cheek impatiently—half a caress, half a slap. "Yes! Now! Hurry up!"

Idris turned away miserably. A dark weight pressed on his brain. He could not rid himself of the subtle, accumulating malaise which obsessed him—something which tugged at his senses, drawing him toward a hidden act of violence.

"No, no," he kept pleading. "Be patient, Hassan."

Hassan shrugged his great shoulders and lay down on his back, trailing his fingers listlessly in the sand. He closed his eyes and started to snore. Idris leaned over and kissed him on the eyelids, then stole back to the heap of ashes and lay down noiselessly beside Ahmed.

11

Morning came; the four travelers were still asleep. Salah tip-toed across the dust and tapped Miss Todd on the shoulder. Some townsmen had come to be cured by "the scholarly madame from the sea." He set a cup of black tea on the ground beside her.

A crystal exhilaration filled the air. The wavelike clang of the bells rose from the town below. Miss Todd peered through the trees. Sabaya lay barren in the sun, white as a heap of sun-bleached bones washed by the sea. Tiny houses clustered along the slope beyond the shore, each built on the edge of the one below; each roof serving as a terrace and a poultry-yard for the house above; so that the village looked like an enormous scramble of stairs, littered with chickens and cats and punctuated by the salmon-pink needle of the minaret. Beyond Sabaya rose the hills. On the edge of the hills rose the castle. Beyond the castle there was nothing but a succession of ridges, rust-colored and empty, vibrating in the sunlight.

The sick and deformed had gathered in the tamarisk grove. There were twenty or thirty, and more coming, climbing in a piteous procession up the narrow path from the harbor. Miss Todd sat down on a rock with her leather kit, Ahmed beside her. One by one the lame and the blind and the ulcerous wandered up, humbly but shamelessly display-ing their ailments. Strange wounds, unidentifiable diseases, not to be found in the medical books: one had a serpent in his brain, one had a stone lodged in his backbone. Ants in the kneecap, water in the toes, a tiny fish trapped in the testes. One child, a beautiful girl with silver anklets, showed a torso covered with great blue stains.

Miss Todd applied antiphlogistine, eye lotion, iodine. She cut a bubo or two, administered quinine and penicillin. The procession grew, gathering pathos and resonance. There was little, almost nothing to be done for most of them. They lay sweltering in the dust, ranged in the fringe of shadow under the trees, shifting their ravaged bodies as the sun moved westward. One man had a terrible wound, splitting his chest from the throat to the navel. One woman was legless and arm-less, borne in the arms of her sons. Another was close to death with elephantiasis. Some looked like skeletons, hollow-eyed grandmothers and children. They all gazed at Miss Todd with reverent, imploring eyes. Finally the ointments gave out. By noon she was close to exhaustion.

Salah brought her a plate of rice and chicken livers, sprin-kled with raisins. She sat under an umbrella on the beach, cooled by a breeze from the gulf, and watched Idris dive into the waves with his spear. Ahmed was kneeling on the ground in front of her, massaging her feet and ankles.

"Your bones are weary, venerable madame!"

"I am old, Ahmed. Too old for Arabia."

"No!" cried Ahmed, solicitous. "Arabia will give you back your youth!"

Miss Todd felt disconcerted, loaded with some ill-defined regret. "You really think so, Ahmed?"

Ahmed looked at her sweetly. His strong brown fingers rolled over her instep. "Are you homesick, madame? So far and lonely?"

"I am never homesick," said Miss Todd, folding her hands.

"You carry your home with you, perhaps," said Ahmed decorously.

She looked at him with a new curiosity. It was the most intense, the most expressive face she had ever seen. But an expressiveness, an intensity veiled by a cool, impersonal gravity. He felt her gaze and lowered his eyes. He was murmuring to himself.

"Someday I shall visit England, madame."

"You won't be happy there, Ahmed."

Ahmed looked troubled. "Will they put me in jail?"

"No, it isn't that, Ahmed."

"Will they scorn me?" His eyes flashed.

"You belong to Arabia," said Miss Todd.

Idris came darting out of the waves, his curls flecked with foam. He thrust his spear into the sand and squatted beside Miss Todd, panting merrily.

"What are you fishing for, Idris?"

"Oh, any old fish," said Idris, rolling his eyes.

"Will you sell them?"

Idris simpered, tilting his head. "No one buys fish in Sabaya!"

"Will you give them away?"

"No one eats fish in Sabaya, madame. They all hate fish."

"Will you eat them yourself then, Idris?"

"No, no," said Idris. "I kill them for pleasure. I stab them" —he made a vicious thrust with his fist—"and send their spirits to join the clouds!"

She felt a strange lambent quality in Idris, warm yet remote. A thread of water was trickling over his cheek and down his shoulder. The full young lips and long lashes cast slate-blue shadows across his skin. He looked gentle as a dove, but a glint of wickedness played in his eyes. He was always gay, always smiling, hoping for fresh calamities.

"You are always happy, aren't you, Idris?"

Idris lifted his eyebrows, preening himself. "Because the Messenger of God has smiled on me. He has given me beauty and strength, madame."

He jumped up gleefully and skipped away, disappearing behind the rocks. Ahmed shook his head and murmured, "He is a squirrelish fellow, I'm afraid." He leaned forward and whispered, "When we reach Mukalla will you leave us, madame?"

"You can come to Aden if you wish, I suppose."

"Idris and I?" Ahmed smiled wistfully. "Yes. We will follow you to Aden. You will protect us, madame?"

"Ahmed! How on earth can I protect you?"

"You have power, venerable madame. You can conquer the demons!"

✿

That evening, outside the tamarisk grove, the men of Sabaya started singing. It was a song of gratitude, of beatification. Miss Todd had become a deity. Her gifts were saintly, beneficent. Akbar looked solemn as he sat listening behind a bush, his bright red beard cocked toward the sunset. A small child brought a pot filled with wilted flowers. Two donkeys were led through the grove, loaded with baskets of dates. Someone set a bowl of wild mountain honey before Miss Todd. She dipped a spoon, a bit hesitantly, in the glassy gold; it had a flavor of legend—opaque and biblical, incredibly sweet.

Finally the ceremonial singers and donkeys departed. The lamps of Sabaya gleamed in the dusk.

✿

A group of elders came strolling up the path. There was something ominous, Miss Todd observed, in their tread and demeanor. They strode in silence up to Akbar, and their spokesman started murmuring, raising his fingers and casting a low, hard glance toward Miss Todd.

"What do they want, Ahmed?"

"They are suspicious, madame." Ahmed frowned. "They think you are trying to plant an evil cult among the people."

"What nonsense, Ahmed!"

Ahmed looked miserable. "They think you are a witch, I think, madame."

The elders reclined in a sphinx-eyed semicircle under the drooping tamarisks. The harangues began. First one side spoke and then another. A tall man in a red *kufiya* got up and raised his hand.

"What have we to gain by disturbing them?" he argued in sonorous tones. "If their cures are sound, let us be grateful. If their cures are false, let us be tolerant."

A stout little man with a sharp, vituperative mouth cried out, "When has tolerance become a virtue, Ali al-Baissa? What have we to gain by helping our enemies?"

"How do we know they are our enemies?" said the man in the red kufiya.

"Can we be sure they are not?" snapped the pudgy one. "Is it wise to take chances, Ali al-Baissa? Better kill fifty friends than spare one enemy and then be destroyed by him!"

"This town," pleaded the tall thin man, "has never been inhospitable to helpless voyagers."

"These aren't voyagers, Ali al-Baissa. These are sorcerers! Unbelievers!"

"We live in a changing world," said the tall man half-heartedly.

"The curse of Allah be on them!" cried the stout one, shaking his fist.

The conference continued. The elders sat in a darkening semicircle, ugly men with huge mouths and black, crafty, close-set eyes. They were obviously enjoying themselves. Their hookahs made an agreeable bubbling noise. A feeling of infinite leisure, interminable patience, hung about them.

Miss Todd called Ahmed over. "What do they want, exactly? Would a bit of bakshish help, do you suppose?"

Ahmed tried to look casual. "Two of the men think you are spies. Three of the men think you are ogres. One isn't sure. One doesn't care. Only one has faith in your goodness, venerable madame."

An elder approached Ahmed with a goblet of yellowish tea and whispered in his ear, peering sidelong at Miss Todd.

Ahmed looked mortified. He beckoned and spoke to Salah. Salah approached Miss Todd with a sheepish air. "The say-yid has decided on a test. You and the elderly sir will obligingly drink this tea, madame. If you are spies or djinns, your skin will turn black." He stroked his beard and added affably, "If you are not djinns you will stay white, naturally."

"You're sure it is tea?" inquired Miss Todd.

"Oh, more or less." Salah coughed absently.

"Please tell the sayyid, Salah, that we will drink his wretched tea if he sips it first. After all, how can we know that it isn't poison?"

Salah bowed. "Very sensible, madame." He waddled over to the sayyid.

There was a whispered, slightly uncomfortable consultation.

The sayyid raised the goblet, wrinkled his nose and squinted, and took a gingerly sip of the amber liquid. He put it down and glared at Miss Todd with an embittered air.

Salah returned with the glass and passed it first to Dr. Moss and then to Miss Todd. They drank grimly. Miss Todd experienced a fleeting doubt regarding the nature of the beverage. She swallowed it quickly and beamed with determination at the assembled elders. The stout little man stared at her hopefully, waiting for her face to change color.

Another of the elders, a spry old dandy in a lilac turban, flung up his hands. He expostulated with the meek, hesitant sayyid. He was gradually working himself into a frenzy of xenophobia. Suddenly he rose and strode over and spat in the doctor's face. Dr. Moss leaped back, stiff with panic. Ahmed jumped between them and waved his hands. The man in the red kufiya raised his eyes apologetically.

The sayyid stepped forward, spreading his arms, as though to demonstrate his authority. Miss Todd sensed a curious unreality in all this turmoil.

Ahmed strode up with a downcast air and relayed the final decision of the village elders. "They are still suspicious, worthy madame. They won't listen to reason, I'm afraid. They want either a large sum or a sufficiently important hostage."

"We cannot afford large sums," said Miss Todd crisply. "And the idea of a hostage is outrageous."

"Just one little hostage," hinted Ahmed.

Miss Todd pursed her lips. "For example?"

"The elderly sir, perhaps, do you think?"

Miss Todd bridled. "Preposterous, Ahmed."

"He looks like a snake-djinn to the sayyid," quavered Ahmed unhappily.

Miss Todd suddenly felt quite weak. The landscape began to tremble; words, faces, trees, Sabaya, the whole labyrinth of mutual suspicions, all went spinning around in a whirlpool. She hardly noticed the coming of dusk, the dying of the heat, the departure of the elders. Their voices faded away like waves on a cliff. She sank to the ground under the tamarisk and sipped at the tea which Salah brought her. The pointed leaves above her stirred in a slow, feathery pattern. From the distance came the voice of a nightingale.

12

At nightfall the village nacouda came up with a message from the sayyid. The elders had arrived at a decision: the four faranchis were to spend the night in the castle.

They rode up the hill with the nacouda in front, and behind them two bowlegged soldiers in yellow kaftans. The castle rose from the top of the hill, blunt, medieval. Four broken turrets clung to the four uneven corners, and a moon oozed out of the roof like a great silver bubble. Black goats were wandering across the white-graveled slopes. They turned and grinned at the procession with their sly green eyes.

Three men came riding through the gate on ivory-haired donkeys. The nacouda introduced them as the lord of the fortress and his nephews—little square-set aborigines with brutish, embryonic faces, quite unlike the long regular features of the typical Arab. They peered blankly at Miss Todd. Ahmed stepped forward and explained; they had come to spend the night, he said politely. They needed food—dates and eggs, a bit of rice, perhaps—and a place to sleep, of course. They would leave the next morning.

The lord of the fortress listened craftily. Then he muttered something in a crude outlandish accent which escaped Miss Todd. She realized bleakly that they were half guests, half prisoners. They were led into the courtyard and through a series of passages and up a cinder-strewn stairway to their rooms. One of the nephews, sullen-eyed, led her through a tangle of corridors and flung open a door. Night had fallen. A tiny hag in a plum-blue barracan dipped through a curtain, set a lamp on the floor, whispered tremulously, "Mar-haba!" and vanished.

Miss Todd lay down on her bed, faint with an ominous fatigue.

The room was gaunt and dingy, but there was a spectral dignity about it, as though for centuries no thoughts had penetrated there except the thoughts of the dead. She watched the nervous arabesque of the lamplight on the wall. The flame died all of a sudden, as though someone had blown it out. But the pattern of light kept stirring gently, like a pale, floating animal. A feeling of peace, of obliteration, began to creep through Miss Todd. She lay on the bed and stared through the window, plucking the familiar stars out of the night. She carefully recited their names in Latin, one after the other, struggling to cling to the banks of her Western habits of thought. But the drift tugged irresistibly; her nerves grew supine and passive; she felt herself carried away on a stream of feeling more reckless, more elusive. New apprehensions, ambiguous reveries crept over her as she lay there. She grew aware of some sly, unsuspected pattern in the flow of events. One more episode, one further crisis, and the shape of the pattern would lie apparent. She gazed at the past, phase upon phase of it, with a wistful detachment. Surrey, Cheltenham, Girton; ivied walls, drizzling hockey fields. Cyprus, Singapore, Calcutta—harbors drenched with humanity. But through it all, untouched, unmodified, moved the obstinate entity of her own routine—the crisp, barren profile of Sybil Todd, exiled from passion.

She buried her face in the cashmere coverlet; her eyes grew blinded with pain.

But peace returned. Distant footsteps echoed across the crumbling terrace. There was a spice in the room, fresh and pungent, like rosemary. The light stirred on the uneven texture of the wall. There was a heightening in the atmosphere. Yes. The room was haunted. She felt sure of it now. But by whom? Not by anything alien, not by a Moslem presence, but by something fragile and intimate and pleading.

She rose and tiptoed out onto the terrace, into the world of the planets.

✿

There was a whisper just behind her. "Are we prisoners, do you suppose, Miss Todd?"

It was Dr. Moss. He stood in the shade of the turret, almost invisible.

"Not in any disagreeable way, I shouldn't think," said Miss Todd with a sigh. She sat down on the broken battlement, faintly dizzy.

Dr. Moss stood close beside her, tapping his fingers on the brick.

"Do you trust these people, Miss Todd?"

Miss Todd felt rather devious. "There is no occasion to trust anyone really, at this point, is there?"

Dr. Moss looked at her acidly, detecting a slur. "I must tell you quite frankly, Miss Todd," he said curtly, clearing his throat, "I have a peculiar feeling about these people. A distinctly unpleasant intuition."

"Yes?" She placed two fingers on her chin.

"Don't you feel something rather odd in the air?"

She smiled thoughtfully. "Are you afraid?"

Dr. Moss gazed at her wildly. "Good heavens! Aren't you?"

"Not in the least, my dear Doctor."

His eyes clung to her like a child's. "Ah. Well, no doubt you are right," he muttered dejectedly.

She felt maternal quite suddenly toward the little professor—a bit worried, a bit bored, but almost affectionate. The light of the stars sloped over his smooth pale forehead. There was a trembling in his jaw, as though he were bursting into tears.

"These people are good, worthy people," said Miss Todd rather indifferently. "But their values are different from ours, please remember, Doctor Moss."

"What are their values, may I inquire?"

"Valor. Piety. Honor."

"Not love?" whispered the doctor. "Not humanity, Miss Todd?"

"Not our kind of humanity," she said whimsically. "Not our kind of love, I'm afraid."

"They are irresponsible," snapped Dr. Moss, gathering courage. "They all border on criminality."

"Criminality, Doctor Moss?"

"You know what I mean, I think, Miss Todd."

"Forgive me," said Miss Todd. She felt her cheeks tingling with a rush of fever. The stars grew blurred; the night swam. "I don't believe I do, quite." She pressed her hands to her shoulders, struggling to keep back her temper. There was something she needed to say. "We must try—we must try to—"

Dr. Moss gazed at her through his tight little pupils; his spectacles gleamed. "Yes? What must we try?"

"We must try to love them," she said lamely after a moment.

She felt that all she had suddenly learned was now eluding her again, drifting away like the fumes from a brazier.

She wandered off, following the narrow black terrace around the roof. The land below stretched into a wind-scarred anarchy.

✿

"Madame! What are you doing here?"

A pale figure leaped out of the shadows. It was Ahmed, coiled in his jerd. He had lain asleep in the cooling breeze.

"Nothing, Ahmed. I've been strolling."

"You should not stroll here alone!"

"Why not, Ahmed?"

Ahmed glanced at the stars and said nothing.

"Allah will protect me," said Miss Todd, without quite knowing why she said it.

"Oh, madame!" Ahmed's eyes welled with love and surprise.

"Nothing evil will ever come to you, madame," he whispered. He sat down beside her on the coal-black mortar. For several minutes they said nothing. She felt his tenderness close beside her; his virile faith, his hard simplicity.

"The elderly sir is frightened," said Ahmed tentatively, guessing her thoughts.

"Yes. A bit, I imagine."

"The Makhfi has crept into him!"

"Mercy, Ahmed! What is the Makhfi?"

Ahmed's eyes were aglow. "The Hidden One, madame. May Allah preserve us! He is worse than all the djinns and all the *sikins*. He is the worst of the spirits. He makes men shrivel and turn purple. And then they die. I tell you, the elderly sir will bring sickness, madame!"

"Perhaps you exaggerate, Ahmed?" The breeze brushed her cheeks. And for a moment a wild, foolhardy gaiety seized her. "My dear Ahmed," she cried, "we're all full of djinns and naughty sikins!"

"No, no," whispered Ahmed passionately. "Don't mock me, venerable madame. They all believe it. The terrible Makhfi has crept into the elderly sir, I assure you!"

Nothing mattered to Miss Todd at this particular moment. She murmured faintly, "Perhaps it is the will of Allah?"

But Ahmed wasn't listening. He was staring at her beads of carved agate. "May I see?" he said, smiling, and opened his palm.

She slipped the chain over her head.

"Are they magic, dear madame?"

She smiled. "A little, maybe."

"Do they keep off the djinns?"

"Who knows? They are yours, Ahmed." The old listlessness was returning, nibbling away at her failing strength.

Ahmed grinned and pressed the beads to his sun-scarred cheek. "Do you long for England, madame?" he said softly a moment later.

"I think not," said Miss Todd.

"Will you be sent back there? When you are dead?"

Miss Todd paused and lowered her head. She felt no horror, no surprise, not even anger.

"No," she said gently. "I don't suppose so, Ahmed."

Ahmed gazed at her with a trembling look. He took her hand and raised it toward his heart. "May Allah shower blessings on you!" he said softly.

13

Soon after dawn Ahmed came and woke them up, one by one.
The air was crisp and transparent as they stole through the
cloistered courtyard. The little guards still lay snoring on
their narrow stone benches, smelling of sleep in their musty,
sweat-clinging *jubbas*. The party hurried down; the light
grew brighter. A voice bleated, "To prayers, to prayers!" And
then from the rooftops came the reedy call of the muezzin.
The new day began, flushed with expectancy. One more hour
and it would turn into merely another day, listless, perfunc-
tory, a day of lounging and loafing and coffee-drinking.

Ahmed guided them toward the swamps, where the fishermen would be waiting to take them around the cape. There,
the following evening, said Ahmed, a larger vessel would pick
them up. The *Guleïfa* had already sailed without them. But
he and Idris would stay with them.

"As far as Aden," whispered Ahmed.

Idris met them at the gate with a sack of rice and a slaugh-
tered kid, and the six of them—two sprightly Arabs and four
uneasy Anglo-Saxons—made their way down the slope toward the stagnant marshes.

Ahmed led them through a maze of turtle-brown hummocks. Their feet sank into the quagmire; an ugly smell oozed
from the ground. Large black crabs crept out of the crevices
—repulsive beasts with claws spread out, covered with a
beardlike growth of moss. They fled in battalions, clacking
their claws as they scampered seaward.

Finally the party came to the beach, which was gray and
muddy and desolate, quite unlike the clear, smooth beach at

Sabaya. White herons were flying high overhead, etched like a cry against the mute indifference of the sky.

Three fishermen were waiting at the edge of the sand with their sambouk—dark young men from Eritrea, or Sudanese perhaps. They rose in front of the strangers and bowed with an elegant solemnity. Miss Todd gazed at them, first startled, then a little preoccupied. They were naked except for their sky-blue loincloths, which brought out the deep, luminous brown of their bodies. They were the most magnificent men she had ever seen. The sunlight shed little scimitars across their muscles, which were shining with oil and dark with indigo. Their hair was like wire; their bellies flickered with light. One of them knelt to sharpen a stick with his knife. Then he rose in a single movement, smooth as a snake's, and slipped the knife under his wrinkled loincloth.

They stepped into the sambouk without a word.

✿

Mr. Maxwell was sitting beside Miss Todd in the boat.

They were heading for the cape, which sank deep cliffs into the salmon sea. Sabaya lay far behind them, bright as a coronet. Ahmed glanced nervously toward the harbor. The air was listless; they were moving slowly.

"Were you in India long, Mr. Maxwell?"

"Three years, Miss Todd."

"In Bombay?"

"Bombay, New Delhi."

"And now?"

"I'll be in Athens for a year or two."

He smiled slyly. She looked into his eyes, disconcerted. His lips were parted, his teeth shone. So simple, so childlike on the surface; so elusive underneath. A typical American? Not quite. Or had she misjudged him? There was irony in his smile. Drops of sweat shone on his handsome face, which was flushed and drawn with the Arabian sunlight.

A beautiful man, thought Miss Todd—but somehow cold,

incomplete. His hair, just graying at the temples, clung to his head like a helmet. His face was still youthful but deeply lined, reluctant. His voice was mild and melodious but oddly restrained, shy, tentative.

"Tell me, Mr. Maxwell, have we changed, do you think? Out here in the wilderness?"

A veil passed over his face. "Do people ever really change, Miss Todd?"

"Perhaps not." Miss Todd folded her hands serenely. "Not at heart, at any rate. Outwardly perhaps. But after all, isn't it better for wickedness to come out into the open? As it does in Arabia?"

David shot a cool, startled look at Miss Todd. "Really, I think—" he began.

Idris waved his arm and shouted, "Look, Ahmed!"

There was the sound of a gun. The spray shot up where a bullet skimmed over the water, a hundred yards or so to the left. The fishermen cursed. Ahmed bellowed, "Treachery!" Another bullet entered the sea. A moment later there were three more shots. The passengers lay flat on their bellies. The boat rocked lazily in the glare of the sea.

They waited ten minutes. The fishermen raised their heads and peered toward the shore. There was a cloud of dust where the horsemen were galloping back toward Sabaya. They waited ten minutes more. Silence hung in the air like a bubble.

Slowly they rounded the cape. Sabaya was lost from sight.

✿

They landed in a tiny natural harbor surrounded by barren hillocks. Here, said Ahmed, they would have to spend the night, unfortunately. Perhaps the following night as well. The passengers stepped across the sand, which was hot and sharp as a bowl of cinders.

Miss Todd felt herself weakening as she limped toward the shade. Something new was in the air—something invisibly but fatefully wrong. Or no—not quite. Something subtly but appallingly right. Things were falling into their neat, appointed pattern. She groped her way through the rocks. The vision was upon her. A black thread started to vibrate in front of her eyes. Everything around her—the silent fishermen, the whiff of tar from the little sambouk—all were pointing in a single, sinister direction. The great thing was about to happen. Some final reconciliation perhaps? No, not yet. Something hovered just beyond her reach—an aura, an emanation.

She called, "Mr. Maxwell!"

The American knelt beside her.

"I have a favor to ask you, Mr. Maxwell." She opened her bag and took out a pigskin case. "Here. Please. These are safer in your hands, I'm sure, than in mine." She opened the case. A string of pearls, a diamond brooch, a sapphire bracelet. "They might be useful, don't you think?" She smiled wearily at the horizon. "One other thing, Mr. Maxwell."

"Yes, Miss Todd?"

"About Sylvia. She is only a child, you know. And then, you see—" She looked swiftly at the American, trying to appraise him. Was she wrong? Was he not quite so perceptive, perhaps, as she thought? "Be kind to her, please, Mr. Maxwell!"

The American stared at her, horrified. He started to speak, but said nothing.

Miss Todd looked away. Idris was crouching among the rocks. Ahmed was building a fire for the midday meal. Sylvia was dipping her feet in the water, and Dr. Moss was wiping his sun-glasses. The fishermen below were bailing out the sambouk.

Miss Todd lay back and closed her eyes, suddenly dizzy with pain.

14

A line of flamingos passed over the shore toward sunset. They floated above the dunes, with their great claws trailing. Then they were gone; the sky grew hollow and lifeless.

Miss Todd turned her head away from the sun. A twinge of pain dug at her neck. Her head shot forward as she gasped for breath. The pain was like a burning wire slowly tightening around her larynx.

The air thinned, and a last mirage went dancing over the plain—a patch of oil which lay squirming like fat in a frying pan.

For one moment, as the light grew vibrant, the sandy hills were flooded with gold, which scattered its brightness like a field of corn rippling in the wind. Then all grew subdued. Light, color, shape, shadow, all withdrew, leaving only a haze of equivocal, dove-gray masses. These too lost substance a moment later, and only stillness remained, the yawning vacancy of the Arabian dusk.

She closed her eyes. Her hold on reality was shriveling away. All was emptiness—a gaping, repellent void. Her senses kept struggling, trying to grasp a human residue. There was none—no passion, no communication. She lay stiff with horror. Nothing was real or identifiable. She felt herself yielding to a force grander, more ruthless than she had ever experienced. The pain grew blurred as it swept through her body. It was like a giant wave sweeping her up.

A minute later it vanished. She felt a surge of relief. Her nerves lay passive, subdued. She let herself flow on a current of images. The forms and colors fell into a haphazard pattern like the chips of glass in a kaleidoscope. A familiar landscape emerged, as though by sheer accident. A small stream flowed through a copse of beech trees and went winding past a meadow. Buttercups danced in the wind, their petals glossy as satin. In the distance rose the moss-gloved walls of the ruined abbey. Swallows dipped through the windows. The air was windless, the grass unruffled. The beeches stood motionless on the hillside, glowing like freshly poured bronze. A distant figure, a young woman's, was waving from the arch of the gate. A bird called. The world seemed caught under a bell of glass.

She sank back into the Hadhramaut. The light was slipping from the edge of the water. A perpetual dusk seemed about to enclose the world. There was no sign of life except for a black-shelled crab which crossed the sand and slid into the oily waves.

✿

Sylvia came up and knelt beside her. Miss Todd felt her nearness without opening her eyes.

"Miss Todd," Sylvia whispered.

"My dear Sylvia. It's been a difficult day."

"Dear Miss Todd! Are you better?"

"Of course. Why shouldn't I be?" She patted Sylvia on the head. "Go and have a nap before dinner, my dear."

Sylvia took her hand and pressed it to her lips. Suddenly she burst into tears. "Miss Todd, Miss Todd!"

"Good heavens! What's wrong, dear?"

"I'm frightened, Miss Todd!"

"Perfect nonsense," snapped Miss Todd. She looked more closely at Sylvia. What was it that disturbed her? "My dear Sylvia," she said softly, "there is nothing to be afraid of!"

"Miss Todd—"

"There. Be quiet, dear."

Sylvia knelt silently beside her. Dusk lapsed into night, and a marshy breeze rose from Ash Shihr.

✿

A little later she woke up again. A white-hot needle shot through her, stabbing her chest and clawing its way toward the tip of her skull. She bit her palm in a fierce, half-crazed determination not to scream.

The pain passed again, leaving her utterly limp. The wind from the gulf played lightly over her face. The air was full of a spicy, mintlike freshness. The sea blazed under the starlight, bright and tremulous, intensely near. She felt she could touch it with her fingertips—like the scales of a trout.

She glanced at the stars, suddenly startled. She realized abruptly that she was dying.

Ahmed crept up beside her.

"Look, Ahmed. The stars . . ."

He cocked his head. "Yes, my madame. The stars are on fire."

"See—that one! Almost green!"

"Ah," breathed Ahmed. "It is the star of Courage."

Miss Todd touched his cheek with her fingertips, stirred by a deep, quaint tenderness. "Ahmed, Ahmed—I wonder—"

"Madame! Lie back! You are weak!"

"Dear Ahmed. I feel quite well."

His face melted in a look of compassion. "Madame," he said in a trembling voice, "I truly love you. If I could give away ten years of my life"—he plucked at his thick brown chest—"I would give them all to you, illustrious madame!"

Miss Todd smiled. "You are a generous man, darling Ahmed." She added abruptly, "How is your snake today?"

Ahmed squeezed his hands gratefully. "Oh, just the same as yesterday. A little bit hungry and bored, I think."

He tucked his hand into his futah and pulled out the snake by the tail. The poor reptile looked disconsolate, with blood-shot eyes and a sagging chin. It curled up in Ahmed's lap, burying its snout under its tail. Ahmed started to charm it, waving his forefinger and humming. "Look! He hears the snake-angels!" The old snake swayed halfheartedly. Then it lay down again with a crushed, dyspeptic air.

Ahmed slapped its neck with his thumb. "Bad, lazy Iuslim!"

Iuslim blinked guiltily and crawled back under the sash.

Everything grew black; Miss Todd's head suddenly fell forward. She lapsed into a deep and dreamless slumber.

✿

She woke up at sunrise, feeling surprisingly well. She turned her eyes and looked toward the sea. A cool, green haze veiled the distant sambouks and the tiny fishermen. Life was straining at the leash, waiting to burst into color. She stared at the sea, feeling the heightening suspense in the air. The light came closer, unfolded. But then something went wrong. Instead of a burst of splendor there was only an air of pause, of indecision. The light shot forth, but a moment later it defeated itself as the brilliance dissolved in a barren overdose of illumination.

Several of the men were down by the water, saying their morning prayers. The surf looked windless, serene. No hint as yet of that globe of heat which lurked in the tawny hills, waiting to explode.

Idris was calling to one of the fishermen. The fisherman called back. Mr. Maxwell was wading through the shallows, taking his morning dip.

Miss Todd was aware that she had something urgent to say to Sylvia, and was about to call. She felt a twinge of discomfort; she decided to wait. She rose cautiously and crept toward the hidden space between two rocks. There she crouched for a minute or two, aware of a dull, gathering vertigo.

She got up and started back. But the world suddenly lurched; the sea shot up at a dizzy slope. She gripped the rock for support and leaned over it helplessly, waiting for the spasm to pass.

And then she grew conscious of a rapid change in her body. She felt her skin growing brittle, like the shell of an egg—under the shell a new awareness was developing, a fabric frail and sensitive as cobweb. The eggshell began to crackle; it was falling away, chip by chip. The light grew feverishly real, as though it were taking on a new dimension, as though the sky were reaching forward and backward into time. She murmured hastily to herself, "Yes. Yes. At last." Her mind floundered aimlessly, caught in a great white web.

"Now," she whispered. "Now, *now*—" The last of her questions was about to be answered. The sky sang, "One more minute!" "Wait! Wait!" cried the sea.

BOOK TWO

The City

15

They crept quietly down to the shore at twilight. The air hung thin, gray, secretive. Gulls were wheeling above the rocks.

The rites had been performed in their own cursory fashion. Ahmed had wept, Idris had prayed. Miss Todd had been buried in a corner of the inlet, where a fan of rock overhung the sand, leaving it in continual shadow. A decorous silence covered the shore; the men squatted among the stones, waiting. The new vessel finally arrived, older and shabbier than the *Guleïfa*. The crew came ashore in the little *youyou,* headed by the captain, Mohammed bin Aissa.

"We must be quick," said Mohammed gruffly. "Or the islanders will find us."

They boarded the *Fatima* at nightfall and slid quietly out to sea. She was a dhow from Oman, perhaps eighty feet long, with a little deck at the stern above the hollow thwarts. The compass was framed in a small brass temple with a lamp inside. There was something in the smallness and dilapidation of the boat which was somehow impressive, antique, heroic.

"How old is she?" asked David.

"Oh, the age of Abdullillah over there," said Saïd merrily.

Abdullillah and Mohammed were the old ones, wise and bitter with the sea, faces hacked like driftwood. They looked like figures out of the Arabian nights with their woolly beards and tattered robes and silver knives thrust in their belts. Nasir and Saïd were the young ones. Saïd was thickset and garrulous, with a pock-marked face and eyes like a deer's. Nasir was a dark-skinned Apollo, aloof and impenetrable.

They hoisted the sails to a whining irregular chant. The men slid about in their futahs, their long thin muscles gleaming like iron. Night fell. The little dhow kept humming as she sped along on the brink of the waves. The hours passed silently. The men lay down and dozed among the bales. David watched the sails move slowly across the stars. Mohammed bin Aissa sang the same little tune over and over, his voice so low that it seemed to rise out of the waves.

David slept and woke up again. Sylvia lay wrapped in Ahmed's djellaba, no larger than a child, her cheeks bright as satin under the starlight. Dr. Moss lay curled up on the opposite side of the deck. The sea rose around them into a wrinkled plateau, while the distances beyond sank into great yawning hollows. The echoing gulf, low, tender, welled all around them. The rich proximity of the sea was like the presence of a slumbering herd. On they sailed, cutting the black, white-bubbled turmoil.

Morning came, thin and pearly, and they passed a group of small islands—volcanic cones rising above semicircular white beaches. There was a derelict squalor about this land-locked water. Shallow lagoons lay filled with idly floating jetsam. The tide was low; the coral reefs were ripe with stench. Waterlogged canoes were drifting through the spreading light. In the deeper transparency the *Fatima's* passengers could see the shapes of giant rays. Along the mirage-studded shore rose great shining steeples which suddenly dwindled, as the boat approached, into drab little fishermen's huts. Some Somali boys were harpooning the rock-dwelling fish with their *harbas*. An old man sat on a rock, smoking his water-pipe.

Suddenly they saw a large *boutre* emerge from the shelter of one of the cliffs and pass slowly southward over the dead brown sea. She was an odd-looking vessel, squat and somehow surreptitious—not quite a fishing boat, not quite a coaster. She passed several cable-lengths to the leeward of the *Fatima*.

Mohammed bin Aissa drew his hand over his chin. Nasir stood by the wheel, pale and expressionless.

The breeze grew gusty. A southerly blow was making up.

The day spread into a pattern of racing clouds. A heavy swell foreboded the violence of the oncoming wind. They passed a new group of rocks, a wild, tortuous archipelago. Then they saw several sails emerging from the silhouetted cliffs behind them, running before the gathering storm.

"Look," said Abdullillah, folding his arms around his bony chest. His fierce little face stood out like a hatchet, the beard cocked impudently at the hidden sun. The men glanced darkly at the mysterious vessel, which now appeared to be following the *Fatima*. She loomed high and narrow, end on, directly astern of them, a snow-white pillar rising from the sea. The *Fatima*'s wake pointed toward her like a broken reflection. She was moving swiftly. The *Fatima* took heart and gathered speed unexpectedly, flicking lightly at the burst of foam as she passed. Now and again a flash of spray flew up at David's face. Sylvia was crouching on the deck, peering like a dwarf through the hood of the djellaba.

Mohammed bin Aissa looked querulous. They were being followed; that was obvious. Was the vessel gaining on them? Ever so slightly, perhaps. The thrill of the race seized their spirits. Now the wind came in great rollicking gusts, and once a spear of sunlight pierced the rolling clouds. They saw the tall white sail flash in the momentary brightness, swaying in their wake like a mighty blade. Then it faded again in the murky shade of the clouds.

David stood behind Ahmed. "Will she catch us, Ahmed?"

Ahmed smiled in his cool, grave way and gazed absently at Mohammed, who seemed lost in the gloom of some private enigma.

"We'll keep our distance till dusk," growled Ahmed. "Then we'll haul off to seaward." The coast emerged and receded as the squalls of rain passed between them. Abdullillah sat on the stern deck near the rudder head, his profile like a gargoyle's against the banners of cloud.

"She's in chase," he croaked. "She's in chase all right."

"Do they know who we are?" said David.

"Know?" snarled Abdullillah. "Of course they know!"

"Who told them?"

Abdullillah squeezed his lips shut and tightened the cape around his neck.

Now the vessel was gaining on them unmistakably—more and more swiftly, it seemed. They shaved the cape. For an instant the sails hung idle to the masts as the wind failed suddenly in the shelter of the promontory. Then the gust returned and filled them again, and the dhow sped along on the smoother water. The *Fatima* seemed suddenly liberated, sweeping along exultantly as the clouds fell apart.

"A bad ship," remarked Ahmed, squatting beside David.

"Who are they, Ahmed?"

"Who knows? Pirates from Ethiopia, maybe."

"What are they after?"

"Ah! Plunder. Gold. Diamonds. Sapphires."

David grew thoughtful. "Tell me, Ahmed. Do you trust these men?"

Ahmed glanced silently across the deck; finally his gaze rested on Nasir.

Now it was growing darker. Again the larger vessel was gaining on them. She looked like a ghost ship to David as she swayed in the *Fatima*'s wake, no longer white but a drab, elephant gray. Night crept toward them. The squall had died. The coast disappeared. The *Fatima* sprang into the sudden darkness like an arrow. The pursuer vanished from sight, but David sensed, under the air of relief, some lingering flavor of treachery.

Mohammed bin Aissa leaned toward Saïd and whispered in his ear; then he beckoned to Nasir and swung his jerd over the bottom of his face.

Nasir walked slowly back and took hold of the tiller. His fine, tense eyes were frozen and clouded.

✿

Suddenly Saïd cried out, "Broken water ahead!"

At that same moment there was a noise under the *Fatima*'s

keel—the scrunching of coral. A quiet shudder passed through the ship.

Saïd screamed from the bows, "The ship is aground!"

Mohammed bin Aissa ran forward. They felt the grip of the hidden rocks on the keel tightening slowly. And then a small, crisp crash as the ship settled hopelessly. The hiss of the water had died. There was a sinister stillness, broken only by the silky whine of the wind. A moment later David heard the sound of a gradual, gentle gurgling—a rush of water and then a quick tense lapping against the inner walls of the ship. The *Fatima* was sinking. Saïd was throwing the deck cargo overboard. The ship swayed, leaned over heavily. She shook with a brittle, splintering sound each time a new wave seized her and vainly tried to shake her loose.

A sharp wail rose, almost human; some new wound had been inflicted. David could see the fish of prey already gathering, darting about in streaks of phosphorescence.

A long deep creaking issued from the heart of the ship, and a moment later the mast came crashing as the poop-deck split and leaped in the air. But the men were already climbing into the youyou, laden with water and rice. David leaned over, lifting Sylvia into the dinghy, and that same moment he caught sight of two dark arms gripping Nasir from the back. There was a bark like a mastiff's as both men shot overboard. The other men, grunting with fear, were all in a cluster, hauling desperately at the little youyou. Saïd was scrambling on all fours. Dr. Moss leaped clumsily. Sylvia called to David, "Quick!" David reached out and felt himself gently, irresistibly tugged from behind; and then something, perhaps the swinging tiller, knocked him over senseless.

✿

He came to in the youyou. It was moving through the shelter of a cove. Saïd and Abdullillah were keeping her straight with their oars. They made for the strip of sand which shone in the moonlight, and presently landed. Ahmed picked up

Sylvia in his arms and waded through the shallow water. Dr. Moss climbed on Idris's back and was dropped on the sand as decorously as possible.

But David was hardly aware of them. The pain in his head felt heavy as a rock. Saïd kept daubing the bruise with a small wet cloth as David lay by the fire.

"Feeling better?" said the doctor presently, settling himself beside David.

"It's nothing," said David, closing his eyes. "Just a nasty little bump."

"Scoundrels," said the doctor. "Absolute scoundrels."

David turned away listlessly. A dark speck swam on the edge of his consciousness. It was like the missing piece in a puzzle. He rehearsed the days' events in his mind, trying to bring them into order. But something kept eluding him. Some crucial fact kept sliding out of his grip. He tried to visualize in turn the plane, the ship, the island, the castle, the harbor, searching for some pungent, revelatory detail; but as soon as an image crystallized in his mind a tiny stain emerged from one corner, spreading a blur across his vision.

The pain in his head grew less. He listened to the embers crackling. A knob of sand dug at his shoulder; he turned sideways and caught sight of Dr. Moss staring into his eyes with a strange, nervous intensity. He shifted his position so that only the sweep of the sea was visible, and fell into a heavy, oppressive slumber.

✿

It was dawn when he woke up again. A scarlet sun was rising, gilding the frail, pitiful wreck which still trembled in the distance.

Saïd brought them their tea, and the Moslems said their prayers. Then they climbed back into the youyou and followed the coast.

16

They reached Bir Barnut at noon. Saïd bargained for two hours with the local nacouda for the men and donkeys to take them to Kumra. No large vessels touched Bir Barnut; it would be best to reach Kumra by land—especially, hinted Ahmed, since the seas were "unfriendly." Abdullillah and Saïd, the cook, would go along, as well as Idris and Ahmed. At Kumra, explained Ahmed, they would take a camel caravan which would head toward Mukalla. Presently the carriers appeared, their torsos dyed indigo, arms hung with silver amulets, and sardonyxes tied to their necks—to "cure wounds," as Ahmed explained, with a touch of envy.

"Greedy tribes!" said Abdullillah disapprovingly, gesturing toward the *soukh*.

"What do they want?" inquired David.

"Ten rupees for each donkey," said Saïd. "And five rupees for the food, and five for each carrier."

"Quite a lot, don't you think?"

Saïd belched. "A very big lot!"

"What is the food, do you suppose?"

"Rice. Dates. Tea. Limes."

"Any meat?"

Saïd pointed noncommittally at two glassy-eyed cockerels which hung jangling against a kettle.

"Three rupees apiece," he said wryly.

"Rather skinny, aren't they?"

"Oh, not very. For three rupees they are sufficiently fat."

Presently the donkeys appeared, and the final preparations were made. David bought a new djellaba for Sylvia, whose dress was in tatters. Dr. Moss purchased a small green skull-cap, embroidered with yellow braid. David felt extremely well; the pain in his head had gone completely; there was only a tiny plaster to mark the bruise. The misgivings, the disorientation of the previous night were gone. Everything seemed, in this crystal air, unusually neat, clear, solid. He reached instinctively toward his pocket. Yes, the little jewel-case was still there. He took Sylvia by the hand, and they strolled through the little soukh, pawing the stray bits of leather and brass and pottery.

The heat of noon died away, and the little caravan started off, heading for the labyrinth of hills which shielded Bir Barnut from the west. Zebra-striped lizards two feet long ran scuttling in front of the donkeys' hoofs. A line of corrugated cliffs rose suddenly to a barren plateau, beneath which yawned the gullies filled with slow, reddish waters. The ancient camel paths went zigzagging past onion-shaped mounds, and as the light grew dusty with evening the contours of the land grew spidery, the rough sprawling shadows grew blue and ghostly. They passed a group of men in the distance, pilgrims to Mecca maybe—naked men with shaved heads, each carrying a black parasol. They moved through the clouds of dust with glazed, vacuous expressions, as though they were floating on little clouds.

✿

The air up in the foothills was pure, pellucid. The sea vanished in the south. They entered the heart of Arabia.

A young boy named Mustafa walked beside David's donkey. He started off in high spirits, but toward dusk he was wincing with pain; his feet were swollen and bleeding. David swung from his donkey and placed the boy in the saddle.

Mustafa smiled, rather uncomfortably.

Five minutes later he climbed off again. "Now I am well," he explained gallantly.

"Look! Your heel is all swollen!"

"No, it is fine," pleaded Mustafa. His spaniel eyes beamed softly at David as he stroked the donkey's mane.

The donkey was a delightful, intelligent creature, listening to every word with his long blue ears laid back. His eyes were full of a liquid, quizzical surmise; his body was as trim as a ballerina's. The staccato of his hoofs was crisp and cheerful, like a spoon in a teacup.

"What is his name?" said David.

Mustafa blushed and said nothing.

"Even a donkey should have a name, Mustafa."

"We call him Queen Victoria, sir."

"But Queen Victoria was a lady!"

"Ah," said Mustafa. "She was a queen!" He grinned delightedly. "The donkey also is a fine, elegant queen!"

They entered the valley, and the hard gray dirt changed to a sucking, slithering sand. A small town clung like a bird's nest to the crest of the hill.

"In three weeks," said Mustafa proudly, "we will have a war with that town."

"Really? Why?"

"The truce expires," said Mustafa, placing his finger against his nose. "It was a two years' truce. Now everyone is all excited about the war."

"*Must* there be a war, Mustafa?"

Mustafa looked puzzled. "It will be a fine war, I think, sir. Sieges. Shooting. Revenge. Everyone is pleased about the war coming."

Dr. Moss was following close behind them. Mustafa turned uneasily. His face grew clouded.

"Tell me, Mustafa—"

"Sh! Sir—"

"What is wrong?"

"*He* is listening!" whispered Mustafa, glancing at Dr. Moss, and scampered ahead on his bleeding feet to walk beside Idris.

✿

They settled for the night at the wall of Qubaida. At sunset the view had spread on every side for many miles, but when night fell the hills closed in like a curtain.

A goat was roasting on a spit in the fire Saïd had lit, and the men lolled lazily in the lap of a dune. The flames were licking at the meat with little blue tongues. They were all in a sulky mood. No one sang; no one was smiling. Dr. Moss was scribbling away in his notebook, and Sylvia sat silently with her chin on her hands, dark and windburned under the hood of the white djellaba.

The meat crackled and was done. Saïd cried, "To the feast, gentlemans!" One by one the men got up and walked to the fire, cut off a chunk of meat, and lumbered back to the circle, munching. One or two of them prowled off with their bones, like dogs, to chew them alone in the darkness.

The fire grew low. The men were dozing. The real world receded. Dr. Moss crept off into the dunes with his rug. Sylvia sat staring into the embers.

"What are you dreaming about?" said David.

Sylvia started. "About Miss Todd!"

"Miss Todd?" said David.

The name echoed faintly, like a pebble dropped into a well.

"I almost feel she's still here," said Sylvia, glancing behind her.

"She loved you," said David. "Very much, I think."

He was watching Sylvia with a new curiosity, as though he were trapping a butterfly. Some subtlety in her nature seemed on the brink of revelation. She drew her fingers along her cheek. The light from the coals played on her face; she looked wild, Polynesian, peering through her long black lashes.

"You are a very brave girl," said David softly.

She glanced at him quickly. "No," she whispered. "I'm not brave. I was terribly frightened once or twice!" She leaned

forward and peered at him anxiously. "Tell me, Mr. Maxwell.
Are they following us?"

"Don't worry. We'll be in Kumra tomorrow."

"Do you think, Mr. Maxwell—"

"Call me David, won't you?"

"Something is wrong. What is it, David?"

"We're Unbelievers, remember. They've been taught to
hate us."

She glanced cautiously toward the dunes, where Dr. Moss
lay curled in a blanket.

"It's—*he*, isn't it?"

David paused. "What makes you think so?"

"The way they look at him. Haven't you noticed?"

"I can't say I have."

"And then—"

"Yes?"

"There *is* something a wee bit odd about him!"

"Poor little man. So out of place."

"They're afraid of him, aren't they, David?"

"Go to sleep, my dear. You're imagining things."

She lay down on her side with a sigh, staring at the ash-
furred embers. David watched her fall asleep. Her arm
twitched faintly, like a sleeping animal's.

He lay back, slightly drugged by the heaviness of the evening meal. One hand lay stretched out on the sand; the other
lay cupped over his pocket. Little by little his consciousness
ebbed from the tips of his body; his fingers and toes, then his
wrists and ankles, then his elbows and knees relaxed into
sleep. His senses nodded; his eyes and his ears and even his
nostrils dozed off. Finally only a small, clear knot in the tip
of his brain still hung awake—a tiny bulb of awareness, afloat
on a sea of slumber like a cork bobbing among the waves. It
was a moment of isolated, accentuated susceptibility. Even as
he lay there he was obscurely aware of its power; just enough
to say to himself, Something is wrong, something is going to
happen. . . .

But then, as far as the visible world was concerned, nothing did happen. The Arabs slept without stirring, the fire gradually died, and the desert grew black as pitch, until at last, very stealthily, like a ferret stalking its prey, a wispy, lemon-bright moon rose out of the dune to the right of the well-house.

17

The next day dawned bright as a crystal, and they started across the *jol*. In the early sun the blunt red mounds cast arrowy shadows, which played like waves on the tortured skin of the limestone.

Three hours later they rode downhill again toward the river-bed. Lean white goats strolled through tufts of *Salvadora persica,* and a tiny shepherdess lurked in the distance, wearing a conical black hat. The sunlight flashed on her hatchet as she chopped the twigs from the fuzzy saplings.

Sylvia waved to her as they passed. The shepherdess gaped at her bashfully and went galloping lightly over the bushes.

They went on riding along the wadi-bed, keeping to the sides of the wadi, under the fringe of shadow cast by the steep corroded shore.

A boy was loitering in the distance with a kite on a string. Idris called to him teasingly, *"Qabunum tayib!"*

"What is he saying?" asked Sylvia.

David wasn't quite sure. He asked Idris, but Idris merely grinned and made an obscene gesture.

An old woman in a purple hood passed by, making her way across the wadi-bed with a watering pot on her shoulders. She stood and watched them, half covering her face.

"How far is it to Kumra?" cried Idris, exuberant.

"Oh, just the throw of a stick," squealed the woman, placing two fingers on her forehead.

A dark figure came riding across the plain. He drew closer through the dust, which swirled about him like a cape, and soon the glittering black mare came prancing alongside the donkeys. The most romantic-looking man she had ever seen, thought Sylvia. His bare feet hung stirrupless; his torn robe danced in the wind; over his shoulder he carried a very old rifle. A bittersweet smell hung about him, like heather.

"Your identifications, if you please," he said in a quaint, ingratiating accent. He reached out his hand toward Dr. Moss.

Dr. Moss took off his sun-glasses. "What on earth does he want?"

"Papers. Passport," said Ahmed.

Dr. Moss dug into his pocket and held out his passport defiantly.

The soldier ran his coarse dark finger through the pages. Then he slid the passport casually under his belt.

"Give it back!" cried Dr. Moss.

The soldier muttered a few hoarse words to Ahmed.

"He says you will get it back in Kumra," said Ahmed, expressionless.

Dr. Moss flung his arms into the air with a cry of exasperation. The soldier sat on his horse and watched him sardonically.

He was glorious, it seemed to Sylvia. There he sat on his sweating mare, his robe furled carelessly around his great brown shoulders, the black hairs spreading from the center of his chest like a silken fan.

Dr. Moss cried in his quavering voice, "Outrageous! Scandalous! I shall put in a vigorous complaint in Aden!"

The soldier flashed a great white smile at Sylvia, turned on his horse, and galloped away. Soon he was lost again in a cloud of dust.

Sylvia watched him dreamily as he vanished across the jol.

"He liked you, mademoiselle," said Ahmed, with a light in his eyes.

"Oh, Ahmed! Do you think so?"

"He thought you were a boy, mademoiselle!"

"But Ahmed—"

Idris was whispering furtively in David's ear, glancing all the while at Dr. Moss. Mustafa was tenderly stroking Queen Victoria's ears.

✿

The distant rocks looked like great razors, carving away at the sky. The gravel cut at the donkey's feet with sharp red edges. Even the light had a cutting edge, giving things a peeled, surgical appearance.

They came to another well, the last one before Kumra, and rested on a carpet of blossoms in the shade of a giant tree. It was the only tree for miles and miles; it looked like the only tree in Arabia. There was an air of the miraculous about it.

"What is the name of this tree?" said Sylvia, leaning her head against the trunk.

"It has no name," said Ahmed. "We call it the tree between Bir Barnut and Kumra."

"There—those small yellow flowers. Do they have a name, Ahmed?"

"They are nameless," said Ahmed patiently. "Just flowers. That's all they are."

He leaned closer and said softly, "Our land is hard and barren. We do not like useless words. We do not have many names."

He winked at her playfully and lay down in the shade and fell asleep.

Suddenly Saïd gave a cry and came running up to Ahmed. "Come!"

Sylvia followed them around the well to a clump of grass on the edge of the slope. A small green snake shot past and vanished. She stepped forward cautiously; a sickening stench of decay swept toward her. The Arabs were leaning over a large dark bundle. Saïd was prodding it with a stick. Idris turned away, nauseated. Ahmed's face had grown grave and preoccupied. An oily stain spread over the sand beneath the dead man's swollen body. He must have been dead a week or more. Saïd gave a thrust. The corpse rolled over; the face was seething with maggots.

"Don't," cried Ahmed. "Don't touch him!"

The men recoiled. Idris seized Sylvia by the hand and drew her back.

Abdullillah flung his jerd over his cheeks so that only his foxy little eyes shone forth, shrill and agitated. "The blue sickness," he kept whispering. "The terrible Makhfi!"

Ahmed cast three handfuls of sand over the body and drew a pattern on the nearby earth, diamond-shaped. In the center of the diamond he placed three little stones, and then he spat scrupulously between the stones.

"To frighten the Makhfi," breathed Idris. "Come, little madame. Bad, bad!"

✿

They rode on toward Kumra and entered a narrow valley, where they met a pious-faced procession. Dark peasants swayed lazily past the trees on their small white donkeys, with maybe a sheep flung over the saddle, or a bag of rice. Two Negro soldiers followed the peasants, wearing only their cartridge belts. Then came a column of women with enormous baskets on their heads, sky-blue trains billowing along on the sand behind them.

"Where are they going?" said Sylvia discreetly.

"To the feast," said Ahmed, squinting.

"What sort of feast?"

"Oh, just a feast. It has no name." He smiled indulgently at Sylvia. "Many things have no name in our land, little madame!"

The old patriarchs filed past them, clad in snow-white, and then a row of dark-hooded folk who kept whispering and chanting. Only their eyes were visible as they lumbered past; and their bony hands, black with the sun, clutching the sacred phials.

18

They rode down the slope and entered a deep ravine. The hardening light of the afternoon drew tiger stripes across the opposite ridge.

Sylvia's bones were aching with the jolts of the donkey-ride. Her skin was burning. The powerful light refracted from the gravel seemed to pierce even the folds of her cape.

"Kumra!" cried Idris.

A line of cliffs shot out of the east, and suddenly Sylvia caught sight of the city perched between two crags—a giant structure of limestone and mud, dented by columns of black-silled windows.

"A holy city," observed Idris. "Bad for the Unbeliever."

"No matter," said Ahmed quickly. "We stay only a night. Two nights at the most."

Three men came riding over a hillock. One of them shook a stick and hailed them briskly. "Are you friends, over there?"

"Friends! Certainly! All of us!"

"Whose friends, may I ask?"

"Friends of the Sayyid of Masna'a!"

"Peace be with you!"

"You too!"

The men rode on.

The path turned, and they saw the cliff looming in front of them like a great ant-hill, with a fringe of lights twinkling in the dusk. The city gradually lost its impressiveness as they drew closer. The proportions seemed to shrink; the houses looked grim and squalid. As they rode alongside the walls the scent of sewage welled up at them. They entered the gate. A swarm of ragamuffins came gamboling through the dust, crying hoarsely. Abdullillah jabbed his umbrella at them; they flew, twittering, into the crannies, like a flock of sparrows.

Ahmed led the way down a winding street and came to a halt by a bronze door. An old man came shuffling up to them, waving his arms and chattering wildly.

"Peace be with you! A thousand welcomes!"

"Yes, you too! God has been merciful."

The light faded rapidly. The walls turned to a deep grape color. The carbide lamps began to glisten. Pale figures tiptoed through the alleys.

It was the world of Sindbad and Ali Baba. One touch of the wand, thought Sylvia, and it would vanish like a soapbubble.

"This way, this way!" cried the old man, with his blue sash fluttering.

They followed him down the street, surrounded by clamor on every side. Long-haired boys in tattered skullcaps kept scurrying around them, clapping their hands. They passed a row of tiny shops no bigger than caves, with the oil lamps glowing on aisles of pottery and burnished kettles, and here and there stray, inexplicable fragments of the West—a hubcap, a bicycle tire, an empty whisky bottle. A thickset patriarch with a face like a walnut and a web of beard reaching down to his belly was tucking his tray of sweets under the carpet. He turned and fluttered his arms.

"Faranchi!" he cried. "Wicked faranchi!"

The inn was at the end of an alley which led through black, towering walls. The donkeys followed drowsily, blinking their eyes. Abdullillah led them, one by one, into the hay-scented courtyard.

The innkeeper sprang out of the darkness, a birdlike creature with a withered arm. He started whispering to Ahmed, glancing significantly at Sylvia.

"They have only three rooms," said Ahmed apologetically.

"That's all we need," said Dr. Moss.

"Three humble rooms," chirped the innkeeper.

"Can you serve us dinner?"

"A humble dinner, sir."

"Do you have fresh water?"

"Ah! Miraculous water!"

"And what do we pay?"

The innkeeper coughed. "Oh, an insignificant sum, sir. Whatever you wish. One tiny American dollar, perhaps?"

✿

The oil lamp stood on a small carved table with a top no larger than a platter. Small white moths covered the ceiling like a fold of lace, and outside the bats were dipping in and out of the eaves. It was a grim, oppressive place, filled with a scent of hostility. Sylvia sat by the window and looked into the night. The valley below had changed its texture; it looked peaceful and pastoral. The sleeping animals in the distance looked like sheep in a moonlit meadow.

She walked to the opposite window, which looked down on the city. A covert excitement was in the air. The streets were garlanded with flowers, and the flames from the oil lamps danced on the mosque. Three boys were playing in the courtyard, beating one another with twigs. Indigo cloths were cast over the wall to dry. A flute started playing. The boys shot through an arch and vanished. The court was empty; nothing stirred; but a moment later two shapes in yellow kaftans stepped through the gate, arm in arm. They paused and whispered, glanced around, and lay down in the darkness. It was a world of males. The women sat hidden in nearby rooms; Sylvia could hear them chattering in their crisp little voices, ticking away like clocks.

Stillness again. The flute stopped playing. A large man stepped through a door and paused directly under Sylvia's window. A ray of light fell on his face. He was a man in his middle forties, with a knife in his belt and a belligerent, tribal look on his face. He called up to her in his soft wild voice and tossed something through the window. It lit on the floor—a paper flower, smelling of sandalwood, with a tiny inscription on each petal.

She placed it on the table beside the lamp.

She undressed and lay down in the bed, which sagged beneath her like a hammock. Her heart was beating violently. Was it excitement? Or exhaustion? No, neither; it was something else, some frail, unfamiliar kind of elation. She tried to sleep, but her eyes stayed open, following the patterns in the sky through the open window, discovering a new, seething brilliance in the arc of stars outside.

She raised her fingers to her cheeks. They were hot and feverish.

Someone knocked; before she could answer, the door opened softly. It was Dr. Moss, carrying a tall white candle in his hand. Something tightened in her throat; suddenly she was on the brink of tears.

"Are you quite all right, Miss Howard?"

"Oh, quite, Doctor Moss!"

"Is your bed clean and comfortable?"

"Yes. At least, I think so."

He stood beside her and leaned down. "I'm in the room across the hall. If there's anything you need, don't hesitate, please—"

She lay still as a feather.

"You're tired, my dear."

"Well, a little, I suppose."

He placed his hand on hers. She quailed; something in the touch of his skin revolted her.

"It's a quaint little spot," he remarked. "Rarely visited. Rather forbidding. Even the Arabs prefer to avoid it. In pre-Islamic times it appears to have been a quite considerable metropolis."

The feeling of repugnance rose in Sylvia; she was close to panic.

"In a way, of course," observed the doctor, taking off his glasses, "it's rather unfortunate that we were forced to stop in Kumra. A notoriously inhospitable town. Distinctly xenophobe. But it's an experience, my dear. You will never regret it, I'm sure. You will have a glimpse into one of the most unfrequented localities of the Middle East, a town of unusual cultural traditions—"

"Doctor Moss—"

"Yes? What is it, Miss Howard?"

"I'm dreadfully sleepy, Doctor Moss."

"Dear, dear. How rude of me. I've been boring you to death. There, go to sleep, my dear. Good night."

The door closed; she could hear another door opening and then closing across the hall.

She kept listening uneasily, not quite sure what she was afraid of.

And then the lamp flickered and died. She fell asleep.

✿

But a little later she woke up again, cold with terror.

For a moment she could not remember where she was. She felt trapped in a prison. But then she knew. She rose and tiptoed to the narrow window. Yes, there he was, waiting—the man with the knife. His thick, brutal face shone in the light from a window. He was singing to her in a catlike whine. The smooth fold of his turban exaggerated his dark, bitten features. His white teeth glistened between his thick, unscrupulous lips. She stood and watched him for a minute or two, strangely excited. Then she leaned out and smiled and drew back instantly, bewildered, not understanding what was happening to her, or why it was happening, or how it would end.

19

Dr. Moss stepped through the door of the serai into the blinding sunlight.

The whole street was a cascade of feverish, improbable colors. A torrent of merchandise flowed out of the shops, which crouched together under a tottering arcade, all shrouded in a vapor of dust that coiled lazily over the silks and sweetmeats. He passed a dark, murmuring cellar and peeped through the grill: some little boys, thin as grasshoppers, were reciting the Koran.

Two beduin girls were filling their goatskins at the fountain beneath the mosque. They turned and smiled at him brazenly, then shawled their faces and moved away, with the bags bulging over their shoulders and their carmine skirts swirling around their ankles.

Two young beduin came up alongside him, with tufts of wool tied under their knees; one with a basket on a wooden yoke flung over his shoulder, the other with two roosters dangling from his wrist. They peered down at him with their bright insolent eyes.

"Can we take you anywhere?" said the older one.

"Up to the fortress, for example?" said the younger.

"Or to the café?" said the other, on whose chin a silky beard was beginning to sprout.

"Yes, thank you. The café," said the doctor affably, and they led him up the hill toward the mosque, a neglected place full of old crumbling columns; and then through the open market, where the sellers sat in rows with great baskets in their laps, weighing chunks of cooked meat in brightly painted scales.

"Faranchi! Faranchi!" the little boys kept crying.

"The fat *haji* will soon be at the café," said the young man with the cocks.

Dr. Moss nodded indifferently. "Oh. Really?"

He added something in his painstaking Arabic, but the boys looked at him vacuously and relapsed into their guttural Aden accent.

"He is an Ingliz," said the bearded youth.

"English? Really?" said Dr. Moss.

"He is as clever as a djinn. He knows everything. He even knows how to make gold!"

Dr. Moss kept nodding briskly as the beduin took him by the hand and led him toward a low gray building in the shade of the minaret. The entrance was low and narrow. They had to duck as they passed through the curtain. The room was so dark that at first Dr. Moss saw nothing. Then he caught sight of an old man fanning coals in a brazier. There was a smell of charcoal and goat-cheese. A row of cushions lay along a wall, and beside them were two low, oval-shaped tables; on each table stood a copper teapot and two tulip-shaped cups.

The two beduin placed their loads on the floor and sat down silently at one of the tables and motioned gracefully to Dr. Moss. The younger one poured him a cup of tea with a festive air. Dr. Moss sank back on the cushion, feeling pleasantly at ease. He watched the glow hovering over the coals, and the soft red light on the old man's face.

No one spoke. The curtain swayed in the heat.

✿

The curtain jangled, and a fat little man appeared in the doorway, pausing a moment on the threshold. Only the silhouette was visible. He was hardly five feet tall. Then he stepped into the room. It was like a fish rising to the surface —the face, the hands slowly emerged. He waddled toward Dr. Moss and sat down on the cushions without a word. He might have been a half-breed. There was something ambiguously

Western about him. He wore a cashmere shawl over his shoulders, and underneath a silk beige gown. He was hideous; a great blue scar crossed his cheek, sleek and swollen. His puckered eyes flashed with a fawning, merciless glitter. He kept panting with asthma; his breasts kept heaving. The bulging nipples and long black hairs clung to the wet, transparent silk.

He poured himself a cup of tea and spread his fingers on the table.

"You're passing toward Aden?" he said in a high, cultivated voice. His eyes kept traveling around the doctor's body, never meeting Dr. Moss's eyes; astute and watchful.

The doctor nodded. "Yes. As it happens."

The fat man smiled appreciatively, as though he were relishing a witticism.

"You live here?" said Dr. Moss.

"More or less!" The fat man smiled, showing a broken tooth. "May I introduce myself? I believe in ceremony. My name is Hirsch. I've been living in the Hadhramaut for thirty years. I know these people rather thoroughly, I may say. I love them, what is more. And at the same time I hate them. I simultaneously respect and despise them. I have taught them to fear me; it's the only way to get along here!"

His English was curt and fluent. He might have been Swiss or Viennese.

Dr. Moss leaned forward and whispered, "Don't you miss the—civilized world?"

"The civilized world!" Hirsch pursed his lips. His eyes grew whimsical, pearly. "My dear sir, one year in Arabia is enough to strip one of illusions! Civilization! What do you mean by it? Mozart? Botticelli? Ah yes, I too used to haunt the museums and concert halls of Europe. I spent my youth in Prague and Budapest. The delicacies of the intellect, the caviar of the spirit—I knew them all! I wrote poetry. I studied Schopenhauer. I joined a revolutionary movement. I believed in progress, liberty, freedom. But Arabia, my friend, is like an X ray. It reveals the skeleton of humanity. Man is still a savage animal. And savage he will remain, my dear sir, for another million years!"

"You are happy here?" said the doctor tensely.

"Yes. Sufficiently. In my own way!"

"You intend to—"

"To die here? Certainly!" The fat man cackled faintly. "I am a legend here, you see—half demon, half demigod. I have been to Mecca. I am a haji. One must not desecrate a legend." He lowered his eyelids discreetly. "Might I be of help to you, by any chance, Mr.—?"

"Doctor Moss. Edwin Moss."

"Moss. Precisely. You are a doctor of medicine?"

"I am an archaeologist," said Dr. Moss.

"Ah. Most interesting. I believe that you—"

There was a pause, a subtle probing, like the stirring of antennae.

"There are three of us here in Kumra," said Dr. Moss. "Our plane was wrecked in the islands."

Hirsch kept nodding. "Yes. We heard about it. Three deaths, I believe. A great pity. We were deeply concerned. And now, naturally, you wish to arrange your passage to Aden. What, may I inquire, are your resources?" His eyes took on a sloping look.

Dr. Moss stared at the ceiling, then sipped thoughtfully at his tea. Finally he reached into his pocket and pulled out his wallet.

The banknotes rippled across the table. Hirsch's eyes grew dull and expressionless. He gazed emptily toward the brazier and poured himself another cup of tea.

Then he plucked the bundle of notes from the table, glanced at it casually, and dropped it again. "This will be more than sufficient, I think, to take care of your passage to Aden. You have no reason for anxiety, Doctor Moss."

He rose ponderously, gathering his shawl about him; he heaved a sigh of apology. "I must leave you, unfortunately. We shall meet again, I have no doubt. I shall inquire about the caravans. And do be careful, my dear Doctor. It would be such a pity if anything went wrong here." He shrugged his shoulders and shot a playful little smile past the doctor.

He waddled back to the door, the curtain tinkled, and he melted into the blaze of sunlight.

✿

The two young men watched the doctor as he tucked the money back into his wallet. For several minutes they sat silently; the brazier crackled. A sense of confidence and well-being spread slowly through Dr. Moss.

Finally the older of the two young men, the more powerfully built, leaned over the table and said politely, "Do you like my friend?"

Dr. Moss blinked his eyes. "I beg your pardon?"

"My friend is very beautiful!"

Dr. Moss cleared his throat and glanced cautiously at the two young men. The older one, the one with the beard, was broad-faced, rather oxlike. His friend was frail and slender, finely boned, with a girlish skin and eyebrows carefully defined.

"You don't care for him?" said the one with the beard, narrowing his eyes as though he were looking through a telescope. His voice grew harsh and covetous. "Do you like me better? I am very strong! I will protect you! I will kill your enemies! I will guide you through the desert."

Dr. Moss wiped his brow.

"My name is Qasim," said the bedu, rising. "I will guide you through the desert tonight."

Dr. Moss felt a thrust of panic. "What did you say?"

The bedu kept jabbing the air with his thumb. "We will visit the desert. It will be very interesting! Very fine! Very lonely!"

Dr. Moss maintained a masklike expression.

"I will come and meet you," said the bedu gruffly, brushing the doctor's shoulder with his hand. "Soon after sunset. At the serai. Until then, much good fortune!"

The two beduin picked up their birds and baskets and crossed the room. The one with the beard glanced back and nodded. Then they stepped through the tasseled curtain.

✿

The sloping light turned the street into a rich hard copper. Fine shadows fell over the walls, sharp as latticework. Dr. Moss threaded his way across the soukh. A hooded man, all in black, was hovering over a heap of beads. A goat-faced boy was buying some coffee husks and chunks of molasses. He dropped them in his shawl, glanced at the doctor, and fled.

A shriveled woman jumped up from a pile of baskets and shook her arms in the air, rattling her bracelets. She snatched at the doctor's shirt and cried, *"Adaryayan! Adaryayan!"*

Dr. Moss tore himself loose and hurried down past the mosque. He felt dizzy; an unfamiliar chill shot through his shoulders. A touch of malaria, could it be? He felt in his pocket for the quinine tablets, paused by the well, and slipped a capsule swiftly between his lips.

20

David lay drowsily on a heap of cushions in the serai garden, listening to the voices outside the wall. Beside him stood a low black table with a small brass teapot, finely designed in the shape of a dragon's head, with the snout jutting out like a tongue. There was a rustle of footsteps down in the street. A bird shrieked overhead.

He had slept for three hours and felt refreshed and at ease. A new feeling was alive in him; his natural leaning toward melancholy had given way to a speculative optimism. Kumra was having a remarkably soothing effect on his nerves. The anxiety of the previous night was completely gone. He had spoken to Ahmed that morning. Everything was running along smoothly. He still had sufficient funds to take care of the passage to Mukalla, which Ahmed had encountered no difficulties in arranging. Lunch had been adequate, if not brilliant. The attack of diarrhea had subsided. Sylvia was well; Dr. Moss had appeared in unusually amiable spirits. The past six days receded into a remote, improbable haze. They would be in Aden in three more days. Adventures like this, he decided, had an invigorating effect in the long run.

Someone coughed. He turned his head. A withered man in a sea-green sash was mincing noiselessly toward him. He paused by the pool of goldfish and bowed ceremoniously.

"The sayyid wishes to extend his gracious hospitality!" He glanced furtively over his shoulder. "You are invited for dinner, Your Excellency."

"Oh—very kind. For tonight?"

"Yes, Your Excellency. You and the lady."

"I see. How shall we—"

"I will fetch you, Your Excellence. In an hour. Will that be adequate?"

"Yes. Of course."

The servant vanished. A distant animation hung in the air. There was a far-off sound of footsteps tripping along the street. A gun went off. There was a hum of voices—but all of it tranquil, preoccupied, like the buzzing of bees in an orchard.

A butterfly lit on David's wrist, its wings stirring lazily and then opening out to gather the last drop of light.

David cupped his hand over the insect and held it between his fingers. The wings were of a watered azure. He ran his thumb over them lightly; it was powdered with iridescent dust. Dreamily, one by one, he plucked the wings from the body. The butterfly fell to the ground, wriggling helplessly, like a golden worm.

✿

The man in the sash led them through the darkening alleys toward the edge of the city. A lamp hung dangling from his waist; the light danced around them. A trumpet sounded. The "great feast" was beginning that very night, muttered the servant. The houses were glowing with hundreds of oil lamps, which dotted the dusk like a swarm of fireflies. Children were scampering along hurriedly, eyes aglitter with anticipation. A row of old men sat by the gate, beating their tambourines. Little by little a soft-footed crowd began to accumulate, following David and Sylvia toward the palace—gay and friendly, most of them, but here and there a querulous murmur, a hand crooked meaningly.

They could see the banners fluttering on the sayyid's palace, above the gate. A row of white-robed elders marched past them, thin, austere in their little skullcaps; and then came a chirruping flock of girls, bright as butterflies in their magenta trousers, bells tinkling on their tiny ankles.

Someone threw a stone suddenly. It went scuttering down the alley, hit a small black boy. Someone else cried out fiercely. There was a pause, a tense expectancy. A voice in the background started shouting.

The servant raised his lantern and called out, "Guests! Guests of the sayyid!"

The crowd vanished like magic, and they walked on undisturbed.

Finally they reached the palace and climbed the steps. The façade was veined with cracks like old china; a frieze of serpentine patterns was engraved on the wall over the entrance. There was an enormous door of carved wood, with hexagonal studs of polished brass. It opened with a groan; a skirted Sudanese stood before them, with a holstered automatic thrust in his belt. His face was covered with great blue scars—from tribal skirmishings, possibly. They entered a passage. There was a smell of balsam. The hall widened, and they could see tiers of brass utensils lining the wall, and a row of carved mahogany chests. An American alarm clock was ticking noisily in the corner.

The old sayyid sat in a large dark room hung with carpets. He was snoring daintily. The servant coughed and hung his oil lamp in the doorway. The sayyid twitched his head, closed his mouth, opened his eyes—small piercing eyes with a humorous, Zeus-like twinkle. He looked sly, wicked, kindly, with his pendulous lips and pouchy eyes.

His fingers danced in the air. "Ahem. Good evening." He got up clumsily, clutching at a table. "Please consider yourselves officially welcome to Kumra, my dears." He spoke in a crisp Oxford accent, choosing his words with a lordly hesitation. "Sit down, please. On the couch. Would you like a cup of tea, little lady?"

"Thank you, Your Highness," said Sylvia, wide-eyed.

"India or China?" said the sayyid wistfully.

"Oh! You have both?" said Sylvia, brightening.

"No, alas." The sayyid sighed. "I have neither, I'm afraid. But it is polite to inquire, don't you think? Here. Have a

crumpet." The servant raised the lid from an enormous pan.
Two little biscuits lay on tarnished silver, dark and weathered
as prunes. Sylvia plucked and bit at one of them; it was hard
as a walnut.

"Sit down," said the sayyid, rubbing his eyes demurely. "Forgive me. I sleep rather badly." He blinked at Sylvia. "You are
English, I believe?"

"My home is in England," said Sylvia faintly.

"Ah," cooed the sayyid. "England, England! I spent two
years in England, long ago. I studied poetry at Balliol. Shake-
speare, Tennyson, Austin Dobson. You have beautiful poetry
in England, I quite agree. Beautiful castles, beautiful forests.
But"—he grinned cunningly—"it is a cold, cruel land!"

"Cruel?" said Sylvia.

"Ah!" said the sayyid, squeezing his hands together. "Everything in England looks soft and quiet. Soft grass, soft clouds,
soft eyes and voices. But within you have souls like icicles! And
hearts like scissors! Yes, my dear little lady, I felt rather miserable in England, to be quite frank about it."

A cymbal clashed in a distant corridor. A curtain parted.
Two little footmen appeared, bearing copper bowls filled with
rosewater. The sayyid dipped his fingers and rose majestically.

"Forgive me," he said, flicking a gnat from his sleeve. "I
have been most ill-mannered, chatting away like this. Come,
my dears. Dinner is ready."

They walked down a colonnade which opened on a cloister-
like garden. Arched doorways, hung with heavy white draper-
ies, opened at the end, and overhead spread a row of semicircular balconies. Pigeons sat in the cornices, above, ruffling
their feathers. In a corner sat a group of girls, sewing away at
a rug. Their faces were hidden; they looked like bats in their
long gray shawls. One of them kept singing softly, and the
others followed the rhythm with their needles. An Arabian
cat, blue and fuzzy, went strolling across the tiles.

21

The city was flooded with an oblique torrent of light and then, five seconds later, sank into dusk. Dr. Moss stepped through the door. Twilight had muted the sounds as well as the colors, but the odors hung accentuated—the scent of smoke, oil, indigo, tinged with centuries of masonry and human refuse. In the distance crackled the noise of an old-fashioned phonograph.

Someone tapped him on the shoulder. It was the bearded young bedu. In his woolly gray djellaba he looked quite different—more shifty, more dandified.

He flicked his thumb toward the southern gate. "Are you ready?" he whispered. He shot a look behind him and took the doctor by the hand.

They walked side by side. The doctor's brief attack of dizziness had gone. Instead he felt a keen, slightly alarming exhilaration. He was wearing his little skullcap; he felt, for some odd reason, unusually dapper, almost rakish. The mountain air, possibly. And, of course, a certain sense of triumph. He would be able to squeeze at least three scholarly articles out of Kumra, which was virgin territory, so to speak, from a strictly erudite point of view. *The Journal of Archaeology* would be only too grateful—"Kumra's Pre-Islamic Remains"; "The Himyaritic Inscriptions of Kumra"; "Some Notes on the Architecture of Kumra." Even this present somewhat equivocal excursion might be made, with a bit of luck, to yield some interesting marginal observations.

The alley curved. A tomcat was wailing behind a wall. They passed under an archway and crossed an irregularly shaped piazza. Two old men sat in a corner under a strip of burlap, smoking their hookahs. A charcoal brazier was burning beside them; there was a smell of burnt almonds.

The street narrowed until it was a black sewage-strewn corridor. The bedu's grip tightened. He was walking more quickly. Dr. Moss heard the hiss of his undergarments as they brushed his limbs.

"Where are we going, by the way?"

The bedu grinned. "Into the desert. Where it is lonely."

His face shot closer. His eyes seemed to dig into the doctor's with a mingling of hate and calculation. "I will guide you. Do not be afraid," he said hoarsely, flashing his teeth in a knife-like smile.

The street ended in a heap of rubble. A stench of garbage rose from the hollows. Two bony dogs were scuffling and snarling among the offal. Beyond shone the desert, bright as ice under the starlight.

The bedu gripped the doctor's wrist feverishly and with his other hand rapped him softly on the back. "Here. This is the place," he muttered.

Dr. Moss came to a halt. Sweat was trickling on his spectacles. A certain recurrent dream had been disturbing him these past few months: he found himself walking through a dark littered alley and arriving at the mouth of a cave, or it might have been the door of a small black hut. A stench of rotting meat came seeping through the door. He knew that something peculiarly horrible was lurking inside, but some irresistible magnetism sucked him through the door into the interior. At this point, unable to face the full bestiality of the revelation, he was seized by a kind of deliberate blindness, and he hurled himself into a pit, or it might have been a well, which yawned beside him. An instant later he invariably woke up in a sweat.

The whole flavor of this dream seemed about to materialize. The bedu's fingernails were digging into the palm of his hand. He paused, breathless with panic, as though a revolver were pointing at his heart.

And his head suddenly cleared. The night spread out with a burning vividness. He gave a cry and wrenched his hand away from the bedu's. The bedu snatched at his shoulder, his eyes sparkling with an almost hysterical cunning. He growled something that sounded like *"Garra! Hamadurra!"* But then his voice disintegrated into a low, harsh gurgle. Dr. Moss tore himself loose, ducked swiftly as the bedu wheeled about, and dove past the wall. He gave a sharp, high scream as the Arab swung his fist, which glanced crisply off the doctor's head.

He started to run, clumsily at first and then faster and faster, with surprising agility. He reached the piazza, where the two old men were still sitting in precisely the same attitude, smoking their water-pipes in the glow of the brazier. One of them turned his head and raised his eyes slightly. He muttered to his companion, who lowered his head and said nothing. There was a sound of hurrying footsteps. A voice sang behind the wall. Dr. Moss darted up a tiny dark street.

A moment later he realized that he had taken the wrong turning. The walls rose high above him, drenched in a fine pale dust, which in the feeble light from the moon looked like a blanket of snow.

The footsteps echoed behind him. He shot through an open doorway and found himself in a small rectangular garden. He sat down on the bottom step of a stairway, panting heavily. He was aware of his body in a new, oppressive way. It seemed hollow and frail, intensely sensitive at every pore. Thick dark flowers hung from a bush, exuding a raw, seminal odor. He closed his eyes, trying to put his mind in order. But a passionate undercurrent churned through his veins, destroying his powers of orientation.

A spider crawled over his hand. He jerked his arm away, horrified. At the same moment a voice behind him murmured lackadaisically, "Come in."

Dr. Moss turned his head, too distraught to be startled. A door had opened, dropping a bar of light over the tiles. A slender shape in a long blue barracan stood silhouetted in the doorway.

She said again, more impatiently, "Come in, if you please."
Dr. Moss rose dreamily and climbed the stairs. He found
himself in a small dimly lit room.

✿

Cushions of spotted brown leather lay scattered along the
walls. A copper lamp dangled over a low, rather unsavory-
looking couch.

"Here. Lie down. You are tired," said the woman, straight-
ening the camel's-hair coverlet.

Dr. Moss sat down on the bed, feeling quite composed all
of a sudden. The woman stepped toward the lamp and
trimmed the wick. The room grew brighter. The folds of cloth
on the bed, the intricate coils of the latticework—everything
looked as though seen through a stereopticon, bright and
frozen.

"Are you weary?" said the woman.

"Not at all, thanks," said the doctor.

The woman stood beside the bed with her hands cupped
over her breasts. She was gazing emptily at the wall. "Come.
Lie down. Here. Like this." She put a small green pillow under
his head.

Dr. Moss closed his eyes; it seemed impossible to keep them
open. Sleep came welling toward him in a huge gray wave. Or
rather, not quite sleep, but a rich, heaving coma in which a
mass of shadows writhed unrecognizably, like giant ferns at the
bottom of the sea.

He opened his eyes again with a violent effort. The lids kept
trying to close, like magnets. Dimly he saw the woman kneel
by the bed, reach across a low black table, and dip her hands
in a little bowl. His eyelids shut irresistibly. But he was aware
of something happening, something obscurely directed toward
himself, and with a panicky thrust of the will he forced his
eyes open again. The woman was staring at him intently; her
pupils narrowed into small red pinpoints. A broad necklace
of silver clung to her throat, each link heavily molded and set

with an egg-shaped amber bead. She might have been forty. Her skin was faintly leathery, but in spite of her age she was unusually beautiful, with a long narrow face and a large but sensitive mouth, and great eyes which Dr. Moss found oddly disturbing—sad yet exultant.

"Please excuse me," he said faintly. "Dropping in on you like this."

"It doesn't matter," said the woman indifferently. "You are a *nasrani*, I can see. There was a young nasrani here eleven years ago. An Ingliz. But not like you. The Ingliz was tall and beautiful. You are small and ugly." She spoke with complete detachment, in a deep resonant voice. "Why have you come? To make love? It's rather late to make love."

"Please," said Dr. Moss frozenly. "I'm afraid you misunderstand."

"You are panting," said the woman, placing her finger on his pulse.

"I—I suppose—"

"You are frightened," said the woman, leaning closer. "Have you killed someone?"

"No!" cried Dr. Moss, appalled. But the question seemed curiously apposite, and for a moment he thought it might even be true. "No, no," he muttered. "I lost my way. That's all."

But the woman wasn't listening. She kept running her finger along his wrist. He felt himself succumbing to a new, furry drowsiness.

"Whenever an Ingliz comes to this city," she said wearily, "there is trouble. Seven years ago there was the drought. Eleven years ago there was a plague of locusts. Why do you come to Kumra? Why don't you leave us alone?"

Dr. Moss was beginning to feel relatively calm again. He smiled apologetically. "We are on our way to Aden. We leave Kumra tomorrow, or maybe the next day. We shan't cause you any trouble, I can assure you, madam."

"Ah!" said the woman, her eyes brightening. "I come from the hills, where the real Hadhrumi live. I have the power of the Hadhrumi, which my mother taught me and also my grandmother. Also my aunt. That was in Shibwa, twelve years ago. I tell you, Ingliz, if you bring any trouble I will change you into a bird!"

The doctor gazed at her with concern.

"Yes! A tiny bird! No bigger than this!" She stretched out her middle finger and thrust it in front of the doctor's nose.

Then she rose and stepped behind a curtain, which seemed to cover the entrance into a smaller room, or an alcove. There was a sound of whispering; a man's voice and another woman's—drowsy, faraway voices that spoke in a melodious rhythm, like a chant. The Arab woman returned, sheathed in dark, tarnished silk.

"Come," she said impassively. "I will make love to you for a little while. Then you must go home right away. It is late. I wish to sleep."

She leaned over Dr. Moss and pressed her lips to his bald, hot forehead. Then she reached down and began to caress him gently, unbuttoning his clothes and skimming his thighs with fingers light and adroit as a pianist's. The touch of her hand, far from seeming crude or lascivious, gave the impression of a casual, serene spirituality. Dr. Moss closed his eyes again. He had never felt like this before. It was as though some stubborn, oppressive knot in his nervous system had been cut, and relief poured through him in a great cool rush. He felt the touch of the woman's lips, and a marvelous lightness seized him and carried him up like a pair of wings. He lay afloat on a soft white cloud.

✿

As he wandered up the alley he was aware of the city drenched in silence, pulsating with sleep. He felt in touch with humanity as never before—through his nerves and bloodstream, so to speak, rather than through the intellect. He felt lighter, more resilient in body than he had for years; and at the same time aware of some continuous undercurrent of terror. It was the terror of a man standing at the edge of a pit, aware of some powerful tug drawing him toward the abyss.

"I must go home," he muttered, in a daze.

He walked slowly toward the inn and knocked at the door.

22

A Negro slave appeared and led the sayyid and his guests through a labyrinth of passages to a long low room, dimly lit by the usual long-snouted oil lamps. A basin was set before David and Sylvia. They washed their hands silently. Then, imitating the sayyid, they crouched crosslegged around a large brass tray. Delicious odors began to filter through the air.

"I must apologize," said the sayyid wryly. "It will be a trifling little meal. What you call pot-luck. Life in Kumra, I must warn you, is rather simple."

Two elderly servants in white robes crept up silently, bearing the dishes. The black boy lifted the lids. There were a bowl of hot milk and a symmetrical array of little wafers fried in oil. The sayyid kept glancing playfully at his guests. His presence dominated the room, tranquil and ponderous, with a subtle charm playing about him like the light of a candle.

"Please, my dears," he kept whispering. "Don't expect Parisian cooking!"

Bowls of sweetmeats were brought, and a purée of dates and figs, and then an enormous kous-kous sprinkled with lamb and raisins, and presently a great dish of rice decorated with slices of sheep's liver. Finally some peppered coffee appeared, and three types of tea.

"Neither India nor China," pleaded the sayyid, running his thumb around the cup. "A tea from Oman, a tea from Java, a tea from Iraq. Quite unimportant little teas, I'm afraid."

David glanced around the room. Crimson hangings covered

the walls except for the space over the doors, which was inscribed with legends in Arabic.

"Texts from the Koran," said the sayyid, catching his eye. "And here and there a bit of poetry. I live on poetry. I am old, you see. Old and decrepit. So I meditate. I read. I memorize. You love poetry too, my friend?"

David smiled hesitantly. "A little."

"Ah. I see." The sayyid leered. "You are young. You have more impetuous tastes. When you are old you will turn to poetry. Poetry, my friend, is like rain. It cools and strengthens and makes things grow. It softens the glare of reality. It draws us back into solitude. There are many kinds of poetry, of course. Poetry about flowers, about clouds. I prefer poetry about birds, as it happens. Especially nightingales."

A shadow passed over the sayyid's smiling face. "More solitude. More meditation. That's what we need nowadays!" He plucked at his ear impatiently. "Look around you, my friends. What do you see? Nothing but people! Everywhere, people. On the hills, in the valleys, thousands of people. Along the rivers and the sea, more and more people. There are far too many people! Far too many cities in this world!" His voice grew mellow again. "There are not enough legends for all these cities, you see. Each city must have its own little legend, its bird. Rome has an eagle. Cairo has an owl. London has a sparrow. Venice has a pigeon. Port Said, as you can imagine, has a horrid black vulture."

"And Kumra?" said David tactfully. "Has Kumra a bird?"

The sayyid's face grew wrinkled with pleasure. "Just a dull, clumsy bird!"

"What bird, Your Highness?"

The sayyid cackled with pride. "An ostrich!"

But then a sadness entered his eyes. "You think I am most old-fashioned, I'm afraid. Alas, it is true. When I was young I believed that the world was changing, that things were growing better and better. But now I have returned to the life of my ancestors." He raised his long withered fingers. "You in

the West! Incurable optimists! You think you can enter
Arabia. You send scientists, explorers. You dig oil, you lay
roads. But you have not entered Arabia, sir! You will never
enter the heart of Arabia! You will cross our deserts like
thieves and creep into our forbidden cities. But you will never
find our secret!" A look of fury was smoldering in the old
man's eyes. His lips tightened; his chin began to quiver.

His glance fell on Sylvia. His face melted again. His eyes
twinkled. "And where, my dear lady, do you go from here?"

"To Aden, Your Highness."

"To Aden!" The sayyid chuckled. "You will be lucky, little
lady, if you ever reach Aden!" He leaned over confidentially.
"The tribes are at war this week, unfortunately. They will
remain at war for a whole season. They will shoot at you.
They will rob you. They will massacre you. Don't go to Aden,
my dear lady."

Sylvia grew pale with alarm. "But we *must* get to Aden,
Your Highness!"

The old man lowered his head. His eyes turned inward discreetly. "Must! Must! My dear mademoiselle, there is no such
word as 'must' in Arabia." He clapped his hands; the curtain
parted. A servant appeared, a young dandy with henna-dyed
hair and mincing gestures. He placed a parcel in Sylvia's lap
and another in David's.

"Open them now, please," said the sayyid with a foxy look.

They drew apart the orange paper. There was a silver sti-
letto for David, razor-edged, with a handle embossed with
Arabic patterns. For Sylvia there was a silver necklace studded
with turquoise.

"These will protect you, perhaps." The sayyid sighed. "Let
us hope for the best. Will you be so kind as to visit the *harim*,
my dear lady?"

The servant waited beside the door. Sylvia rose politely,
fondling her necklace. She glanced at David with a flicker
of apprehension. Then she followed the henna-haired dandy
into the corridor.

✿

The sayyid led the way into the adjoining room, a kind of loggia looking over the hills. It was a surprisingly modern room, with low divans and English sporting prints and shelves of leather-bound books. David glanced at the titles: *Aurora Leigh, The Sorrows of Satan, Lady Ashville's Revenge.*

"Sit down," murmured the sayyid. "Would you like a cigar, my dear sir?"

David sank back on the divan and drew a cigar from the box. It gave out a dry, cinnamon-like odor. He glanced at the band—a golden ostrich engraved on a bright red oval. The sayyid beamed. "Made especially for me! Shipped from Bond Street!"

He smiled proudly, rolling an enormous bloodstone in the palm of his hand.

"An English lord once told me one should always have cigars for a guest. I keep waiting and waiting for a guest who will smoke a cigar. Pray smoke!" His fingers fluttered with joy. "You are the first guest in seven years, my dear sir, who smokes a cigar!"

He lapsed back, suddenly mournful. "Ah, here we sit, chatting. We chat of poetry and birds, we smoke cigars, we become friends, but alas! we will never understand each other, I'm afraid." He sighed profoundly. "You come from a new world. I come from a lonely little old world." The sweat was gradually washing the kohl from his eyes. A large black pearl flowed down his cheek. "Sometimes, frankly, I feel full of misery about Arabia. Everything goes down the hill. The incense trade crumbles apart. Cities fall into decay. Tribes squabble but do not fight. Valor declines. Wisdom declines. Only Islam still holds, but even Islam makes concessions, and I see nothing but muddle, muddle, muddle."

"There are worse things than muddle, perhaps?" suggested David.

"No. Nothing is worse than muddle," snapped the sayyid.

The palace had sunk into stillness. Clouds of mosquitoes welled in through the lattices. A baby bat swooped into the room, darted about in a panic, and then shot out again. Somewhere in the distance a child began to cry.

The sayyid kept murmuring in low, monotonous tones. David's mind strayed helplessly; the old man's sentences slid through the air and fell noiselessly to the floor, like withered leaves. Certain phrases recurred: "The soul of Arabia," "the life of our ancestors"; but their import grew more and more nebulous. The sayyid's head sank forward. He had fallen asleep. David rose and looked through the window. He could see the line of the jol, and the nearby cliffs, white as salt in the moonlight, and the moon itself, no more than a shred of light swathed in mist; it seemed to be evaporating. There were dark hollows among the cliffs—the old caves where the shepherds dwelt. A patch of firelight shone on the slopes.

David stepped back from the window and tiptoed across the room. The sayyid was snoring. The cigar smoke was spiraling toward the ceiling. A long knife lay tucked into a bright red book. David glanced at the title—*The Mysteries of Paris.* He picked up a small jade elephant from the coffee table, held it against the light, and put it down again. Something, he knew, was going to happen. It might be an earthquake. Or merely a gnat biting his cheek. Or perhaps it would happen without his ever realizing it. But it would happen. Of that he was sure. A breath of wind stirred the shutters. A pink feather fell from the table, hung floating, fell to the floor. The sayyid's eyes opened hazily. He began to smile. The curtain billowed in the breeze as a door opened behind him.

The servant came shuffling forth with a lantern.

"Don't be nervous, my dear young American," said the sayyid impenetrably. "Don't be afraid in Kumra. You're quite safe, I assure you. The young lady is waiting. Hamadullah will lead you home. Good night, my friend!"

23

A boy servant in a green kufiya led Sylvia toward the harim. They passed through a little courtyard filled with birds in cages—parrots and parakeets, lovebirds, tiny birds no larger than dates, drowsy birds and frantic birds, dainty birds, dilapidated birds. One of them started clawing at the wires with a strangled look, crying, "Marhaba! Marhaba!" The passage turned abruptly; they climbed a blue-tiled stairway. The boy raised a percale curtain, and they entered a large cool room. Bowls of light burned in the corners, casting a confidential glow. The air was dense with a kind of listless femininity.

The ladies swam about like goldfish in the flamelit gloom, sparkling with brocade and anklets, three earrings dangling from each ear, and lime-green handkerchiefs tied over their heads. They gathered about Sylvia, whimpering faintly with surprise, spreading their painted fingertips with pleasure. Their monotonous black eyes shone like large, inquisitive beads. Some were beautiful as camellias, some were coarse and pock-marked, but all were somehow formalized into a crystalline prototype. They radiated the pure, impregnable essence of Woman. The heat was suffocating; the floating odor was that of a beehive. Sylvia caught that wavering whiff of female power, so much older, more majestic, more intimidating than that of mere man.

A middle-aged lady, powerfully built and matriarchal, emerged from the columns like an Assyrian priestess, wearing a red silk barracan and amber bracelets that clicked like castanets.

"My name is Zubayda," she announced in formidable tones.

She took Sylvia by the arm and led her to one of the cushions. Her long henna-stained fingers reached into an onyx bowl and then dropped a small green fig into her mouth. She leaned closer, snapped her fingers, and poured out a cup of bitter coffee.

"I am a poetess," she declared. "The sayyid, you see, is rather drowsy. He needs to be soothed, invigorated. I recite three poems for the sayyid every day!"

"How very interesting," said Sylvia.

"He is a highly spiritual person. He prefers poems about death," said the poetess with a piercing look.

"Oh, really?" said Sylvia anxiously.

"Shall I recite a poem for you?" demanded the poetess.

"Please," said Sylvia, lowering her eyes.

The poetess leered at Sylvia. "A poem about love?" she inquired rather grimly.

Sylvia blushed and nodded her head.

"I shall recite you a poem by the great Yazid ibn Maqsam Assafadi." The poetess groaned, lifting her chin, and her voice subsided into a wavelike rhythm. The other ladies gathered about her silently, folding their fingers in dainty triangles. The poem rose and fell, the words wandering about like flotsam on the massive undulations of her voice. Her exquisite Renaissance face was pale, strong, elongated; the damp curls falling over her forehead made her look more like a man than a woman.

There was a tense, slightly intimidated silence when the poem ended. The room had darkened. Sylvia felt the eyes of the assembled ladies fixed upon her, the lamplight hovering in their great black pupils. A touch of panic seized her as she felt the touch of these probing eyes, nibbling away at her person like a school of fish.

"Very beautiful," she said faintly.

The poetess nodded. "But very sad. It concerns the cessation of love and the blowing of winds and the departure of birds and the coming of winter. You are going to Aden, mademoiselle?"

"Yes," said Sylvia. "I hope so!"

"Tsk, tsk," said the poetess, stroking her earrings. "An evil journey!" She reached for Sylvia's hand and gazed at her palm. Her brow grew furrowed.

"You read the future?" said Sylvia thinly.

The poetess nodded, crooking her forefinger.

"What do you see?"

"A bad, black journey," said the poetess, tapping her chin. She leaned toward Sylvia, leveling her gaze. "Stay with us, mademoiselle!"

"I should like to," said Sylvia uneasily.

"I will teach you the poems of Nasr ibn Sayyar!"

"How very kind of you," said Sylvia, quailing.

"You will stay?" cried the poetess, rattling her beads.

"I must go to Aden," pleaded Sylvia.

The poetess reached out and touched Sylvia lightly on the arm; her hard, hawklike eyes were swimming in tears. Outside there was the sound of footsteps clattering across the courtyard. A plate fell and crashed. A boy servant cried softly, and suddenly the birds started screaming, first the parrots and then the parakeets, and then the tiny green birds, all chirruping in a panic of vituperation. The poetess glanced across the room, drew Sylvia suddenly closer, and in a swift beaklike motion pressed her lips to Sylvia's cheek.

"Good-by, my dear mademoiselle."

"Good-by," said Sylvia. "Thank you for the poem!"

"It was nothing. Nothing at all," said the poetess rigidly.

"Good-by, good-by," squealed the little ladies, gathering about in a flurry.

Their voices tinkled along the corridor as Sylvia hurried back to the garden, where Hamadullah was waiting with his long blue lantern.

24

The following afternoon Dr. Moss visited the fortress. A self-appointed guide, a scrawny boy in a tattered fez, led him down the slope toward the western quarters. Here everything was squalor. An open sewer ran down the middle of the street. Thousands of cats prowled through the arches, dozed in the windows, leaped into the cellars—skeletal beasts, pink and yellow, with a sly, jaded air; ancestral cats, thought Dr. Moss, like those engraved on Egyptian tombs.

"Here! This way, Your Venerableness," cried the boy in the fez.

They crept over a bridge which crossed a moat, and scrambled up a flint-littered slope toward the fortress. Here the boy came to a halt, pointing proudly. There was a Himyaritic inscription on the wall, cut in massive strokes on the pockmarked stone. It had to do, so it seemed, with a ceremonial visit by the Governor of Cana. Dr. Moss knelt down scrupulously and started copying it in his notebook.

The sun shifted. Sweat was pouring down the doctor's cheeks. He wiped his glasses, then drew his fingers over the stone. It felt curiously smooth and alive, like the hide of a beast. A ripple of gooseflesh ran down his back. Some fleeting innuendo from the past? Something more eloquent than the tale of the governor's visit? There was a hint, in that Himyaritic scrawl, of the impenetrability of the human mind; and at the same time of its warm, inextinguishable intimacy, as though the flesh of past centuries were still stirring under the hot wild sunlight.

Dr. Moss grew aware of a certain restlessness in the air. The boy in the fez tapped him on the shoulder. A crowd had gathered on the slope. An old cripple crept up and peered into the doctor's eyes, muttering under his breath. Dr. Moss finished his transcription calmly. Then he tucked his notebook in his pocket and strolled back to the bridge.

Someone came running up behind him and tugged at his coattails. It was the boy in the fez.

"Your Venerableness! The white haji wishes to see you!"

He took the doctor by the hand and led him in a roundabout way, through a series of kasbah-like tunnels and up circuitous stairs, toward the crowded part of the town. Dr. Moss followed meekly. He felt listless and weary, depressed by a certain hostility in the atmosphere of Kumra.

They came to a small café, similar to the one he had visited before. Was it the same one perhaps? He wasn't quite sure. The curtain over the entrance parted, and they entered the leather-scented darkness. A group of bearded, hilarious elders were drinking coffee. There was a passageway on the left where a row of men lay sleeping on thick rush mats.

He took off his sun-glasses and peered across the room. No one seemed to be looking at him, but he felt, rather uncomfortably, that he was being scrutinized.

"Sit down, my dear Doctor." A pudgy shape loomed over the table.

Dr. Moss sank down on a cushion not far from the entrance.

"I have asked you to come without delay. Please excuse me," murmured Hirsch. His mouth played about in his sagging face like a fish caught in a net. His tiny pupils grew piercing. "It is a rather urgent matter, Doctor Moss."

Dr. Moss stared at his fingernails. "Yes? What is it, Mr. Hirsch?"

"It has come to my attention—regrettable as it may seem, and even preposterous, I dare say, to a Western mentality— that there are certain rumors current in Kumra. Well, not to make too fine a point of it—" He pressed his thumbs together; his gaze grew indulgent.

"Certain rumors?" said Dr. Moss, frowning slightly.

"You must try to understand, my dear Doctor. These people are not accustomed to foreigners. You are the first in seven years to penetrate the walls of Kumra. There was the eminent Swedish archaeologist, Doctor Svensson, who unfortunately died of cholera here in Kumra. And several years before that Sir Basil Kennedy, the explorer, disappeared mysteriously in the outskirts. There is a suspicion among these people that foreigners bring misfortune to Kumra. Pure superstition, needless to say. But traditions are powerful in this part of the world, Doctor Moss."

Dr. Moss tapped his knee impatiently. "Won't you come to the point, please, Mr. Hirsch?"

"Alas!" Hirsch sighed. His eyelids flickered unhappily. "I wish there *were* a point. But there isn't unfortunately. Things are never so simple as that in Arabia. There is no black, there is no white. There is only a muddled, wearisome gray."

"You asked me to come," snapped Dr. Moss. "Was it for a discourse on philosophy?"

Hirsch ran his tongue over his lips. A gleam of amusement lurked in his eyes.

"Not quite, my dear Doctor. You must cultivate the art of patience, if I may make a suggestion." He sank down on the cushion beside the doctor and ran his palm along the edge of the table. "A serious occasion like the present one deserves a certain flavor of decorum. The crises in life must not be handled too brusquely. One must not simplify! As your own profession has undoubtedly taught you, Doctor Moss."

Dr. Moss sank back in his cushion. His attention was beginning to wander. The coffee drinkers were engrossed in a game of dice. The curtain tinkled; a serving-boy appeared with a copper tray. A thread of sunlight fell on his face, which looked brilliantly happy, almost ecstatic. He knelt down and poured the tea into the cup. Dr. Moss felt an esoteric undercurrent in the air, as though the men in the café were all members of a cult, engaged in some intricate ritual.

"What are these?" he inquired sulkily, pointing to a tray of pastries.

"Maize biscuits." Hirsch sighed. "And honeyed dates. Local delicacies. Please, please."

Dr. Moss sipped at his tea.

The serving-boy tightened his tea-stained sash and stretched out his arm as he lifted the plate. A golden bracelet sparkled on his thin brown elbow. Under the bracelet Dr. Moss detected a row of small pink abrasions, slightly swollen, like the bites of an insect.

Hirsch folded his arms and leaned forward. His face looked suddenly venomous. "Doctor Moss, I feel I must inform you that you are in mortal danger. The people of Kumra do not like you. They are afraid of you. They have been watching you night and day. They are of the opinion that you are—how shall I put it?—an evil spirit. A man possessed. A demon, in short. They are waiting for an omen—a sick goat, for example, or a case of epilepsy. When that omen occurs, Doctor Moss, they will in all probability—" He shrugged his shoulders and sighed compassionately.

Dr. Moss felt strangely indolent. "They will do what, Mr. Hirsch?"

"They will kill you," murmured Hirsch.

"I see," said Dr. Moss.

"You are a man of character, Doctor Moss. I realize that the threat of death does not unduly disturb you. But I should add that these people occasionally seize on rather eccentric methods of capital punishment. There was the case of a young adulteress a year ago, for example— Well, I shan't distress you with the details. Doctor Moss, do me a personal favor!"

Dr. Moss raised his eyes to the ceiling. "What kind of favor, Mr. Hirsch?"

"Leave Kumra tomorrow, my dear man. How much cash do you have with you?"

"Two hundred and fifty American dollars, approximately," said Dr. Moss.

"Any jewels? Or gold?"

"Nothing of consequence," said the doctor crisply.

"You're quite sure?"

Dr. Moss pinched the tip of his nose rather thoughtfully.

"A bit of jewelry would be very useful," hinted Hirsch, lowering his voice. "Sapphires, for example."

"I have no sapphires," said the doctor limply.

"Well, think it over, Doctor Moss. Please bear in mind the importance of the occasion. My boy will accompany you back to the inn. I will expect you here at five. Bring me the dollars and the sapphires, and I shall arrange your immediate departure. I have no ulterior motives—not even charity, I'm afraid. Merely a wish to avoid unpleasantness." His lips curved in a cherubic smile. "One last point, if you will permit me. Don't think too badly of Kumra, my dear sir. They are fine people in their way. It is merely that they have certain deplorable prejudices!"

He rose and extended his wet pink hand. "Au revoir, Doctor Moss. I have, in my own way, thoroughly enjoyed our brief acquaintance. I regret that we haven't found time to converse on mellower topics!"

He waddled back to the corner where he had been sitting before. The game of dice continued. There was a clinking of coffee cups.

A dry little man sat crouched in a corner with his jerd covering his chin. Dr. Moss gave a start. Those glittering foxy eyes: could it possibly be . . . The man turned quickly, whisking the jerd across his cheeks.

The curtain over the doorway parted. The boy in the fez stood silhouetted against the light. He was beckoning gently to Dr. Moss.

25

Sylvia stepped through the raffia curtain into the garden of the serai. The fireflies were dancing their evening quadrilles, weaving a pattern of polka dots in the sea-green air. All uneasiness vanished; a gentle longing came over Sylvia, a nostalgia focused neither on the past nor on the future but on some indeterminate point outside of time. A small owl started hooting in the direction of the mosque—some sort of sad, Arabian owl, with a sharp brassy voice.

She tiptoed across the tiles. Idris was leaning over the edge of the pool, watching the goldfish.

"Look," he whispered, drawing Sylvia toward the pool with his long warm hand. "Do you see that little fish?"

"There? Under the fern?"

Idris nodded. "That is a ghost fish, madame. Reach into the water and he vanishes!"

Sylvia dipped her fingers into the pool. The fish flicked his tail and was gone.

Idris gazed at her teasingly. "You are a mischievous little madame!" He leaned over and plunged his face in the water, then rose again, streaming. His teeth were flashing. "Tonight is the night of the Queen of Yemen," he whispered, scooping the drops from his forehead. "She is the greatest ghost in Arabia. All other ghosts are afraid of her. Tonight is the night that she crosses over the deserts of the Hadhramaut, from Maida all the way to Ras Fartak and Salala. She walks backward, like every ghost, but faster than any ghost in Arabia, so fast that you see her for only a moment—first her back as she

hurries toward you, and then her face as she hurries away
again. All the other ghosts watch her from their secret hiding places. That is why the ghost fish is so nervous. He is
frightened to death of the Queen of Yemen!"

"Do you really believe in ghosts, Idris?"

Idris looked shocked. "Believe in ghosts? Certainly not, my
dear madame. I believe in Allah, and in Mohammed his
prophet!" His voice sank to a whisper. "But ghosts exist all
the same. It can't be helped. It is not my fault. Look, little
madame!" He raised his hand and held it against the moon,
which was shedding its silver scales on the far-off minaret. "We
are all only ghosts, just helpless, worried ghosts. We were
ghosts before we were born and were sprayed into our moth-
ers' wombs, and we are ghosts again after we die, frightened
of the powerful phantoms." He thrust his face close to
Sylvia's; she caught the scent of his breath, sweet as milk.
"You think you are looking at Idris, madame. But no. You
do not see the real Idris. The real Idris is a ghost; perhaps he
is wandering over the sands of the Rub' al Khali, perhaps he
is floating in Qamr Bay. Who knows—perhaps he is up in the
moon, or even in London! Idris is far, far away. What you see
is only a bit of skin and a lock of hair wrapped around a bone.
The real Idris will visit you someday in your dreams, my
madame!"

He smiled festively and raised his brows. "Would you like
to see the Queen of Yemen?"

Sylvia nodded, tingling with pleasure.

"Come with me," said Idris.

✿

Crickets were singing down by the date palms at the bottom
of the hill. Three lonely houses lay on the outskirts of the
town, just beyond the fortress. Idris pointed. "Every house in
Kumra has its own private ghost," he said solemnly. "We beduin know all about them. Do you see that yellow house with

the ibis horns? It belongs to the widow of a former sayyid. It has a very distinguished ghost—a shriveled lady in a silver *tobh,* who sits in the kitchen with a harp. And that little house over there on the right has a fox who creeps into the beds—a very bothersome ghost, I think. And the lonely house with the blue windows—look at it carefully, little madame!—has the best ghost in Kumra—a sad young Ingliz who creeps about with a knife in his heart!"

In the distance shone the jol, cold and desolate, like a sea of salt.

They came to a well-house at the edge of the desert. "You must sit here to see the ghost," said Idris stealthily.

The door of the well-house opened, and a wrinkled man with a cane stepped forth. Long gray locks fell to his shoulders; wisps of hair grew from his nostrils. He was leading a nannygoat with a bell around her neck. He stepped back with alarm when he caught sight of Sylvia. Idris spoke to him soothingly. "Don't be nervous, Salim. This isn't a ghost. It's only a lady from the land of the Ingliz. She won't harm you. Don't be frightened."

"Are you waiting to see the queen, by any chance?" said Salim.

"It could be," fenced Idris.

"Well, she passed an hour ago," snapped Salim.

"You're quite sure?" said Idris. "She passes at midnight, doesn't she?"

"She was early this year, I'm afraid," said Salim, sniffing. "Stay if you wish. Don't let me discourage you. But I saw her whizzing by just an hour ago, as it happens."

Idris looked piqued. "What a pity. Good night, Salim!"

"Peace be with you," cackled Salim and shuffled away through the sand.

Sylvia sat on the step of the well-house and listened. The night was bubbling with little noises. Something—a lizard perhaps—was rustling in the jujube bush. Night-birds flitted about, small and velvety as bats. Some beduin had camped on the edge of the jol; they lay scattered across the sand like egg-shaped boulders.

Was this a dream? Squatting in the Arabian wilderness, waiting for ghosts? Lost in a world of lizards and bats and superstitious beduin? A rush of amazement passed through Sylvia, fanned out on the desert air. The whole world seemed suddenly quite fantastic; not merely this haunted valley of Kumra but everything she had ever seen—the whole universe, from the distant, half-remembered shores down to the crickets chirping among the palms.

Idris plucked at her thumb. "There! Look, little madame!"

A haze of light shone over the wadi. It swam indecisively, like a thread of yellow ribbon. It might have been smoke from a hidden fire or the glow from a swinging lantern. It passed behind the fortress and disappeared.

"You saw her?" Idris gasped.

Sylvia stared wistfully at the distant walls.

"It was the queen! The murdered queen!"

Sylvia felt a pang of disenchantment.

"Now you have seen an Arabian ghost!" said Idris, triumphant.

Sylvia gazed at him thoughtfully. "Thank you, Idris. It was a lovely ghost!"

✿

They wandered silently into town. She followed Idris through the narrowing alleys, which now were completely unlit, unrecognizable. All of Kumra had gone to sleep. Even the cats had vanished. The iron stakes in the marketplace threw a crisscross pattern on the walls of the mosque. Two empty jugs stood beside a sleeping donkey, and behind the donkey lay a sleeping child. It looked very thin and sickly. Sylvia knelt down and touched its cheek.

She called, "Idris!"

No sign of Idris.

Her voice echoed across the marketplace, thin and bizarre, like the voice of a cricket.

She drew a ring off her ring-finger and slid it into the palm of the sleeping child.

Then she sauntered dreamily toward the serai.

26

David strolled over the tiles. A flurry of cloth lay tossed by the goldfish pool. He recognized Ahmed's djellaba and a moment later he saw Ahmed himself, knee deep in the pool, splashing water up at his thighs.

He called softly to David. "Sir! Come! I am bathing."

David knelt at the edge of the pool and sank his arms in the cool black water. Ahmed grinned, covering his groin with one hand and splashing his belly with the other.

"I could not sleep." He sighed, wrinkling his face apologetically.

"Isn't it early for sleep, a bit?"

"No! It is late!" said Ahmed darkly. "It is the night of the ghosts. All men should be asleep in their beds when the ghosts come flying!"

David sensed a new intimacy in Ahmed's voice. A touch of playfulness? Or anxiety, perhaps? Ahmed stepped out of the pool, tossed his feet to shake off the drops, and flung his djellaba about him.

He squatted beside David, sniffing at the air. "Do you smell them?"

"The flowers?"

"No! The ghosts!"

The spice of the vines hung heavy—and a more elusive fragrance, like wild cranberries.

"The night is full of them," confided Ahmed. He pointed toward the moon. "Even the moon is a ghost tonight. The soul of the Great Warrior has slipped into the moon. Let me tell you about the moon, sir, when it looks like this, shaped like a tusk. Camels go mad in the light of the tusk-shaped moon. Women turn into witches. Men grow violent and murder other men. And do you know why? Because the djinns have built their home up in the moon."

Ahmed leaned closer. "Even kind, gentle folk turn into traitors by moonlight. Even the beduin. Even the wise and experienced elderly beduin."

David glanced toward the west, where the top of the mosque gleamed over the innyard wall. The dome hung floating under the rain of stars like a phosphorescent umbrella.

"Whom do you mean, Ahmed?" said David quietly.

Ahmed smiled. "When things are delicate, sir, we do not like to use names in Arabia."

He folded his arms and peered quizzically at David. "Are you waiting for the little madame?"

"Is she asleep, Ahmed?"

Ahmed smiled knowingly.

"Have you seen her?"

Ahmed grinned. "Ah. You love the young madame!"

"I hardly know the young madame."

"But you love her," whispered Ahmed. "Because the elderly madame willed it before she died. She willed that you should marry the Ingliz lady. Isn't it true?"

"Of course not, Ahmed."

"Then you do not love her?"

"She is only a child—please, Ahmed."

"You are a strange man, Sir Daïd," said Ahmed, folding his arms around his belly. His eyes twinkled ironically. "You are a strong, beautiful man. You look like a warrior. You are frightened of nothing. But—forgive me, Sir Daïd!—there is a ghost troubling your blood. You hide your soul behind a smile. Is that how it is in your country? You smile to hide your loneliness?"

"You are a clever man, Ahmed."

"No, not clever. I am a bedu. I have traveled." His eyes

grew subtle. "Tell me, Sir Daïd. Why is it that you are afraid of love?"

"What is love, Ahmed? Do you know?"

"Love," said Ahmed, "is everything! Nothing else matters to the man who loves. The rest of the world does not matter, and only the kiss of the beloved matters. When you are in love, my beautiful sir, you would chop off your arm, you would walk through fire, or swim through the Gulf of Aden. All this you would do to win a kiss from your beloved."

"Have you ever felt like that, Ahmed?"

"Twice, sir." Ahmed's eyes flashed; his lips were shining. "Once with a man and once with a woman." He paused, waiting for David to ask a question.

"Were you happy, Ahmed?"

"Ah, my admirable sir! We must never look for happiness; only for peace. Let me tell you exactly how it was with me. My love for the man was a hard, violent love, full of terror and jealousy. I felt weak and a little crazy. I thought of death very often. My love for the woman was a peaceful love, bringing strength and self-forgetfulness. Love for a woman is like a flower. Love for a man is like a knife."

They sat silently for several minutes, looking at the slow-rising moon.

"Where is she?" said David suddenly.

"Ah! With Idris, I think."

"Where, Ahmed? Do you know?"

"By the well-house, maybe," said Ahmed placidly.

He grew pensive and added, "Or perhaps she has lost her way. Idris is such a careless, frivoling fellow!"

"Ahmed!"

"Sir?"

"Did you allow this?"

"It is nothing naughty, sir! You misunderstand! They are only waiting for the ghosts to pass."

David sprang across the garden and flung open the gate into the street.

✿

He hurried through the marketplace, past the row of little shops, which were blind and bolted for the night. The whole town seemed deserted. He imagined Sylvia wandering helplessly through the labyrinth of alleys, groping her way through the filth and decay of Kumra.

A light shone at the corner where the alley joined the walls of the town. An old man with a cane was hobbling up through the gate, leading a goat. David strode up and seized him by the arm.

"Have you seen a young Ingliz lady?"

The goatherd stared at him with an empty gaze and shrieked, "Nasrani!"

David shot past him toward the gate. There was a grotto-like cavity in the massive wall. A lamp shone dimly through a curtain of old burlap sacking which hung over the entrance. There was a bubbling of voices. David drew aside the curtain. Three young beduin sat crouched over a teapot which was gurgling softly above a brazier.

"Has an Ingliz lady passed by here?"

The men turned and gaped at him. A glitter of alarm crept into their eyes. Their fingers slid slowly down toward their sashes.

David dropped the burlap curtain and hurried around the corner. A long street led toward the palace, which was silhouetted on the brow of the hill.

He called, "Sylvia! Sylvia!" His voice echoed back. He started to run.

✿

An iron lamp hung over a door; under the lamp a boy was squatting. David touched him on the shoulder. He was panting with worry and exhaustion.

"Did you see a lady pass by here? An Ingliz lady?"

The boy peered at him cunningly. He pointed to the door. "In there. She is waiting for you."

David found himself in a low-ceilinged passageway. There was a smell of slime-covered mortar. He heard the splashing of water directly below him. A winding stairway, completely dark except for a tiny flame tucked in a bowl of glass, led down into a rambling, soap-scented catacomb.

A fat, female-breasted Negro knelt in front of a fire, fanning the coals. Steam was rising from a black octagonal basin. David felt the sweat beginning to run down his chest. The Negro waddled up to him with an absent-minded air and without a word unbuttoned David's garments, which he hung fastidiously on a rod in the wall. A row of futahs, jubbas, and kaftans hung from the other rods. Silver ornaments, bracelets, and talismans lay glistening on a stool beside the fire.

David stood naked in the middle of the room. The stench of steam laden with sweat and camphor filled him with a sudden languor. He forgot why he had come here; he forgot the whole outside world. He felt mesmerized almost, with fumes of steam circling around him.

The Negro cast a towel over David's shoulders and led him into the neighboring room.

27

Sylvia wandered on dreamily. The street took a familiar turn, and she looked for the brass-studded gate of the serai.

But there was no gate, no serai—only a long black wall.

She had lost her way, she now realized. Here the houses were of a drab dark mud, monotone, unlightened by whitewash. The city dissolved in a honeycomb of tunnels. She ran quickly under an arch, following a narrow alley that went winding along the base of a tower. Every house looked alike. Every window was black. Everywhere lurked that insistent odor of Kumra—half cinnamon, half excrement.

A furious itching crept over her body, as though she'd been lying in a bed of nettles. Arms, ankles, the base of her spine—what was wrong? Had some insects slipped into her undergarments?

She glanced up. A light shone behind a battered curtain. Was someone beckoning? She climbed the steps and entered a courtyard, hoping it might lead to the serai. A medieval lamp hung in a niche, under a pair of horns. She crossed the court toward a gate at the opposite end. Through the grillwork she could see the pattern of shadows: a ring of tiles, a tiny pool. She sighed with relief. It was the garden of the serai. She tugged at the gate, which squealed softly and swung open.

The familiar fragrance fell about her—the mossy pool, the deteriorating mortar.

She sank to her knees beside the pool and drew off the top of her dress. Carefully she cupped her hands in the water and let it trickle over her breast. The coolness brought relief. She dipped her face in the pool, feeling the clean fresh touch of the moss on her cheeks.

When she looked up again the walls of the house seemed somehow blurred, unfamiliar. She crossed the garden. A small red lamp hung over a door, and above the door hung a little balcony. A shadow was stirring behind the latticework.

Suddenly she realized she had made a blunder. This was not the serai after all; and the very fact that the scene was so similar was curiously unnerving to her.

A slim young man in a pale gray cloak stepped out of the shadows and walked noiselessly past her, bowing gracefully. The light falling through the grill of the balcony cast a shadow over his cheeks. He had a scar over his eye, which gave him a frowning, piratical air. Black hair hung in wet little coils over his forehead. He was young—eighteen perhaps— but with an old, metallic glint. His face was leathery, almost black with the years of the desert.

Had she seen him before? In one of the shops? Or maybe—? He came to a halt and raised two fingers, about to speak.

One of the shutters squeaked up on the balcony. He turned his head quickly and ducked it so that he was entirely in shadow. He was panting with excitement.

"Why are you here?" he said in a nasal tone, which might have been threatening or conciliatory.

"I lost my way," said Sylvia. "I thought—"

"Where are you going?"

"I was looking for the serai!"

"You are alone?"

"Yes—well, no. I just happened to—"

He looked at her furiously. "Go away now! Quickly!" He reached forward, about to touch her; his long dark hand hung over her arm. "You are a faranchi. Go from Kumra!"

His eyes were abnormally brilliant, piercing. She had never seen eyes so intensely black, so passionately alive. He muttered something which she did not understand and hurried soundlessly through the pointed archway. Sylvia stood motionless by the gate, touched by an inexplicable sense of loss, of something perilous and fiery floating out of her life. Should she call him back? She might never see him again. She raised her arm. No. Too late. The garden was empty and still. He was gone forever.

She hastened back to the gate. It had fallen shut. She tugged; it wouldn't budge. Was it locked? Who had locked it? She called softly. No one answered. The house seemed deserted. Carefully she placed her feet in a coil of iron and started climbing over the gate. The gate shook under her weight and trapped her thumb in the hinge. She cried with pain; a trickle of blood ran down her palm. Tears sprang to her eyes, but an instant later she was seized by a feeling of defiance, abandon. She crossed the garden and slid through the narrow black archway under the balcony.

✿

It was black, still, spicy with a mintlike fragrance in the corridor. It curved to the right and then divided, one branch leading into the dark, the other toward an open patio. She tiptoed along a colonnade of spiraling pillars, bright with mosaics under the filtered starlight.

She halted, breathless. A paw of darkness slid over the walls of the loggia, then vanished. There was a tap-a-tap behind her, a stealthy tread, like an animal's. She stepped into a nook of shadow and pressed her back against the wall. There was a stirring among the pillars; the shape drew closer. She recognized him by instinct before she even saw his face— something in the grace of the walk, the flow of the pale gray garment. He walked past without seeing her; she could have touched him as he passed. He ducked through a door at the end of the patio.

Sylvia's blood was tingling with a rush of recklessness which was more than curiosity, which was stronger than fear. She glanced behind, then stepped noiselessly through the columns and crossed the patio.

She paused outside the door.

Her hand rested on the thick bronze doorknob; it squirmed under her palm like a snail. She pressed softly. The door swung open. The room was dappled with the light of the moon, which fell through the latticework. Nothing moved; it seemed empty except for some cushions which lay strewn on the floor. Then she caught sight of him, lying motionless in the dark. He'd thrown off his djellaba, which lay crumpled on the tiles. One arm was flung out on the flagstones, the hand grasping a flake of moonlight. The rest of his bare body lay blurred by the mottled shadows.

A curtain parted. Someone else stepped into the dark—a slender shape in a dark robe. A woman, could it be? There was a low harsh muttering. The air grew alive, as though struck by a firecracker. The man twisted about and leaped to his feet. His shoulders shone in the light from the window; his belly was sprinkled with flecks of brightness. A flash of panic shot through Sylvia. This was something she had sensed, had dreamed, had been told about but never dared to visualize—the phallic rush of the male. He looked slightly grotesque as he stood there, almost deformed. The dark barracan fell from the woman's shoulders; only a gauzelike sheath still clung to her. She looked luminescent and fragile beside the hard black bulk of the man. They stood for a moment face to face, without quite touching. Then he hurled his arms around her, and they sank to the floor.

Sylvia pressed on the knob; the door gave behind her. She stood in the doorway for one last moment, feverishly watching the lovers. There they lay, ensnarled in a monstrous little mazurka.

✿

She ran down the moonlit colonnade, through one door after another, and suddenly found herself in the narrow, ill-smelling street. She could see the dome of the mosque at the end of the soukh.

Someone tapped her on the shoulder gently.

"Idris! Oh, Lord!"

He smiled dolefully. "Little madame!"

"Where have you been, Idris?"

"All over Kumra! Looking for you!"

Sylvia's lips began to quiver. "I lost my way," she said hoarsely.

"Madame, I was frightened! The Queen of Yemen might have—"

Two great tears rolled from her eyelashes.

"Don't be sad, little madame! Now you are safe. Come home quickly."

She took his hand and nodded disconsolately. The alley dipped and then rose again. Idris kept gazing at her with his doelike eyes as they climbed the filth-littered flagstones.

28

It took a minute or two for David to grow used to the darkness of the *hammam*. Dark-skinned Arabs were sitting around the edge of the pool, lazily soaping their thighs, dangling their feet in the tepid water. The atmosphere was thick with steam. Nothing was distinct. Light, temperature, sounds, and odors—even the dark-skinned bodies—all were veiled, limbo-like. A lamp hung dripping from the ceiling, lost in the clouds of steam. Everything was cracked and crumbling. Flakes of plaster hung from the wall. Great cockroaches went scurrying over the tiles.

David sat down at the edge of the pool. The men around him seemed hardly aware of his presence, in spite of the fact that he was conspicuously blond in this assembly of black-haired nudities. The man next to him belched apologetically; his paunch hung drooping like an enormous sack. The rest of the bathers—beige, bronze, chocolate, écru, coffee-colored, most of them hideously fat or frighteningly thin, two or three of them superb as statues—all seemed lost in daydreams, lolling their heads, murmuring aimlessly.

David began to see more clearly. A group of men lay sleeping on mattings laid out in an L-shaped alcove. Nearby, on a marble slab, some men were being massaged. Now and then someone emerged from behind a black felt curtain, dripping with sweat, and sank with a groan into the milky water.

A bowlegged boy ran up to David and began rubbing his back with a brush. He tugged at David's arm. "Here! This way, please!"

David followed him through the curtain into a room still

hotter, still more aromatic. A feeling of well-being was seeping through David, and at the same time a wave of repugnance that bordered on nausea.

Steam was rising in the center of the room from a little hole about the size of a saucer. An old man crouched on a ledge, pouring water over the bathers. David stepped closer. An enormous bowl was emptied over his head. He cried out; it was cold as ice. His skin quivered with the shock.

"Sir! Over here, please!"

He dropped on the marble slab. A great jellyfish of a man poured amber oil over his body and started kneading his chest. He closed his eyes. He heard nothing but the rhythmical patter of flesh. The masseur's hands went bouncing over his belly, soft as rubber balls. David's nerves were melting away in a trickling stupor. His body lay spread like a harmonica into separate layers of sensation—arms, legs, shoulders, and hips, all lay floating in a sea of oil. The masseur turned him over and started slapping his buttocks. Waves of pain shot up his spine, spreading into a cool, bright relief. He felt his neck being ground, his thighs pinched and pounded. Finally he rose in a daze and groped his way through the alcove.

"Here! Lie down, sir."

He found himself in a kind of tunnel filled with couches. A row of small pear-shaped lanterns shone on the disarray of cushions, towels, and hashish pipes. The sea-blue light made the place seem vast and uncanny, blurring the contours, bringing a vibrancy to the motionless bodies. Most of the men were fast asleep; some stared vacantly at the ceiling. In a nook at the farther end of the room could be seen, through a haze of smoke, a knot of dark, heaving bodies. David listened: gasps of pain, sobs of hashish-ridden pleasure. A hand moved slowly up his back. He recoiled, terror-stricken. A man was kneeling on the bed beside him, a bird-faced man with a little beard and intelligent, glittering eyes—an Arab from the desert, wiry and lean-waisted, with thick gray feet, all callused, like an elephant's. He flung his arms around David's waist with a grip of steel. David struck out in a rush of panic. The man shrank back, muttering, "Aya!" Another man raised his head and started waving his arms. A thin little voice cried, "Faranchi! Faranchi!" David ran through the hammam, past the pool into the dressing-room. The Negro was squatting beside the fire, lazily fanning the embers. He stared blankly at David, then rose with a groan and whisked David's clothes from the rod in the wall.

❖

Taurus and the Pleiades hung shining above the minaret. A haze of oyster-gray light, like a fan expanding, hid the horizon. In the distance, through the city gate, the thorn trees were already silhouetted against the east, but on the opposite side, where a caravan lay sleeping in a hay-strewn courtyard, all was black except for a row of water-bags, white and fleecy as sheep.

Idris was waiting at the serai entrance, grave and sleepy-eyed.

"In the garden, sir—the little madame—"

"Is she back?"

Idris nodded.

She was sitting beside the pool, talking placidly to Ahmed. Ahmed glanced up as David approached, and dipped tactfully behind the trees.

"Sylvia! Good God!"

She smiled innocently.

"Where on earth have you been?"

"Looking at ghosts, my dear!"

He sank on the tiles beside her. She raised her finger, as though listening. What was it—a distant bell? No, it was more like a faraway drum. Was the caravan gathering, perhaps?

Her forefinger fell on his wrist. "There. Did you hear it, David? The moon is calling! Idris told me about it. The ghosts are hurrying back to their homes!"

He took her hand. "Really, Sylvia—"

"You think I am silly, don't you, David?" She pinched the air with her fingers as though she were squeezing a butterfly. A bird called—a wavering, plangent sound like a clarinet. She cocked her head, straining to catch the sound of the little night-bird. In this cool, swimming light she looked almost beautiful. Her cheeks were aglow. Her eyes were luminous, ecstatic.

"Do you realize that you've been extremely naughty, Sylvia?"

"Oh, David! I'm not a child any more."

"Sylvia, listen to me."

But she wasn't listening. Her eyes shone with a secret triumph. "Kiss me, David!"

He leaned over and kissed her on the forehead, very lightly.

She drew back and rose, drawing her fingertips over her forehead.

"Sylvia, you must promise absolutely—"

"Good night, my darling!"

She went floating across the garden with sly, glittering eyes.

29

Clouds of smoke filled the café. No lamps had been lit, and the only light was the haze seeping in from the soukh.

"The haji is waiting," said the boy with the teapot, lowering his blue eyelids and filling the cup for Dr. Moss. The rest of the drinkers, squatting on the cushions along the wall, turned their heads. Their eyes watched the newcomer with a sly, coppery glitter.

A moment later Hirsch appeared, suave and ingratiating, wiping his brow. He loomed over the table like a Hindu idol, many-breasted, exuding a whiff of cloves. He smiled wistfully as he counted the money, bill by bill, and tucked it into his shirt.

"And the sapphires?" he asked patiently.

Dr. Moss placed a folded white handkerchief on the table.

Hirsch opened the handkerchief, peered at the bracelet, and sighed augustly. "Thank you, my dear Doctor. My boy will accompany you to the caravan. The caravan will conduct you to Raïda. In Raïda arrangements will be made for your trip to Mukalla. The ship calls at Mukalla in eight or nine days. *Bon voyage!*"

He stood in the doorway for a moment, gazing benevolently at Dr. Moss. His shirt clung to his chest, translucent with sweat. He waddled into the street and entered the soukh, where he soon was lost in the crowd of white-robed figures.

Dr. Moss sat alone, staring dejectedly at the coffee drinkers. The glitter of eyes, bemused, narcoticized, shone like beads through the veil of smoke.

Little by little, as he sipped at his cup, he noticed a change coming over his senses. He could see everything in the room with abnormal exactitude. His brain worked with a strange new insight and clarity. He drained the cup and rose wearily. The eyes of the coffee-drinkers were fixed on him, watching his movements with a kind of mesmerized curiosity. He stepped through the door. Even the twilit soukh, even the lines of the jol in the distance, still faintly discernible through the scalloped roofs, hung poised in front of his eyes with a microscopic precision. He noticed a tiny *ilb* tree on a mound in the distance, just to the right of the fortress; the web of branches was etched against the sky, sharp, minute as the blood vessels in an eyeball.

The copper utensils spread out in the little stalls caught the light. The bolts of indigo cloth shone with a deep, rich stillness. Everything looked supple, lustrous, as though he had just set foot on a bright new planet. He felt a clutching expectancy, a deep inner animation. But outwardly, as he groped his way past the stalls, he seemed numb and helpless, almost robot-like.

The scrawny boy in the fez came running behind him. "Here! Here!" He gestured fiercely. "This way, nasrani!" Dr. Moss followed him down the alley. They crossed the market square toward the gate: first the boy, loping nervously on his thin scabby legs; then Dr. Moss, walking rapidly, eyes glazed, head thrust forward.

✿

Some peasants were trotting along on their donkeys. The smell of ripening maize filled the arcade. Dr. Moss and his guide wandered down toward the caravan road, where the hoofmarks drew a pattern into the far-off sands, fine and clean as the pattern of birds' feet.

They walked into the hills and entered a rock-littered valley and presently came to a crossroad. The boy in the fez

pointed to the left—"To Ash Shihr!" Then to the right—
"To Raïda. Here you wait for the caravan."

He paused, his eyes growing brittle, attentive. Finally he
muttered, "Bakshish!"

Dr. Moss leaned closer. "What did you say?"

"One dollar," said the boy. His voice grew rasping and
ugly.

Dr. Moss stared at him bitterly. "Go away, please. I have
no more money."

The boy leered brazenly at the golden wristwatch.

"Go away," said the doctor stonily. He sank down on the
sand, faint with heat. His forehead was throbbing miserably.
He reached toward his pocket for the aspirin, but even as his
hand touched his pocket a great indifference came over him;
the presence or absence of pain seemed a matter of no consequence; all that mattered was this great heaving brilliance
which surrounded him, this acceleration of the senses which
made the air seem electrical, which gave such a rainbow-
colored splendor to the curving horizon, which gave to the desert stillness the grandeur and immanence of a symphony.

He cocked his head and gazed at the sky. Three stars
started twinkling. A sound of bleating rose from the shrubs
on the other side of the valley.

"Is it true what they say?" said the boy, squatting in the
sand, arms akimbo, making water in the Arab manner.

"What do they say?"

"That you can change a man into a turtle."

"Sheer nonsense," snapped the doctor.

"Can you make gold? Like the haji?"

Dr. Moss smiled wearily. "I wish I could!"

The boy stood up and tugged at the doctor's sleeve. His
eyes grew vicious with cunning. "You are a djinn," he whispered.

Dr. Moss shrugged his shoulders. "No. I am not."

"They all think so. Everyone in Kumra thinks you are a
djinn!"

"They are mistaken."

"The men in the caravan will think you are a djinn," said the boy. He opened his hand and stretched it meaningly toward the doctor.

"No matter," said the doctor casually.

"They will not take you if you are a djinn."

"I am not a djinn!" screamed Dr. Moss, flinging his arms in the air.

The boy stared at him with sudden terror. He cried, *"Sarra, sarra!"* and started running down the path, heading for the cliffs of Kumra. Dr. Moss watched him gravely—scampering over the sands like a baby ostrich, growing smaller and smaller in the gathering dusk.

✿

Now it was dark. The gravel along the edge of the jol changed its color. It looked blue and transparent, streaked with a furrowing white like a glacier.

The lights of Kumra had vanished. The only light now was the gleam of the early stars and the soft, translucent afterglow of the desert. An air of sealike loneliness was cast over the dunes. There was no wind, no sound; only a faint smell of sheep and the clean dead smell of the sun-baked gravel. Dr. Moss crept toward the jol. He moved as in a dream, lulled by the spaciousness and stillness.

The glowing hues of the Arabian nightfall shone forth for a moment or two: the glowing violet of the eastern cliffs, the fierce maroon of the western plains, and over all the diaphanous half-light of the darkening sky. All around, east, west, the world of people sank into darkness. The smell of humanity died. Only the jol remained. Dr. Moss felt like a last survivor. A great panic gripped his heart. Was it too late? Was everything lost? He stretched out his hand, clutching at a fistful of dry blue air. A sickening dizziness seized him; he almost screamed. Something took him by the throat and sent him staggering across the gravel, lurching blindly, like a drunkard.

But then gradually he grew calm again. His mind was drained of confusion, as though a great clot had been washed through a funnel. He walked on carefully, making his way along the edge of the jol.

Something in the sand suddenly caught his eye—a black splinter, like a chip of obsidian. He knelt and plucked it out of the sand. Curiously heavy, hard as a diamond—it looked like an arrowhead, whittled to a razor-like sharpness. It bore the unmistakable imprint of man. He pressed it to his lips, feeling the sharpness dig into his flesh. A tiny drop of blood trickled along his chin. He tucked the stone into his pocket and started strolling down the caravan road.

An odd effect of repetition lurked in the landscape, as though each mile mirrored some previous effect down to the last detail—rocks, hillocks, even the arc of the camels' hoof-prints. Several knolls rose in the south, pale, drab, thimble-shaped. A flurry of dry shrubbery dimmed the long plateau in the north.

A stab of pain stung suddenly at the hollow between his ribs, as though someone had struck him in the solar plexus. He sank to the ground, gasping for breath. His eyes grew watery. For several minutes he lay quite still, waiting for the spasm to subside. It went as suddenly as it had come. He lay panting with relief. Then he got up again, bleary-eyed, and looked around for the road. Night had fallen. The edge of the Hadhramaut lay black, indistinguishable. He sauntered along aimlessly, looking for a familiar landmark. There was none. Even the cliffs of Kumra had slipped from the horizon. He decided to turn back and look for his footprints. Not a trace. They had died away like ripples in the sea.

"Never mind," he murmured.

The moon was rising. A chilly light fell over the desert. He caught sight of two egg-shaped domes on the brink of a hill and started walking toward them. They were *qubbas,* holy tombs. He scanned the whitewashed walls, instinctively searching for the usual inscriptions. The place looked utterly neglected. Rocks and rubble were strewn around. Strips of elaborate carving and scrollwork surrounded the windows; but from close up they looked coarse and shabby.

He entered the tomb on the right. Two small coffins white with dust lay side by side under a cobwebbed niche. Local saints, probably. He ran his hand along the top of a coffin. Relatively recent, he decided—a hundred years; possibly less. He groped his way out through the open doorway and entered the smaller tomb, the one on the left.

30

Sylvia crossed the soukh, feeling the sunlight whip at her
arms. She passed a stall in which some rice-cakes were sizzling
away in a pan of grease. From the leather shop rose the
stench of goat-hide, mingling with the perpetual tang of
urine and the sweeter, mellower aura of camel dung. She felt
herself floating in an olfactory world.

A dog came sniffing at her heels. She bent down to stroke
its ears. But then she saw with disgust that its snout was seething with vermin.

Two young women hurried past her, faces hidden under
their veils, only their eyes black and sharp with antagonism.

The seller of beads shrank back as she leaned over the stall.
He started crying something that sounded like *"Murra,
murra!"*

What was wrong? Beneath the timelessness of Kumra something unusual was stirring. A pock-marked boy was fanning
an old man who lay panting beside his corn bowls. Two small
children were carrying a bucket of filth down the street.

At that moment someone started to scream from the re-
cesses of an alley.

Sylvia stood motionless, fixing her eyes on the end of the
street, where a tower stood perched on the city walls. A
woman was standing motionless in front of the tower. Her
skin was dark, almost Negroid, and her dress was long and
black. A silver chain hung over her forehead. Her arms were
rigid at her sides. There was an odd, somewhat sinister majesty in all that blackness and stillness.

Suddenly she flung out one arm. Something fluttered

under her robe. Was she beckoning? Sylvia looked back uneasily. The woman in black kept on staring—neither at Sylvia nor at the street nor at the walls; not even into space. It was a stare without meaning in destination.

The woman began to lumber toward the soukh, carrying a basket under her barracan. She started to pant uncontrollably as she staggered up the alley. Once again she came to a halt, fingering the wall for support. Was she blind, perhaps? She suddenly dropped her basket, and a bevy of figs went rippling across the pavement. Her mouth fell open in a noiseless shriek; a rope of blood shot forth, streamed down over her breast. She keeled over and lay flat on the pavement, arms flung out, quaking with pain. Sylvia shouted for help, but the entire soukh seemed mysteriously deserted. No one appeared. Sylvia ran toward the dying woman.

A voice behind her called, "Wait, madame! Don't touch her." Idris came darting through a café doorway.

He flung his scarf over his chin. A fig came rolling across the dust. "Here! Quickly! Come!" He tugged at her arm and led her swiftly through the empty streets.

✿

The bell on the minaret kept ringing. On it rang, on and on, while the evening veiled the jol and the light on the far-off ranges grew dusty. They were sitting on the roof of the inn, breathing the cool dry air—Sylvia and David and Idris, who was fingering his talisman.

"There! Do you see them?" said Idris, pointing.

A straggling procession was passing through the gate. The exodus had already begun. People were rushing to leave the city before the sayyid ordered the gates locked and the city quarantined. Hand in hand they wandered into the desert in their cobalt cloaks, carrying bags on their shoulders, leading their children and donkeys. On the opposite side of the town, down by the fortress, they were chanting their prayers. A fire was burning in the little valley where the first of the corpses were being burned. One by one the black bundles were dragged on ropes through the dust and then dropped over a ledge into the flames. The women prayed rhythmically, raising and lowering their arms. The sound of their prayers was hoarse and monotonous, broken occasionally by a cry or a lamentation.

A door opened behind them, and a tall pale figure stepped onto the roof. It was a moment before Sylvia recognized him; he wore a jerd around the lower part of his face, covering his mouth and nostrils.

"It is all arranged. The guards have been paid. We leave tonight," said Ahmed. His voice was unusually solemn.

David looked at him sternly. "Do they think we brought the plague to Kumra?"

"No, no," breathed Ahmed. "It isn't we."

"Tell us the truth, please, Ahmed."

"We are quite safe," pleaded Ahmed.

"And the elderly sir?"

"He has fled."

"Fled!"

"He has gone on the caravan road to Raïda, sir. He will join us in Mukalla." He glanced at Idris uncomfortably. "He paid the haji. It is all arranged."

There was a troubled little silence.

"Tell me, Ahmed," said David carefully. "Who brought the plague to Kumra? Do you know?"

"No one *knows*," said Ahmed, blushing.

"It might have come on the *gibli* from Africa," hinted Idris.

"It might have come in the sacks of incense shipped from the mountains," suggested Ahmed.

"In any case," said Idris, "it is the will of God."

Ahmed nodded. "It is the fate of Kumra."

"How long will it last, do you suppose?"

"Thirty days, Sir Daïd."

"When do we leave?"

"Two hours after sunset." Ahmed's face grew suddenly

cheerful. His hands danced busily. "Before the moon is high. Idris will fetch you. We meet the caravan by the southern gate."

"The caravan to Raïda?"

Ahmed looked furtive. "No, the caravan to Raïda left three hours ago. This is the caravan to Ash Shihr, which joins another caravan to Mukalla. There are many nice, dependable caravans these days," he added thoughtfully.

He beckoned to Idris; they stepped through the door, and three minutes later Sylvia saw them hurrying through the garden, laden with bundles.

✿

It was nearly dark. Sylvia sank back on the cushion and stared at the sky.

A host of blackbirds went fluttering overhead, spreading and circling as they reached the fortress. They sank down and settled among the crannies and grew still. Five minutes later, when the gloom of the dusk had swallowed Kumra, the bats came out and went zigzagging through the serai garden, dipping down over the roof, almost brushing Sylvia's hair, casting quick little stains on the starlit tiles.

"Are you worried?" murmured Sylvia.

"Not really," said David, expressionless.

"What will we do about Doctor Moss?"

"Poor old doctor," said David dourly.

"David, do you think—"

"Let's not think! Let's hope for the best."

"He's such a helpless creature, David."

"Not so helpless as all that, my dear. I might as well tell you that he slipped Miss Todd's sapphire bracelet out of my coat this afternoon while I was asleep. Ahmed saw him entering my room."

"Mercy! How odd. But maybe Ahmed—"

"I trust Ahmed completely."

"Well, I shouldn't have thought—"

"He had his reasons, I'm sure. Only I can't help wondering whether he's been very far-sighted. But in any case there's nothing we can do about it, is there?"

He took her hand and pressed it to his cheeks. "How warm your hand is!" He kissed it gently and gave it back to her. "Dear little Sylvia. We all become very wicked in Arabia, don't we?"

31

Two men lay in the qubba, fast asleep—an old man and a young man.

Dr. Moss crept closer. The old one lay on his back, snoring. The young one lay with his face buried under his elbow, like a dog. Both had their djellabas spread out under them, the edges rolled into pillows. He could smell their flesh, furtive and musty—men from the wilderness.

Should he wake them up? Better not. He thought of lying down beside them. No; no telling who they were—pious pilgrims or dangerous brigands. Or maybe just beduin on their way to Raïda. A spirit of cunning came over the doctor. He thought of searching their garments for a knife or a gun.

He knelt down beside the old one. A small black beard bobbed up and down, ruffled faintly by the sleeper's breath. Dr. Moss felt soothed by a momentary sense of power. One slight gesture, one clutch of the thumbs on the gullet— He reached for his arrowhead—one sharp little jab at the jugular. A flash of lucidity came over him. He had cast off his past, he suddenly realized, like a worn-out garment; and with it his habits, his values, his scruples.

Through the low round door he could see the moon rising, the icy light touching the outspread fingers of the sleeping bedu. The old man's eyelids began to flutter. He let out a groan, twisted his head, gaped at the doctor, and cried, "Mahmoud!"

The young man turned over on his back and sighed. The old man jabbed at his ribs. "Mahmoud! Wake up!"

"I beg your pardon," breathed Dr. Moss. "I hope I am not intruding."

The old man gave a snort and screwed up his eyes. He peered at Dr. Moss with a mingling of fear and calculation. Mahmoud belched drowsily. Suddenly he sensed the air of panic; his hand shot to the knife in his belt, and he snarled at the doctor.

"Who are you?"

"An innocent wayfarer," pleaded the doctor.

"You tried to kill us!" squealed the man with the beard.

"Not at all," said the doctor primly. "I am waiting for the caravan to Raïda, that's all."

The men stared at him, incredulous. The old one whispered in the young one's ear. The young one, a powerful thickset fellow, rose and groped his way through the tomb, lunged into the night, and disappeared.

"Where did you send him?" asked Dr. Moss.

"To signal the caravan," said the bedu. His manner had grown obsequious, fawning.

For several minutes neither spoke. Dr. Moss felt calmer. The flush of uneasiness was followed by an instinct of trust and serenity. There was a dignity, a spirituality in the old man's face. Or was he really so old? The desert had withered and worn him; he might really have been no more than the doctor's own age. The moon sprayed its brightness through the door of the little qubba, and a feeling of subtle kinship crept over Dr. Moss, as though this bedu had something profoundly in common with himself—something elusive but fundamental, which only a difference of circumstances had veiled.

The bedu leaned closer and tapped him on the shoulder. "Are you hungry?"

"Not much." Dr. Moss sighed. Then he realized his lack of manners. "Certainly," he said. "Thank you kindly."

The bedu pulled at his futah and drew out a slice of coal-black meat. The whole tomb stank with the sickening smell of dried shark. "Here," said the bedu, breaking the slice in half. Dr. Moss felt nauseated as he raised the fish to his nostrils. He held his breath and chewed feverishly. The flavor of decay flooded his tongue like an acid. He almost vomited as he forced the salty flakes down his throat.

The bedu looked appeased. He stroked his beard. "Did you like it?"

"Delicious," said the doctor, quailing.

The bedu smiled noncommittally.

"You look like a scholar," he observed, watching the doctor from the corners of his eyes. "I can see it in your nose. All scholars have thin, thoughtful noses. I too am a scholar. Let us talk," he purred, "about the glory of learning."

"Learning is an excellent thing," said Dr. Moss wanly.

"There are three kinds of learning," declared the bedu with a ghost of a smile.

"Yes? What are they?" asked the doctor, brightening.

"Medicine, religion, and astronomy. The study of Men, of God, of the Stars. That is all. All other knowledge is vulgar and trivial."

The doctor nodded, peering anxiously through his glasses. There was something in the old man's face that thrilled and fascinated him—as though the bedu had passed through every conceivable type of experience, as though his body and instincts knew infinitely more than a man could know with his brains. The teeth shone brilliant. The small black eyes gleamed like a rattlesnake's. Dr. Moss leaned forward, pressing his hands together tensely.

"And there are three kinds of men," continued the bedu, picking at his teeth.

"What are they?" said the doctor.

"Men of fire, of water, of air." The bedu sat back and grinned playfully at the doctor. "Men of fire are quarrelsome and brave—kings and heroes, for example. Men of water are astute and practical—merchants and the like. Men of air are spiritual, meditative—like you and me, shall we say. Mahmoud, unfortunately"—he sighed significantly—"is a man of fire. He is very impulsive."

They sat in silence for several minutes. Dr. Moss lay down on his back, limp with fatigue. He lay very still, feeling the pungency of the bedu's nearness, sly and shifty and yet at the same time peaceful, harmonious. The stillness of the earth expanded beneath him, a stillness so intense that it seemed to palpitate—the panting of the globe, it might have been, slowly revolving on its axis. A strange excitement grew in him. He opened his eyes again; the desert stars were shining into the qubba. All the enormity of the world seemed to lie concentrated like an essence in the little tomb. There was something familiar, reminiscent about the scene, as though he had caught a glimpse of it long ago, in early childhood. For the first time in his life he sensed the unraveling of destiny, the gradual fulfillment of a drama already plotted out to the last detail. The black sky, the white qubba, the darkness of the Arab's face and the whiteness of his robe—it reminded Dr. Moss of a negative emerging under the chemical.

32

"This way," said Idris, bright-eyed with excitement. He led David and Sylvia through a maze of alleys toward the southern gate, where Ahmed had promised to wait for them. The bells stopped ringing. The city was steeped in an evil hush. A smell of ammonia came seeping through the half-closed doors. There was a twitter of night-birds from an unlit garden; a dog snarled, tugging viciously at a small wet parcel which lay festering in the gutter.

"Let's hope that we can pass through the gate!" said Idris.

They hurried across the empty soukh. A scrawny silhouette emerged from the shadow of the mosque and walked rapidly toward them. "Abdullillah!" whispered Idris. He drew the other two quickly into the shade of a doorway. Abdullillah hurried past them, his parrot-like profile jutting forward, and darted into the alley which led toward the serai. "The scoundrel," growled Idris.

"Why? What's the matter?" said David.

"The filthy little scorpion!"

"Oh! Was it Abdullillah who—"

"Ssh!" said Idris. "Quick! Before he runs to the sayyid!"

They waited for Abdullillah's footsteps to die away, then hurried, almost running, toward the two blunt towers that rose on their left. They turned the corner toward the city gate. Two soldiers in turbans stepped from a barred enclosure.

"The gate is closed!"

Idris paused. "A friend is waiting at the gate," he said in a dull, tense voice.

The soldier stared expressionlessly. "There is no one at the gate."

Idris tried to brush past, but the soldier seized him by the arm and shook him gruffly.

"Let me pass!" snarled Idris. "I have a permit."

"No one passes except the dead. The city is locked."

"The sayyid has spoken for us," said Idris, panting. He snatched a slip of green paper out from his sash and flashed it at the guards.

They frowned and stared at the little card, muttering uneasily. At that moment Ahmed came hurrying from the shadow of the gate.

"Marhaba!" he said firmly, rushing up to the guards.

The soldiers glowered at him with sullen eyes. "Marhaba," said the older one, stroking his chin suspiciously.

Ahmed squeezed four little coins into the soldier's hand. The soldier looked puzzled and wrinkled his nose. Ahmed signaled toward the walls, and the fugitives hurried through the gate, which creaked on its hinges as it opened through some invisible agency and then closed behind them again, bolting the rest of the world from the plague-stricken city.

✿

The caravan was waiting down by the edge of the wadi. Everything was rustling in a fever of preparation; ropes were bound, bags were laden, bottles and kettles were tied to the camels' tails. Ahmed had chosen the mounts with care— sturdy beduin camels, inured to thirst and ceaseless marching, as Ahmed explained, with cheeks aglimmer; rather than the more agile, more fashionable Batinah camels, which, according to Ahmed, grew fussy and petulant in a crisis. A spare camel was brought along for the reserves of food and water. Disguises were produced for the fugitives: a pair of voluminous white pantaloons for David, covered by a long white shirt and girded with a dagger and a cartridge-belt. A white kufiya was wrapped around his head.

"You must go barefoot," insisted Ahmed. "No one must see that you are a faranchi."

For Sylvia a pair of pale tight trousers was unfolded, and than a kufiya was cast over her shoulders, flapping loose over her head. A black handkerchief was tied over her hair, and a thick red scarf, a woolen *hazaam,* was wound tightly around her waist.

"Where are we going?" whispered Sylvia.

"To Bir Ali," said Ahmed. He added patiently, "And then to Suqa. And finally Mukalla."

"How long will it take, Ahmed?"

"Not long." He smiled prankishly. "Two days to Bir Ali. Four or five days to Suqa. Two more days to Mukalla. Nine days, mademoiselle."

"Nine more days! But, Ahmed—"

"Maybe less," purred Ahmed. "Or maybe a trifle more. Still, it always seems to take nine days to Mukalla, no matter where we start from."

Now they were introduced to the caravan leaders, Hussein el-Hamri and Yusuf Qamish.

"Bless you," chirped Hussein el-Hamri, a plump little man with birdlike eyes. He mounted his camel, gasping nervously, and finally sat perched on a yellow box, pointing his rifle, his face half covered in the folds of his jerd.

Two black Sudanese, gorilla-like men with sweet low voices, raised Sylvia and David gently aloft. The camels rose one by one. The caravan uncoiled. The six laden camels followed Hussein el-Hamri's. There was a shuffling and tinkling as the camels stretched their legs.

"*Alura!*" cried Yusuf Qamish.

Hussein waved. They started off. A little foal came trotting clumsily alongside the last of the camels. Sylvia sat huddled under her cape, stirred by some supple exhilaration, breathing the medley of spices that fluttered about her like gauze.

Behind them rose Kumra, clifflike, intense. The limestone seemed alive in the brightening moonlight. Smoke was rising from an unseen hollow. A row of figures was passing along the edge of the wall. A quick stench assailed them as a gust of wind ran down from the fortress—burning flesh, burning bones. The bells were ringing again. A strange regret gnawed at Sylvia. It seemed cruel and sad, all of a sudden, to be leaving this godforsaken place, this city filled to the brink with decay.

Finally Kumra was lost in the hills. The caravan turned westward, and they entered the sea-blue indifference of the jol.

33

A shadow blocked the door of the qubba. Dr. Moss turned his head. It was Mahmoud, the sturdy young bedu. His eyes were sparkling like glowworms in the darkness.

"Are you ready?" he whispered.

Dr. Moss lay motionless, trying to evaluate the look in Mahmoud's eyes.

"Come," said Mahmoud quietly. Something in his tone made the doctor rise and step out into the open, where Mahmoud stood beckoning.

"The men of the caravan are waiting," he said, cocking his head toward the wadi, where the distant glow of a campfire was shining behind some rocks.

They started down the slope, which was blocked halfway down by a row of boulders. Mahmoud slid rapidly across them, supple as a snake, but when the doctor tried to climb them he slipped and fell to the ground. A sharp pain struck at his instep.

"Here, here," growled Mahmoud.

Dr. Moss limped after him, grinning with pain. The air in the wadi was heavy and stagnant. They stepped down over a ledge and walked along the dry basin, which crumpled under their feet into a fine black powder. In the distance he heard a high, flutelike sound. Once he thought he heard a man shouting, but he wasn't sure. It scarcely occurred to him to wonder where Mahmoud was leading him. In some odd way the sensation of danger seemed to collide with and melt into the yearning for rest, for oblivion. They plowed through the dust of the wadi-bed, which welled about them in clouds, and climbed down a stairway of rocks which at rainy periods must have been a waterfall. A thicket of camel-thorn enclosed them. The air grew tight, laden. A hint of moisture rose from the depths of the waterfall. Mahmoud plucked at the doctor's hand. They made their way along the side of the cliff and finally reached the bottom.

Here the air was like an oven. Clouds of mosquitoes churned about. Dr. Moss felt his cheeks suddenly itching beyond endurance; he tore at the flesh with his fingernails, snarling with impatience. They stepped through the tangle of withered shrubs and saw the firelight flashing among the rocks directly in front of them.

Mahmoud halted and placed his hand on the doctor's wrist. "Now," he said, panting with the heat.

A group of men—eight or ten of them—had gathered around the fire. He could see them leaning closer, passing the hashish pipe. Three of the men rose up and began to dance—a primeval sort of jig, more African than Arabian. Himyaritic, perhaps, thought Dr. Moss, aglow with curiosity. He stepped closer. The dancers were almost naked, with bracelets flashing as they moved. Talismans jangled about their necks. Their eyes were glazed with narcotics. They might have been men, it occurred to the doctor, of the notorious Ba Qutmi tribe.

One of the men began an incantation, swaying his hands like an orchestra conductor. Dr. Moss listened carefully; it was a dialect that eluded him. All he grasped was the word "Ingliz" steadily recurring, and once or twice the word "nasrani."

"Is this the caravan?" said the doctor bleakly.

Mahmoud nodded. "They are waiting for you."

"It doesn't look like a caravan," said the doctor in a feverish tone.

Mahmoud turned and smiled at him indulgently. "Come," he said, tugging briskly at the doctor's arm.

The older tribesmen sat in a circle around the fire, shriveled as lizards, little fluffs of white hair shining around their nipples. The three young dancers jerked their way back and forth in front of the flames, eyes burning under their lashes, torsos shimmering with oil. Dr. Moss, crouching behind a rock, began to tremble as he watched them. The old men were swaying, raising thin, rootlike fingers. They looked like old hags, dry-breasted and wispy-haired. A dreadful suspicion crept through the doctor's brain.

"Come," said Mahmoud. "It is time."

Dr. Moss whispered, "No! No!" He tried feebly to break away. But Mahmoud's grip was like iron. He forced the doctor down to the ground, twisting his elbow around his back until he cackled with pain.

"Wait, wait!" the doctor kept panting. "I have something to tell you!"

"What?" said Mahmoud with a hollow look.

"Be my friend! I will help you!"

"I *am* your friend," said Mahmoud, expressionless.

"Take me away. Take me back to Kumra!"

"They will tear you to pieces in Kumra."

Dr. Moss rose to his knees and clutched at Mahmoud's arms. Tears welled from his eyes. "Please! Help me!" He pointed to his wristwatch. "I will give you this! And many other things! Pearls, diamonds! Take me away!"

Mahmoud's eyes were twinkling with amusement. "Are you afraid?"

Dr. Moss stared intently at Mahmoud's dark, sensual face. He felt almost hypnotized by the animal beauty of the eyes.

"No," he said. "I am not afraid." Merely saying it seemed to calm him.

"They will kill you," said Mahmoud gently. "You brought the Makhfi, and now they must kill you."

Dr. Moss looked emptily up at the hills.

"It is not because they hate you," continued Mahmoud almost beseechingly. "It is not hate that they feel." He placed his hands on Dr. Moss's wrist and cocked his head sideways. "You must forgive us, sir. We do this only to gratify the djinns."

Dr. Moss whispered hoarsely, "Is it the will of Allah?"

Mahmoud lowered his eyes uneasily.

"There is no God but Allah!" said the doctor tensely.

"Ah, that is true," said Mahmoud, with guilty eyes. "But there are other spirits too, wicked sand djinns and water djinns."

"And you fear them?" said the doctor.

"Don't be angry with us," pleaded Mahmoud. "If we kill you it is not because we hate you. We do it to destroy the bad turtle-djinn who has crept inside you and spreads the sickness!"

Mahmoud's face grew tense, agitated. Beads of sweat hung on his brow. He leaned over and clutched the doctor's hand; his voice was a rasping whisper. "Come—come."

Dr. Moss glanced around. He was barely conscious of Mahmoud's presence. The air was rapidly cooling. Brilliant moonlight covered the slopes in the west, which seemed coated with snow.

The men by the fire were still dancing. The rhythm had quickened. The three youths were writhing about spasmodically. Suddenly one of them fell to the ground, foaming at the mouth.

"Come!" snarled Mahmoud. He jerked violently at the doctor's arm, drawing him up.

Dr. Moss felt a surge of power run through his muscles, as though the hidden forces of a lifetime were suddenly being poured through a funnel. He tore his arm loose and sent two fingers spearing into Mahmoud's eyes. The enormous Arab swayed, blubbered; his arms struck wildly at the doctor's face. The doctor ducked like a squirrel and jabbed his knee into the Arab's groin. Mahmoud sank to the ground, doubled up, snapping for breath. Dr. Moss reached swiftly into his pocket and drew out the arrowhead, hurled himself astride Mahmoud, and dug his fingernails into Mahmoud's cheeks. An uncontrollable frenzy shook him. The stars shook, the desert quivered. He snarled with excitement as he hacked at Mahmoud's neck with the arrowhead. Mahmoud squealed like a rat; his teeth started chattering. He snatched at the air with both hands, then flung his head back with a muffled roar. Dr. Moss thrust one fist into the Arab's mouth and, with the arrowhead in the other, slit the veins in his throat. Blood came bursting like a fountain. There was a hot, mossy odor. A great spasm shook Mahmoud; his knees shot toward his chin and froze tight. His eyeballs rolled white as his breath gave out and his heart stopped beating. Then everything went limp. His young face, pale as a mask above its collar of blood, gazed at the sky with a look of cowlike indifference.

Dr. Moss started running along the edge of the wadi.

34

He ran on and on. His brain was empty of thought.

Clouds crept out of the plateau and rose wispily toward the moon. The gravel rattled; the wind went whining and stuttering among the boulders. A small avalanche of sand went rolling down into the river-bed, sending a spray of snowy dust behind it. The ground gave way under his feet; he leaped like a cat. Mosquitoes swept after him, cloud upon cloud. He climbed over a mound and stumbled on a broken twig, scraping his knee. "Oh, Lord," he whispered. He glanced back, tense with an awareness of ambush, of hidden enemies lurking among the rocks. The moon winked through a cloud like an idiot's eye. He rose and staggered across the hillock. Just below him was an ancient well-house, a derelict *siqaya*, half hidden by a growth of thorn trees. He half crawled, half rolled down the sandy slope and lurched into the shelter of the little hut. Everything was black here, water-scented. The coolness was wonderfully assuaging. He knelt by the well, which loomed below him, black and bottomless, ringed with slime.

An uncontrollable thirst took hold of him. He dipped his face in the well and lapped at the sweet thick water, which had a faint tang of coffee. He reached up and snatched the tube of aspirin from his pocket. The tablets crumbled between his fingers as he plucked them out. He scooped up the powder with trembling hands and sprinkled it on his tongue, then leaned down and gulped greedily at the ink-black water.

Finally he sank back and muttered, "There. At last. There's nothing to worry about."

He was drenched in sweat. He tore off his coat and shirt

and splashed his bony chest with water. The drops rolled heavily down his skin, cool as marbles. He began to shiver uncontrollably.

"Am I sick?" he wondered mechanically. "Malaria, could it be?"

And then abruptly he slid to the ground and fell asleep.

✿

Even before he opened his eyes he felt the presence of crisis. The smell, maybe? Or the hush of a footfall, almost inaudible? Or perhaps it was nothing more than some telepathic thread that went arrowing through the dark and punctured the stillness of his slumber. He opened his eyes. For a moment he thought he was still in the qubba. Then he recognized the smell of the stale water in the siqaya.

All was black. Only a thin slab of silver hung by the door. A crack of moonlight, it might have been. But it wasn't; he felt sure of it. He smelled the odor of blood-lust, thick and sullen, like the smell of iodine. The gleam of the knife crept closer, slow, patient as a snail. He caught the scent of a man's breath. There was the stink of shark-meat. Now he knew who it was. He lay still as a stone. He closed his eyes for a moment, but then the terror was even greater. It was like falling into a snake-pit. He stared at the door, trying to see some trace of a silhouette. But the moon had gone again; the night was black as tar; all he saw was a patch of shadow crouching in the deeper black of the hut, hardly stirring, yet intensely alive, hot, imminent.

The old bedu crept closer. The doctor's eyes grew blurred. The knife hung poised over his belly, scarcely three feet away. His brain shot into the air, piercing the sky like a hawk, until the earth seemed to glow beneath him, infinitely far away, small as an ember. On he swept, higher and higher, his great wing-beats bearing him on through the aisles of time.

The knife fell. Dr. Moss gave a little cry. His body leaped and then sank again on the still cool sand.

BOOK THREE

The Desert

35

When morning came they were crossing the hills that shielded the wadi from the south. Everything was drawn by the morning light into a kind of hard, dead stillness. No life was left in the earth. On the mouse-gray rises lay scattered the shells of empty houses; down in the hollows lay the mounds of long-deserted wells. Only a few miserable peasants still lurked about here and there, trudging across the slopes like mummies, naked and dusty.

Then the sun exploded. Everything shot into flames. The frozen stillness began to seethe. The sand seemed to flow in great cascades. Then that too died, and the desolation of total light fell over the scene.

After the hills had been crossed the scenery grew baroque— no longer that smooth, clear deadness. There was a look of lawlessness, delinquency—ridges bitten by wind and sandstorm, crazy lumps of coagulated earth. Wandering shepherdesses peeked at the caravan through wisps of brushwood.

"Look!" cried Idris. "There it is!"

They had come to a siqaya. The little dome shone through the rocks like a thumb of snow. They halted. One by one they reached through the mud-wrought latticework and drank from the dipper, which was tied to the wall with an iron chain. It was the sweetest, coolest water that David had ever drunk —as though the crystal freshness of the night still lay concentrated in each drop.

The men stripped off their futahs and splashed the water over their heads. They squealed with delight as the cold green beads ran down their spines. Character, habit, even the landscape lay mirrored in their bodies. Ahmed's body was tense and wiry, already a bit corroded by the desert. The older men were bowlegged, lean-shanked, sway-backed with the life of the caravans. Only Idris was straight and symmetrical, with hard thick breasts and arrowing belly curving toward the flat, smiling groin. They were all circumcised in the Moslem fashion, and most of them were almost hairless, but Yusuf Qamish was shaggy as an ox, speckled with tufts of blue-black hair.

They lay and slept for several hours to break the heat of the day. Strips of burlap were soaked in water and draped like a marquee to shelter the sleepers.

The land grew dented and craggy as they wandered westward through the afternoon. The air grew cooler; flowers shone among the blood-red gorges. There were tufts of fuzzy pink, like rhododendron, and sweet-smelling clusters of white, like oleander. There was also a curious creeping plant which the Arabs called *batata:* dragonflies went zooming from blossom to blossom on wings of lapis lazuli.

"What is this flower?" said David, pointing to a flower which looked like a blue nasturtium.

"Tsk, tsk!" cried Idris. "Don't touch it! It's a wicked flower, Sir Daïd."

"Is it poisonous?"

"It's haunted!"

"Haunted by what, Idris?"

But Idris wasn't listening. He had disappeared among the bushes, chasing a gold-spangled butterfly.

"*Ya bayya!*" called Ahmed. "Idris! Come back!" He turned to David confidentially. "Idris is a butterfly-brain, sir. Do not listen to his silliness. That flower is a nice, respectable flower. Even the camels eat it."

They halted in the shade of a gorge, and the beduin made a fire of dry camel-thorn. They set up their tent of goats' hide and hung a blanket to cut off the wind. Then they lay beside the fire while the pots bubbled and sang to the sound of Yusuf Qamish's little viol, which he called a *rababa*. And the Arabs, so incredibly patient on the road, so calm and tena-

cious in hardship, now in the hours of leisure grew wanton
and volatile. Ahmed started reciting ballads. Idris did a Jav-
anese dance. One by one the men grew drowsy and disappeared
behind the stones for a nap.

And all the time David felt a curious stillness inside him.
He spread out his fingers and watched the glow of the fire
shine through the skin.

✿

"How strange it is!" said Ahmed, his powerful eyes aglow
with the firelight. "Yesterday we were in Kumra, surrounded
by people. Today we are in the hills, surrounded by stones.
Life is a wandering thing, isn't it?"

"You love wandering, don't you, Ahmed?"

"Ah, yes, only wandering is real," said the bedu. "To stay
in one place becomes unreal. One forgets what the world is
really like. Look, Sir Daïd! The stones and the wind and the
flies, and this piece of broken rope, and my left arm itching—
all that is real. But those hills beyond the jol are real too,
only I do not see them. And Qamr Bay is real, though I do
not see it. And Persia and Russia are real. Even London is
real, I suppose. I must always keep on wandering or I forget
that other places are real. The world is not real except for
the man with a wandering heart. Just think! Men are sitting this very moment around a fire somewhere in Russia, or
even London, listening to a rababa and watching the camels
sleeping."

"You are happy to be a bedu?"

"Happy beyond all happiness!" Ahmed looked at David
absently and took David's hand in his own. "We desert beduin
possess the world. The desert is mine! These cliffs are mine!
Even the stars are mine! Our lives belong to one another.
We have no secrets, like the city men—no shames, no worries.
Why do men in the cities hide their lives, sir? And pretend to
be other than what they are? Does it bring them happiness to
hide? I am a bedu and I do not think so. All we ask of a man

in the desert is that he fight bravely against his enemies, be
generous and loyal, abide by Islam, and love fine horses. All
else is trivial. Let him make love as he wishes. Let him dress
as he wishes and kill as he wishes. A man is a man. All men
are forgiven, except he who is frightened of his own true
self. Such a man is empty and false. Little by little he turns
into a ghost!"

There was silence for several minutes. Ahmed gazed into
the coals. He had never spoken as much as this. David felt
touched, vaguely honored. The firelight accentuated the
bedu's expression—the fervor, the poise, the calm nobility;
even the sly animal innocence.

Ahmed turned to David. "Why did you come to Arabia,
sir?"

"You know why I came, Ahmed. A plane fell out of the
sky, and I was in it!"

"Yes, yes," said Ahmed, frowning impatiently. "But there
was a reason behind it. It was destined that you come to
Arabia. The falling plane was just an excuse. There was some
reason in your soul that made you come to Arabia!"

"You think that everything in our lives is destined,
Ahmed?"

"Mm." Ahmed smiled. "Every hair on our heads."

"Then we are helpless?"

"Oh! Utterly!"

"Then why do we struggle?"

"We are destined to struggle! Always and forever, Sir Daïd.
It is the will of Allah."

✿

The last of the flames were dancing in the boughs of camel-
thorn. Sylvia climbed over the stones and curled up next to
David.

"Look at the flames," she murmured, touching his wrist
with her forefinger. "What do you see there, darling?"

David stared. "I see horses galloping over the sand."

"I see a humming-bird fluttering, I think."

"And now I see a fox crawling under a fence."

"Look. There's a snake climbing a tree."

David tossed a pebble into the fire. "We're turning into children, aren't we?"

"No, no," said Sylvia, looking mischievous. "We're turning into Arabs!"

She glanced at her toes, which were red and swollen with the long day's journey. "Tell me, darling," she murmured. "Do you think you'll ever fall in love?"

"I try to love everyone a little," said David. "That's more sensible, don't you think?"

"Is it?" Sylvia sighed. "Do you really think so?" She poked at the fire with a broken twig. Suddenly she turned to David with great, beseeching eyes. "Am I very ugly, David?"

"You are very pretty, Sylvia. You have beautiful eyes."

Sylvia shook her head miserably. "No, no. I know better. I'm dreadfully plain. Look. My mouth is too big. I'm bony and scrawny. My hair is all in a tangle. No one will ever fall in love with me."

"Don't be impatient. You're still very young, my dear."

"I'm not a child, David. I'm a woman! Listen, I already—" She blushed; then she whispered, "David, tell me. Do you think you'd ever want to sleep with me?"

David looked at her quickly.

"Someday maybe? When I'm less homely?"

"What would you like me to say?"

She tossed her head. "I don't care!"

"Then why do you ask?"

"Oh. Merely curiosity." Her lips trembled, her eyes flashed. "I know what you think. You think I'm a virgin!"

"You're not a virgin?"

"Certainly not!"

A creeping tenderness rose up in David. "Listen, Sylvia. I have something to tell you," he began.

But at that moment Yusuf Qamish came rushing up to them, waving a blanket.

"What's wrong, Yusuf Qamish?"

Yusuf Qamish looked agitated. "Bandits, sir! From Raïda."

"Where?"

Yusuf waved toward the north.

"Who saw them?"

"Ismaël!"

Ismaël was the cook of the caravan, a leathery old man with eyes like a salamander's, which he closed by raising the bottom lids.

The camels were growing restless; they sensed the alarm in the air. "Come," cried Ismaël, scurrying about to gather the pots and kettles. "Kill the fire and let's leave. One more hour and we'll be in the plains."

The camels rose, and they started off through the dawn for Bir Ali.

36

In Bir Ali the vines were already in flower. Blossoms clung to the foliage like great azure butterflies. Under the boughs seethed the honey-bees in a golden cloud. Off in the east the old shepherds sat crouched on the rocks, gnawing away at strips of bark, small gray beards fluttering wispily. Naked boys were playing leap-frog under the date palms. The caravan passed an old cemetery. Small pink tombstones, cracked by centuries, were sprinkled at random behind a well—medieval warriors, said Yusuf, who had been buried as they fell in battle.

They arrived at the inn, which was surprisingly pleasant and hospitable.

They entered the gate, and the camels were led to the camel court. The guests were ushered into the shady wing of the serai. Carpets and cushions had already been put out for the unknown visitors. It was late, almost dusk, but the cook went scampering down to the kitchen, and soon the delicious odor of barbecue welled through the patio. Sylvia was led through an arch to a little room hung with curtains. A hook-nosed servant brought an oil lamp, trimmed the wick with her fingers. A tongue of light shot from the snout; suddenly the night closed in.

"I am Jamila," said the maid, rolling her ostrich-like eyes.

She flung open a door into a hexagonal patio. Sylvia caught the hard, brisk scent of Arabian vegetation. Jamila came up beside Sylvia and carefully drew off her clothes, and Sylvia stepped into the pool, which was tiled in black, no larger than a bathtub. A glow of well-being passed through her nerves. The water slid over her skin; the ache and the weariness were gone.

A cymbal sounded—dinnertime. The servant led her back through the patio, and she entered a long cool room covered with rugs and cushions. David was waiting for her, freshly bathed and barbered. Hussein and Yusuf Qamish bowed solemnly; they were wearing clean white kufiyas. They dipped their fingers in a copper basin and moved toward the other end of the room, where a majolica bowl stood on a bowlegged table—a giant kous-kous seasoned with sugar, almonds, figs, and raisins. They ate with quick, gingerly gestures, dipping their fingers in the kous-kous and rolling the grains into yellow balls, grunting and belching politely. A curtain parted. An impressive personage walked slowly into the room—some sort of sayyid, perhaps, or a village dignitary. To Sylvia he looked magnificent and terrifying, with his shaggy beard and flashing amulets and wild, libidinous eyes.

A whole sheep, freshly roasted, was ushered into the room and laid on a circular mat among bowls of rice. Platters of dates dipped in butter were passed around, and a succulent silence fell on the guests. The smoke from the oil lamps grew thicker. Sylvia felt vaguely drugged. Footsteps rustled outside the window—the townsmen were gathering for a dance, apparently.

"A war dance," said the local dignitary. "Bir Ali is famous for its warriors!"

A copper ewer of tea was brought, and a basket of figs.

The conversation continued. Yusuf Qamish praised the figs. The local dignitary spoke in favor of aristocracy. Hussein el-Hamri condemned the Turks, the French, and the Jews. Then Yusuf Qamish praised poetry. The dignitary spoke in favor of nightingales. Hussein el-Hamri condemned tobacco, homosexuality, and communism. The dignitary disagreed, dipping an almond cake in his teacup. Communism was deplorable, tobacco was unclean, but sodomy was a blessing to women, who would otherwise be in a perpetual state of pregnancy. Yusuf Qamish replied with a discourse on *imsak*—imsak being the Arab technique of contraception, the retention of semen by the male during the orgasm. The dignitary spoke airily in favor of chastity and decorum. Hussein el-Hamri ended by roundly denouncing the Egyptians, the Lebanese, and the Abyssinians—the first for their venality, the second for their ugliness, the third for their lack of personal hygiene.

Sylvia sat listening, wide-eyed. She hardly understood what the men were saying. Their low, unscrupulous voices were like an incantation. The smoke from the lamps, the rustle of footsteps, the glittering eyes of the bearded dignitary—she felt trapped in a shaggy, carnivorous world of males.

A musket went off. Shouts rose from the village soukh. The dance finally began to the sound of chanting and strumming. Fireworks flashed over the date palms, and the scent of gunpowder seeped through the latticework, mingling with the cozy fumes of roast mutton and incense.

✿

Sylvia returned to her room, feeling slightly dizzy.

A curtain had been drawn aside in the alcove, revealing an old brass bedstead of equivocal European origin, draped with disintegrating tulle and a spray of artificial rosebuds. Jamila smiled with a dainty pride as she drew off the coverlets. A Venetian mirror, cracked through the middle, hung in a small green niche. Jamila vanished. Sylvia gazed intently at the mirror. She was shocked by the change. Her face was dark with the sun, like an Arab boy's. Her cheeks were bolder, her mouth firmer, her eyes deeper and more alert. She drew off her tobh and placed two fingertips on her nipples. A sting of yearning shot through her, spreading puckers of gooseflesh across her back. She was passing through a menstrual period; a depressing indolence took hold of her suddenly; she sank onto the bed and buried her face in the pillow.

Something brushed her thighs lightly, like a silken thread. She glanced down. A small object had lit on her belly, blue and furry, like a cornflower. It stirred, leaped suddenly—an enormous spider. She jumped up and seized the cushion. She saw that the bed was alive with spiders; they were lurking in every fold; they came popping like corks from the satin coverlet.

She screamed. "Jamila!"

The lamp swayed, the shadows shifted, and she saw that the walls were seething with vermin, spiders and centipedes hanging in garlands from the crumbling plaster.

She shook with panic. "Jamila! Jamila!"

Jamila ran in from the patio, hands fluttering.

Sylvia was staring at the walls, speechless with horror. "Ah," Jamila purred, flinging a shawl over Sylvia's shoulders. "Don't be upset, madame. They won't bite you." She picked up a spider and looked at it tenderly. "They bring luck! They protect you! They are the souls of earlier wanderers who have stayed in the inn."

She led Sylvia to another room, which gave out on an oval courtyard. A brand-new room, explained Jamila. No wanderers had ever slept here. She sighed reproachfully. "No souls to protect you! Sleep peacefully, madame."

Outside Sylvia's window, the click-click of the domino-players kept her awake. Somewhere in a distant part of the inn there was the scraping of records on a worn-out phonograph. Outside the window the vines looked white and thin, bending in the wind. A bearded man stood under the tree, making water against the wall.

She lay down in the bed, filled with terror—not of spiders this time, but of something mightier, more immanent. The room revolved like a whirlpool. Then everything came to a halt. A strange rigidity possessed her. She longed to cry, but the sound clung to her throat. Nausea rose up in her in gradual, peristaltic waves. She jumped out of her bed, raced into the courtyard, and vomited.

She knelt in a corner of the patio, feeble and bleary-eyed. The world had splintered into triangles like a broken mirror.

Nothing made sense. The frame had crumbled. The future and past were nothing but fog, through which the present loomed indistinctly, like a fluttering scarecrow.

She cried softly, "David!"

A bat came dipping out of the roof. She fell asleep without warning, sprawled out on the urine-scented flagstones.

✿

Once she woke up for a moment or two. The air had cooled; leaves were rustling. A boy in a futah leaned over her, touching her forehead lightly.

"*Mallalah*," he whispered, and ran his fingers over her belly.

Then he whispered something else, which sounded like, "*Sadra! Sadra!*" and tiptoed into the darkness of the loggia.

The following morning she woke up in the arms of Ahmed, who was carrying her back into her room. Her malaise had gone; she felt cool and refreshed. Through her latticed window she could see the village soukh, already crowded with the bustle of caravans. Bearded men with the appraising, wistful look of far horizons stood about in solemn groups. Laden camels were barking from the camel courts, eager to be off. In the middle of the soukh sat a juggler in a green kimono, tossing knives. An old snake-charmer was unraveling the snakes from his basket and plunging their heads into his mouth like a row of cigars. Cocks were crowing, dogs were yelping, a flurry of blackbirds swung over the cornfields.

Sunlight fell on the dome of the mosque. The muezzin called. The Arabian day had begun with a shrill, clownish cheerfulness.

✿

Jamila came to take Sylvia for a visit to the harim.

It was a modest little harim, much smaller than the one in

Kumra. The ladies sat by their balconies with inquisitive painted eyes. The wives in favor were cheerful and opulently dressed, tinkling with necklaces of silver, trailing feathers of perfume; those out of favor had lapsed into a kind of slovenly dejection. An elderly *sherifa,* an aunt of the sayyid's, opened a large straw trunk and drew out a cataract of dry, wrinkled satins.

"Have you brought us gifts?" cooed the sherifa.

Sylvia blushed. "No. Forgive me."

"Little bottles? Full of smells?"

"I'm dreadfully sorry," pleaded Sylvia.

She drew off her silver bracelet and dropped it into the sherifa's palm. There was a hum of appreciation. The sherifa reached into the trunk and chose a gift in return—a long purple cape with gold-braided sleeves. A young woman with beady eyes sidled up casually and ran her fingers along Sylvia's arms, patted her buttocks, pinched her nipples. She shook her head disapprovingly. "Hard! Thin! Like a boy!"

The shriveled sherifa flung the cape over Sylvia's shoulders. "The color of love," she said, fluttering her tiny fingers.

She plucked at a row of multi-colored beads along the collar. "Green," she chirped. "Green is for courage. Yellow for joy. White for innocence. Black for patience. Red for desire. And gold for pride. You will need all of them, my child. All of them!"

"Thank you, madame," said Sylvia, bashful.

The sherifa gazed at Sylvia searchingly, cocking her head. "You are unwell, mademoiselle," she whispered.

Sylvia looked away quickly. "It's been a difficult journey, I'm afraid."

"You have been too much with men," said the sherifa, pursing her lips. "You have lost your delicacy. Your beauty."

"I was never beautiful," said Sylvia, sad-eyed.

The sherifa ruffled her shawl. "My dear child," she began. Her eyes were hard and greedy, like a magpie's.

A bell tinkled; Jamila ran up, waving Sylvia's djellaba. It

was time to leave. The camels were strolling through the archway.

"Farewell!" cried Sylvia, raising the thick white curtain from the doorway.

The sherifa stared at her with melting eyes and nodded swiftly, three times.

37

"This way," said Yusuf Qamish, "takes six days to Mukalla. We go down the wadi south of the hills. It is not long. The land is peaceful."

"And the other way?" said David.

"Five days only. But the land is troubled."

"Bandits?"

"No. Not exactly."

"Hostile tribes?"

Yusuf leered. "Go the peaceful way, sir, and pay the men for an extra day."

"How much do we pay for five days?"

"Thirty thalers. Three for each man and ten for the food."

"We will pay them in Mukalla, I suppose?"

"They are nervous. They want it now."

"I have no thalers, Yusuf Qamish."

Yusuf sighed. "They won't go."

There was only one thing to do. "I have some pearls, Yusuf Qamish. Will you buy them from me?"

"Let me see the pearls," said Yusuf Qamish.

David opened the pigskin case. There were forty-four pearls on the chain. He broke the chain and drew off one, two, three little pearls.

Yusuf Qamish smiled disparagingly. "I am sorry, sir. Three pearls are nothing. A pearl is worth three thalers in this part of the world. Not a penny more."

David drew off seven more pearls. "Thirty thalers," he said.

"And how do we go? The peaceful way?" said Yusuf Qamish.

"Come. We are leaving," said David angrily, beckoning to Ahmed. "Go the troubled way if you wish. We want to get to Mukalla."

✿

The gazelles down in the wadi were almost tame, gazing limpidly at the passing caravan. A flock of sheep grazed nearby. Shepherds were gamboling among the hillocks, surveying the roving flocks. They called out merrily to the travelers and began to play on their pipes. Long after they had vanished the sound of their pipes still hung in the air, lonely and unanswerable, like a cry of longing.

A deep gully ran through the foothills, and in it a thread of water moved lazily, pausing in cherry-red pools, gurgling and trickling into the shadows. A wooden bridge bound with rope spanned the gully. First Ahmed crossed, stepping gingerly over the planks. Then came the first camel. It paused at the edge with an insulted air, then crossed, raising its hoofs like a ballet dancer. Then the rest of the camels crossed, never more than one at a time. One of them stumbled—a weary old naga. A water-bag broke from its halter and fell into the gully. The planks swayed and creaked; the ropes crackled ominously. Finally David and Sylvia crossed with Idris on foot, and the empty bridge rocked behind them in a haze of dust.

They met some pilgrims, pious men from the shores of Oman. The older, wealthier men were jogging along on donkeys. The young ones walked barefooted, tugging at their umbrellas in the fitful wind. A group of Negroes followed the procession, husky fellows who had crossed from Massawa on sailing boats, brisk and smiling in contrast to the grim, fanatical Arabs.

"*Keif halak,*" they muttered as they passed, nodding their enormous heads.

Some carried heavy-handled swords of the type carried by the Crusaders; others wore little daggers strapped to their biceps. More and more of the pilgrims gathered, hundreds and hundreds, and finally they came to a halt at the edge of the gully. They trod their way over the sandstone, which blazed in the sun, bright as topaz. A sacrificial feast was prepared in the shade of the cliffs, and soon the rocks were spattered with the blood of the goats. Hearths were hastily built, rings of stone filled with charcoal, and over the embers stones were laid on which the meat began to sizzle. Columns of smoke drifted skyward. The old men sat clicking their rosaries and chewing bitter myrrh, to prepare their stomachs for the heavy feast. They sat on cushions of sheepskin, while the naked butchers skipped about, brandishing their knives, their bellies dappled with sprays of blood.

The prayers began to rise. *"Allah illa Allahi . . ."*

Three silver planes passed overhead through the glare of blue. Strangely powerful they looked, more real and yet at the same time more dreamlike than the land below and the praying Mohammedans. One shaggy-browed man shook his fist toward the sky.

"What is he saying?" inquired David.

"Some sort of curse," said Ahmed casually. "Floods. Hurricanes. Explosions. The usual sort of thing."

"Against us all?"

"No, no." Ahmed grinned. "Only against the land of the evil bird-men!"

✿

Two hours later an ugly wind was creeping up from the south. Slowly they felt it drawing closer, its power still hidden, its fury muted. The sky grew veiled over the southern horizon; a sheet of dust sprayed over the dunes.

Then they heard it—a delicate whine, which broadened into a dull, hoarse rumble. The air grew stale and nerveless; the heat smelled like potassium. A wall of dust enclosed them, and the men flung shawls over their faces. The path dipped, and they entered a valley, and the wind went galloping off to the north.

A young Arab rode over the dunes, a black filly loping behind him.

"Keif halak!" cried the caravan.

"*Taiyib, Taiyib*," replied the rider and halted his horse beside Hussein, who kept glancing nervously at Yusuf Qamish. It was a lovely Arabian mare with bloodshot eyes, flanks matted with sweat and nostrils distended. The little filly kept prancing about with sudden, uncertain curvets. A falcon sat on the rider's wrist, feathers shabby and frayed, with a bloodthirsty look in its wild, hacking eyes. It rocked gently as it sat there, head thrust forward, beak clenched, but something in its stillness hinted at the love that existed between the rider and his bird.

"What is its name?" said Ahmed.

"Zurayda," whispered the rider, his face lit up by a huge, sweet smile.

He looked like a dandy as he sat there in his high-pommeled saddle, which was decorated with tassels and tanned with mimosa; the one black rein hung loose from his outspread fingers. He wore a camel's hair cloak over his cool silken dress; his eyelids were painted dark blue, and a heavy scent spread from his body. A rifle swung negligently over his chest.

He frowned and whispered to Ahmed.

"He wants us to follow," said Ahmed dourly.

There was an uneasy consultation between Hussein and Yusuf Qamish.

Then Hussein nodded, and the caravan curved to the north, following the rider.

✿

The tribesmen sat in a circle, smoking their tribal pipes. Ismaël came up and placed a basin of camel's milk beside them, and then a bowl of barley and a kettle of tea. The tribesmen began to gossip, appeased by the prospect of further offerings.

"Whom did you meet on the way?" said one.

"What is the news from Ash Shihr?" said another.

A third said, "What is the price of dates in Mukalla? And of silk in Mocha? Do you happen to know?"

Two bedu girls sat plaiting the young men's hair, which hung down to their nipples, bright and powerful. It was being washed in camel's urine and oiled with sheep butter and then spiced with mercury, to kill the lice. They were incredibly vain, these young men, sprinkling their bodies with incense and rubbing powdered antimony over their eyes. It was the girls who were fresh and stalwart, the men who were puffed up like turkey-cocks.

Finally the bargaining began. The tribesmen wanted gold. They had no gold, said Hussein obsequiously. Silver, then, insisted the tribesmen. Ninety thalers, and they could continue. Hussein quivered with humility. Ninety thalers! What did they imagine? This was a poor, inadequate caravan, and they had no gold, no silver, not even silks or incense. What did they have? inquired the tribesmen darkly. The price must be paid; if the price was not paid they would have to take over the camels. Hussein winced. A few pearls, that's all they had, he said miserably, wrinkling his crafty little eyes.

Finally the price was established and paid. Twenty pearls were slid from the chain and dropped into the palm of the oldest tribesman, who rolled them about greedily, peered at them, sniffed at them, and finally tasted them with the tip of his tongue.

Ismaël came waddling up with new trays of food. The tribesmen were all in high spirits by now, clapping their hands and jingling their talismans. Idris brought out his mizmar, and one of the girls leaped up to dance. The excitement kept rising, fanned by the fumes of the hashish pipe. The old men clapped their hands in an accelerating rhythm. Idris's wrist danced like a bird along the edge of his flute. Eyes sparkled, lips shone; feet started to quiver. The bedu girl swayed to the music, supple as a stoat. She was unveiled; in the oasis all the women had been veiled.

A strange unease filled the air. One of the boys sprang toward the firelight.

"Look, look!" he cried, swelling his biceps and breaking a knife between his fists.

"Look!" cried another, lifting a huge, smoldering log out of the fire.

"Look at me!" cried a third, ripping his loincloth from his body.

Others rose one by one and joined the onanistic dancer. A rhythmic chant began: "Oom-oom . . . Oom-oom . . ." Eyes were glittering with drugs; bellies and thighs shone with sweat. The scent of sex, pungent and peppery, joined the odor of woodsmoke. Idris was swept into a maelstrom of naked bodies, and the last that David saw, as he stole with Sylvia back to their tent, was the bedu girl flung through the air, sleek as a mackerel, and trapped in a flurry of long brown arms.

38

The following day brought the "phantom lands," as Ahmed called them. The air at dawn was still chilly. The men were shivering under their sheepskins as the sun rose in a yellow mist. Gusts of acrid brown smoke were wafted from the camel-dung fire, and finally Ismaël brought them the tea which drove away weariness.

Then they rose and rode into the harsh morning freshness. Paleolithic flints lay strewn on the ground, flashing in the sun. A shattered, derelict land, as though a hammer out of the sky had sent it splintering into fragments. Slowly, impalpably, like time itself, the shadows of clouds flowed over the *tufa*.

"No faranchi has ever passed those hills," observed Hussein. "These tribes hate the faranchis. They think whiteness means treachery. The white faranchi, they think, has brought turmoil into the land."

David looked quizzical. "Maybe it's true?"

"Ah, who knows?" Hussein belched. "Turmoil and misery are the will of God. Even the white faranchi, with all his cleverness, can do nothing against the will of God."

He tugged meaningly at David's sleeve. "Yesterday's tribe allowed us to continue. That was the Ram Taqid tribe. But tomorrow's tribe, the Ruquda tribe, is far more pious and dangerous!"

The clouds died. A new onslaught of light began. Even his muslin clothes grew oppressive to David. Instinctively the camels moved toward the patches of shade, but even in the shade the heat was suffocating. His eyes stung under the sweat, and a headache hammered at his skull. The ground burned at his feet through the thick-soled sandals. The grains of sand sprayed up by the hoofs burned his skin like flying embers.

Tiny circles of white-hot thread kept spinning in front of his eyes. They grew larger and larger; they turned into fiery turbines churning in a sleek, swollen void. He listened: it was like the roar of a great Niagara. Through the rush of waters the wheels kept singing, "Something will happen . . . something will happen . . ."

A tiny cloud shaped like a razor floated across the sun.

Never mind, he thought, forcing his nerves into calm. Nothing will happen.

At noon the sun blazed over a lifeless world. The real desert was beginning, the periphery of the Rub al Khali—no shrubs, no watering places, not even a hill as far as the eye could wander or the mind imagine. There was an air of terrific newness about the earth, of light and space freshly cast in a white-hot mint.

✣

"Hamdullillah!" cried Hussein and slid off his camel for the noonday prayers. Ismaël huddled under his pea-green parasol and opened a tin of sardines.

"Where are we exactly?" said David.

"Nowhere exactly." Yusuf sighed. "This place has no name. It is too empty even to have a name."

Ismaël glared from the corners of his eyes. "Tamr lies to the north."

"There is water in Tamr," admitted Yusuf.

"Should we go to Tamr, perhaps?" said David.

Yusuf rested his bearded chin on the knob of his cane. "We *should*." He nodded. David waited. Something had been left unsaid.

"Is it too far?" suggested David.

"Perhaps," said Yusuf enigmatically.

The gravel flamed under the light. A vivid mirage danced on the brink of the plain. A flood of green water was flowing over the empty sands. The backs of the camels bounced like dolphins among the heat-waves, and the dunes were a foaming blaze of surf. They mounted imperceptibly. The intensity of heat declined, and they entered a tableland with ripples of slate running westward.

An hour passed. The tinted earth gave way to a blinding white limestone.

Another hour went by. It was time for their evening prayers.

"Haya alla sala! Haya alla fellah!" Their voices broke through the air, bleak and plaintive. They spread out for a nap, planning to continue by starlight. A fire was built, and two of the drivers droned out verses from the Koran, a lulling monotonous sound which sent David to sleep.

When he opened his eyes again the stars were on fire.

39

They rode on through the night. Their footsteps died in the snow-soft sand. Sylvia looked at the stars, those burning asters with Arabic names, which shone over the land as though they had grown out of Arabia: the Scorpion, Aqrab, Deneb the Tail, Altair the Flyer, and Aldebaran, who was the Follower.

Distant volcanoes appeared in the north, drawing smooth black outlines across the horizon. The paraffin lamps swayed noiselessly, the voices of the camel-men were crooning, the saucepans tinkled against the shanks of the camels, and Ahmed kept humming the ninety-nine names of God, to keep awake.

The strange pain in the bottom of her throat had gone. The throbbing behind her eyeballs had gone too. But something else had come instead—a feeling that everything was unreal, that these camels and men prowling across the sand were just dolls dangling in space: they weren't real, they weren't even moving; everything she saw was a mirage, and the only reality was this strange dark fever welling around her. It was a fever that sang like the sea; it moaned and echoed like a great surf breaking.

"No, no," she kept whispering. "Don't listen to it. Don't listen to it."

Once they paused for a nap. They ate their last remaining rations of roasted meat, and the renewal of strength brought a renewal of pain and discomfort. Sylvia lay on a sheepskin, Ahmed beside her, and they stared at the stars while the rest of the beduin lay sleeping. Soon the brilliance of the night diminished; morning was drawing near. The stars shone down on them with a dove-gray coolness.

She laid her head on Ahmed's arm. "We're friends now, Ahmed, aren't we?"

"Friends of iron, my little madame."

"Ahmed." She looked at him tensely. "Tell me something." His face grew expressionless.

She wavered. She did not ask what she wanted to ask. Instead she said, "Tell me, Ahmed. Will we ever get to Aden?"

Ahmed's eyes grew stern and distant. He knew she was thinking of something else. "We live on hope," he whispered.

She pressed her face into Ahmed's powerful, bristling neck and began to sob.

"Yes. I know," said Ahmed tenderly, stroking the hair back from her forehead. "You love him. And he is cold. Be patient, dear little madame."

✿

Idris tapped her on the shoulder and woke her up before dawn. His teeth were flashing in a catlike smile.

"Is it time to go?"

"Almost!" He took her hand and held it against his breast. "Do you feel my heart beating?"

She nodded.

"Never has my heart beaten so strongly!"

"Are you in love, Idris?"

"Ssh, madame!" He placed his finger on his lips. "It is forbidden in the desert to speak of love!"

She drew her hand away, troubled. "Love doesn't exist in the desert?"

"Not a love that has a name. Nothing in the desert has a name. One must speak of nothing in the desert that cannot be seen with the eyes or touched with the fingers!"

"Idris, listen. Sometimes I see things that can't be seen with the eyes. Sometimes I'm afraid of things I don't understand, Idris."

"Don't be afraid," purred Idris. "All will be well. No Arab will ever hurt you. Not even a bad bedu!" His voice grew courteous, circumspect. "To the bedu you are not beautiful. Unusual, yes. Mysterious, yes. But not at all lovely. Look. Your hair is straight as the wind. Your eyes are like a boy's. Your mouth is a boy's. Your hips are slender, your buttocks are small, your breasts are no bigger than figs! You are not for the bedu. Unless, of course—" He smiled at her mischievously.

"Unless what, Idris?"

"Get up, madame! It is almost light. Look, there goes Ismaël with his teapot."

✿

Tamr lay just over the hill, but it was "an angry, God-loving town," said Yusuf. So Ahmed was sent discreetly on foot through the early dawn, to fetch food. He took Ismaël's basket and parasol and disappeared over the dunes while the rest of the men started packing their goatskins.

Then they sat in the shade of the tent, waiting for Ahmed to return. He crept through the mouse-gray dunes, vanishing and reappearing, a tiny black spot in that limbo-like emptiness. They waited two hours; Idris grew nervous. Yusuf told for the seventh time the tale of the thief from Medina, and Ismaël recited for the third time the ballad about the ogres from Mocha. They kept straining their eyes. No sign of Ahmed.

Idris climbed to the peak of a hillock.

"Can you see anything, Idris?"

"No. Not yet. Soon, I think."

And then: "Anything in sight, Idris?"

"Not yet."

And finally: "Look again, Idris!"

"The sun is blinding. I see nothing at all."

Idris grew sulky and melancholy. He spoke of Ahmed with a sorrowing reverence, as of a long-lost parent. "He has what only the greatest of men still have, my friends. He has both *irdh* and *murnah!*" He explained to David. *Irdh,* or honor, meant power and nobility of character. *Murnah,* or manliness, meant loyalty, courage, and generosity.

The stillness of the hills was a waiting stillness. The air had the glaze of a telescope. Iqbal, who was a cousin of Yusuf Qamish and the youngest one in the caravan, started tying the last of the bags together. They were considering a four-hour detour to Tamr to fetch Ahmed, leaving Sylvia and David behind with Idris for the rest of the day.

But then a bright green beetle came crawling over the dunes—Ahmed and his parasol.

He was weary and irritable when he finally joined the caravan, carrying a baby lamb and a jug of honey. The camels rose, and they started off toward the west, with their shadows wandering lazily in front of them.

40

"Tariq!" cried the camel-boy. The camels rose, grunting petulantly. Slowly they entered the zone of the volcanoes.

They passed into a huge, rocky amphitheater. In the distance lay the scallops of a range, rolling like waves in the foaming light. Men and beasts, with their goatskins dangling, looked curiously bright and biblical. The camels paused to nibble some frail volcanic flowers which clung to the rocks.

"Tariq! Tariq!" cried the camel-boy. The camels obediently proceeded.

On they rode, gradually entering a new kind of dreariness —hard gray hummocks, on which the hoofs left only faint little marks, like commas, and a wadi below them which had been parched for decades; its dryness was sadder than the usual desert dryness, with cracks dividing the earth into great octagonal tiles. Above them shone the irregular crests of rock —chunks of obsidian, smooth as glass, radiating a whole spectrum of colors.

The camels moved along, supercilious as dowagers. There was something grand about these patient, dour, arrogant creatures. Man's link with the desert: the drabness as well as the pride, the indignation of the desert. Young Iqbal loved his camel with a deep, unuttered love. He walked close beside it, stroking its belly now and then.

Once three shadows appeared, moving in single file along the ridge. They looked like men from the Ruquda tribe, remarked Hussein—brightly decked, dressed in black. They paused for a minute or two on the ridge and disappeared on the other side of the hill.

"They are devils," said Yusuf. "Those men from the Ruquda tribe."

"Devils?" said David.

"All in black! With souls like midnight."

"Do you also have angels in Arabia?"

"Yes. The angels are all in white." Yusuf grinned.

"Look," said David. "Idris is wearing a white futah. Is Idris an angel?"

"Today, yes," said Yusuf philosophically. "Tomorrow, who knows? Idris is too nervous to be an angel for long."

As the heat grew worse the camels grew sullen and unpredictable. Their eyelids grew droopy, cadaverous-looking; the old naga was panting like a motor. When David touched her belly it felt hot as an oven.

✿

In this extremity of the desert David felt his senses changing their hues, like a film exposed to the light. Into this barren world now crept a strange variety of sensuous effects—of color and temperature, of scent and sound. Everything changed its consistency. Everything partook of the opposite. The sun looked black; the stillness grew clamorous. The wind seemed solid, steady as a wall, and the rocks grew tenuous and vibrant, like the wind. The heat was like a great white bandage clinging to his flesh.

At ten o'clock the sand blazed and billowed like lava. At eleven the eyes of the camel-men were sunken and purple. At noon the world was aflame, and they crawled into the darkness of their tents, gasping for breath.

"Two more days like this will be the end of us," said Yusuf miserably. "Such heat has never existed. Bad luck with the water, bad luck with the weather. Now, who knows, there'll be bad luck with the Ruqudas!"

"An evil spirit is pursuing us," hummed Idris, tapping David's arm.

"Yes? What spirit?"

"The elderly sir!"

"You think he has turned into a spirit?"

"He is dead! And his ghost is following us!"

"What nonsense, Idris!"

"Only an angry ghost could bring such heat!" His voice grew wistful. "Once, Sir Daïd, we had a *good* spirit."

"What spirit was that?"

"The elderly madame! She protected us from our enemies. Now she neglects us. She prefers Sabaya, where it is cool."

"Who knows?" said David halfheartedly. "Maybe she still protects us, Idris."

Idris snuggled his head on David's lap, like a kitten. "I have a sadness, Sir Daïd."

"What is your sadness?"

Idris sighed. "I do not belong with my people."

"Why not?"

"Look!" He pointed to his eyes. "There is blue in my eyes. I am not a pure bedu. My father was a stranger. Perhaps from London."

"Where were you born, Idris?"

"In Mukalla. In a brothel, sir."

"You're very dark. I don't think your father was an Englishman, Idris."

Idris pouted. "I have the soul of an Ingliz. Sensitive and elegant. Don't mock me, Daïd!"

He plucked at David's wrist. "Take me to America with you, Daïd. I will be your slave. I will follow you everywhere. If you ask me to chop off my arm, I will do it!"

"That would be rash, wouldn't it, Idris?"

"Ah, perhaps. But all beduin are rash," growled Idris.

✿

They entered the night again. The paraffin lamps were lit, and the camels, unable to see any shrubs to distract their attention, began to move more swiftly and placidly. The men sang in unison. *"Shey latif! Ma salaam!"*

David took hold of Sylvia's hand as they paused in the dunes for their nightly tea. "You look sleepy!"

"No," she whispered, snatching her hand away. "I'm wide awake."

"You need a rest," he said. "You need sleep. Be patient, my dear. Four more days, and we'll be in Mukalla."

She looked at him gravely, listening, with her huge, vague eyes.

A shooting star crossed the horizon, and he whispered, "Sylvia! Make a wish!"

"I made it long ago," said Sylvia in a trembling voice.

"Make another then. Quickly!"

"It won't come true. I know it won't."

"If you wish it hard enough it will come true, perhaps."

She looked solemnly at her fingertips. "Can one wish for happiness, do you think?" Suddenly she twisted her head around and cried, "Why are these people so happy? In this awful land?"

"Who knows? They love life, even when life is rather unpleasant."

A moment later she whispered, "What has happened to Doctor Moss, do you suppose?"

"Nothing, probably. We'll meet him in Mukalla," said David uncomfortably.

She shook her head. "No, we won't. You think what I think. What they all think." And suddenly she cried, "Oh, we've all become so wicked, David! We've turned into savages!"

✿

As he lay there, half asleep, the past unrolled like a great map. His mind reached back through the convolutions of India, the shadowy gullies of Japan. It crossed the Pacific and rambled over the great Wyoming hills; it wandered eastward and finally came to rest on the shore of a river, where the birches shone through the clear cool glow of a summer evening. Black-eyed susans speckled the fields; sumac flowed over the hills. A dusty path led up past the cornfield, which swayed lazily in the ruddy air, rosy tassels dangling like manes through the crisp, fluted ears. There was a barbed-wire fence along the edge of the orchard. Hornets buzzed over the rotting crab apples; grasses stirred over a passing snake. Dragonflies bright as mica went zooming down to the banks, where the cattails bristled in the soft gray mud. A family of turtles lay dozing on a trunk that floated by. Not a sound, except for the humming of insects, and the far-off call of a whip-poor-will. Dusk gathered, the air grew filmy. And suddenly from the western hills rose the whistle of the freight train on its way to Prairie du Chien. Then stillness again; the sweet, harsh stillness of the inarticulate. Leaves came drifting down from the birches, bright as goldenrod, and tufts of thistledown lay floating in the windless air. This was the past which had shaped him; this was the intensity which lay buried in him. As his mind reached into the darkness, trying to grasp the nature of his loneliness, to touch the roots of that shapeless anxiety which never left him, what he saw was the vast, haunting savagery of an entire land—a land where desire hung like an aura in the very smell of the woods, where it fell and withered like the little crab apples in the grass. Was this the specter which haunted him? This perpetual yearning of a land that had grown too fast and had flung the mantle of power over a raw, barbarous body? The shore darkened. The river flowed past the tawny sandbars. Fireflies danced in the raspberry bushes, and down by the Devil's Nose a kingfisher dove—one quick splash, a flurry of blue, then lost in the peace of the autumn night.

41

Now the land grew undulating, with giant waves rippling toward the west. The gravel had turned to a coral red, soft as heather to the nostrils but sharp as a chisel to the feet and the eyes. They paused before noon, and Iqbal built a *zariba* out of matting to protect them against the wind. There they lingered in the troubled shade, drinking tea out of rusty tins.

Old Ismaël sat close by David, his pale blue turban stained with sweat. David could smell the sagelike scent of his wise, wilted body.

"Tonight," said Ismaël, with a stormy look in his joined black eyebrows, "we pass the Ruquda tribe. We of the Ruashid have a blood feud, as it happens, with the Ruqudas. Sometimes the authorities come and try to put an end to the feud. But hate is easier than love, and war is livelier than peace."

He paused, drawing his fingers over his nostrils.

"Once a young man of the Ruashid, a distant cousin of mine, was passing through this region with three merchants from Shibwa. It was late in the day, and they saw two horsemen riding out of the west. The men followed in the distance but never drew close. Night came; the strangers vanished. But when my cousin woke in the morning he saw two of the merchants lying in the sand with their throats cut wide open."

"And the third merchant?"

"Vanished! And the money too!"

"He killed the other two, I suppose, and ran off with the money?"

"Possibly. But we prefer to think otherwise. We prefer to

think, contrary to the evidence, that it was the men of the Ruquda tribe who did it. After all, vengeance is sweeter than compromise."

"And so you of the Ruashid started a feud with the Ruqudas?"

"Precisely!" Ismaël's eyes glittered. But then he lowered his lids discreetly. "I bore you, I'm afraid, with all my chitter-chatter."

✿

They started again at dusk. The climate was changing. The extremes were more violent, the winds were more brutal. And the mental climate changed too, grew suspicious and irritable. The light of the moon was a light without gentleness. And as the hours moved past them the passage of time grew equated with the passage of landscape, and David felt a sense of the numinous rising around him. Here at last it seemed absurd to think of time as measurable. Space was vast, darkness infinite, but above all it was time that took on grandeur in this ocean of sand. The churning of turbines had gone; the sound of the cataract had died; all that existed was a gulf of emptiness, like a bowl carved into the sea. The night passed in a daze. When day broke they were lame and weary. He felt his knees swollen with pain and a whittling ache at the base of his spine. They all climbed down and rolled up in their dirty camel rugs and lay among tufts of grass which warded off the whip of the wind. Dawn rose with a pink flush. The Moslems turned wearily toward Mecca, bad-tempered with rheumatism, and washed their faces in the sand, muttering huskily, *"Allahu Akbar!"*

✿

Sylvia was still asleep when he woke up.

He knelt beside her and looked at her face. Sun and sickness had left a fine, swollen web around her eyes. He remembered how she had looked the first time he saw her, when they stepped on the plane at Bombay—shy and prim, with her smooth black hair tied neatly behind her head, her cheeks plump and rosy, her eyes alert as a setter's. Now she looked like a gypsy, dark and tousled and weather-beaten. Even as she slept he could see the change: her girlhood had gone. A hot glow shone under her skin, like a flame shining through a sheet of parchment. He laid his hand on her burning forehead.

She opened her eyes and stared at him with a touch of fear, which instantly died.

"Is it time to go?" she whispered.

"Not yet."

"Why did you look at me?"

"I watched you dreaming."

"Could you guess what I was dreaming?"

"About bandits, maybe?"

She shook her head.

"About England, possibly?"

"I've already forgotten. Tell me, David. Have I changed very much?"

"We've all changed, I think."

"Am I older?"

"Yes. A little."

She smiled wanly. "Someday I'll be old enough for you to love me!"

It was well after noon, and the air was hot and breathless. Half-naked figures were hauling water out of the well for the camels. This was the last well, said Ismaël, for a long, long stretch. They filled the water-bags with the ill-smelling fluid, and Idris started to boil the tea. Food was low; they were living on dates, milk tablets, chocolate, sardines.

As the afternoon deepened the light created new images. All things seemed laden with significance—a ring of stones, the skull of a camel. Petrified trunks of trees suggested a remote antiquity. And the men, masked with dirt, bearded and brittle-haired and sullen, looked like neolithic wanderers as they lay in the shade of the camels.

"It is dangerous to start early," said Ismaël dourly. "The Ruquda people are watching us. They will shoot as we pass their hills."

"It is dangerous to start, in any case," said Yusuf, scowling, "but it is more dangerous to wait. These are nasty lands."

So they started off again while the sun still hung over the horizon. One by one the camels rose, and the caravan uncoiled. That evening David caught sight of an unusually brilliant mirage. A great scimitar cut through the air, like a distant mountain. As they drew closer, just at the point when the sun was setting, a dazzling gyration of rivers and palm groves unfurled, and a beautiful vista of deep blue pools. Everything began to quiver. The leading camel lost its outlines; it turned into a tower and then a great umbrella; then it narrowed into an obelisk and for a moment vanished. Finally they reached the defile. The sun sank. The mirage faded. A sultry blue covered the land, and the hills drew back into shadow.

A voice called from the hills. They turned and looked and saw no one. Ismaël called back angrily and wanted to halt. But Hussein ordered the men on, and they continued, sore and dust-ridden and quarrelsome.

A shot echoed in the distance. Their lethargy left them like magic. Their eyes sparkled. Ahmed drew out his gun, and Idris shook his arms delightedly. They led the camels behind the dune. Then Ahmed started firing. Two guns replied. Idris got out the old Berdane rifle and cocked it gleefully. The firing from the hills stopped. The camels yawned with nervousness. Ismaël cried out at the top of his lungs, "Cowards! Idiots! Pigs! Centipedes!" But only an echo replied to his quavering old voice.

A fit of recklessness came over Idris; his eyes flashed with joy, and he started running up the slope, brandishing his rifle.

"Come back, Idris!" cried Ahmed.

"Don't be a fool, Idris," called David.

But a .wild young daring was alive in Idris. He shouted defiantly at the hills.

The men conferred; Ismaël was arguing stubbornly with Ahmed. And then another shot rang out and Idris gave a sharp little cry. He sank to the ground, wailing bitterly; a bullet had entered his thigh.

✿

An hour later they were under way again. Night had fallen. The stars were blazing.

42

The chilling night was followed by a hot blinding day. Light flooded the landscape like a boiling wave. The wadi-bed was strewn with clusters of shriveled grass and stunted camel-thorn. Here and there shone dark green hollows, where water had lain two months ago.

They climbed the jol to an area of stone which lay spread on a plateau. Chips of flint lay scattered about, split by some ancient cataclysm into the blood-red spatulas. Then they crept down again. The gullies shimmered with heat. A carpet of dust was wandering over the dunes, which were patterned like a tiger-skin. Finally they reached a smooth, canary-bright plain—no plants, no birds or insects; not even stones. Only a gulf of gravel. The world lay transformed into a burning disk, ceaselessly quivering. Once the mirage of water grew so convincing that their hearts rose in hope. But then the mirage rippled away again, revealing a sand-worn skeleton.

"Where are we?" whispered the young boy, Iqbal. "Do you know where we are, Yusuf?"

Yusuf nodded. "There, to the north, lies Aq Medla."

And an hour later Iqbal cried, "We are lost, Yusuf!"

But Yusuf pointed to the south and said, "There lies Jebel Mullah. We aren't lost."

The undercurrent of fever kept growing. Danger wandered beside them like a shadow. So much depended on so little. So little was enough to destroy. A broken water-skin, an ailing camel, a moment of uncertainty in Yusuf's bearings—any of these might be fatal, so slim was the margin of security. Not an inessential ounce of luggage, not an extra footstep could be afforded. Most of them were walking. Only the wounded Idris and Sylvia were riding; and now and then, for a rest, old Ismaël, the cook. Yusuf insisted on doing eleven hours a day—thirty-five miles or so, at the rate they were going.

' And now the desert brought out the intrinsic flavor in each character. Triviality and pretense fell away. Laziness, lechery, all fell away. Iqbal turned into a grown-up man, full of a strong, fervent dignity. Ismaël turned into a youth again, wayward, resilient. Yusuf was touched with a kind of fatalistic pride. Ahmed showed a loving, confident calm. And Idris, wounded and feverish, grew strangely tender.

But even so, dangerous tensions were developing under the surface.

✿

The wind turned around and blew southward from Shibam. Comets of sand shot from the hoofs of the camels. On they trudged in a brainless rhythm, borne by nothing but a sheer blind passion for survival.

"Three more days," Hussein kept chanting. "Three days, and we'll be there."

"With luck, maybe," growled Ibrahim, the black one.

"With or without," sang Hussein with a parrot-like glare.

"Courage," moaned Yusuf. "In Suqa we'll find water and fruit. And in Mukalla we'll find riches and fleshly consolation!"

Sylvia rode on the small she-camel. David poured ointment on her blistered feet. The diet of dates had given her a splitting toothache; he kept giving her aspirin in spite of the heat.

Ismaël came up beside her and glanced up in his sweet old way. "Women are weak!" he said whimsically.

Sylvia gave him a thin, sad smile.

"Once a month," said Ismaël, "they are *very* weak. The rest of the time they are *somewhat* weak." He looked deep into her eyes; his wrinkled face grew solicitous. "Do you have your monthly sickness now, madame?"

Sylvia blushed and glanced toward the hills. "Not quite," she said. "It is over now."

Ismaël nodded understandingly. "One must be careful." He sighed. "It is wearisome to be a woman, dear madame, isn't it?"

✦

Once they saw some small red flowers nestling beside a rock. But when David reached down to touch them they turned out to be lifeless, petrified.

The men now looked like a band of ruffians, ragged and surly. The camels had grown very thin, and the strength and sweetness of their souls now emerged in the hours of hardship. They wandered on, waiting for the coolness of night to gather them, the merciful night, which was like a river on which they could float to oblivion.

Finally the territory dipped; a whiff of freshness shot toward them. An edge of sand was tufted with coarse gray brush. Lizards went scuttering into their holes.

"There was a well here three years ago," said Yusuf thoughtfully.

They halted, turning the camels to graze in that inhospitable growth; the two boys spread their scarlet rugs in the dying sunlight. Then the men said their prayers. Ismaël set the water to boil for tea and started cooking their last bit of rice on a brushwood fire. Iqbal and the black, silent Ibrahim began digging for water.

"Is it moist yet, Ibrahim?" Ismaël kept calling.

"No. Not yet," growled Ibrahim.

Idris lay down beside David and drew off his loincloth, inch by inch.

A slate-blue spot shone in his thigh. David washed it lightly with disinfectant. But the bullet-hole looked ugly. There was a sleekness around it, like a stain of oil running across the groin.

"Here it hurts badly," whispered Idris, pointing to the testes. "But here I feel nothing," he said, pointing to the heart of the wound.

"You will save me, Daïd, won't you?" he cried softly and buried his head in David's arms.

✿

Ismaël woke up Sylvia presently and poured her tea from the battered kettle. Ibrahim had finally discovered a few drops of brownish water.

The pain in her eyes had gone down. Her toothache had gone as well. All she felt at this moment was a kind of groping amazement. She felt herself hanging in midair, suspended on a fine silky thread. The earth below her looked like the bottom of a chasm. She looked up and tried to follow the thread into the sky. It went up and up, soaring into the empty blueness, but, as she watched, it started to tremble, about to break.

She raised the cup and held it to her lips; her hand shook against the rim.

Night fell. She saw Ahmed sitting motionless in the starlight, staring at the sky. His face looked somber and sad under the great white turban.

"Look!" he said to her, pointing.

A shooting star flashed over the desert—a rosy arc, quick as a humming-bird, then lost in the dark.

"To us," said Ahmed, "it means an omen."

"To us it means a wish will come true."

"Make a wish!" said Ahmed, touching her hand.

She made a wish—the same as before, with one slight difference.

"What was your wish?"

"I can't tell you, Ahmed. Or it won't come true."

"I think I know your wish," said Ahmed. He added quietly, "When a star shoots in the north it means a camel will die."

"But this one shot in the south, didn't it, Ahmed?"

"That means—" But he didn't finish his sentence. He gazed patiently at the ground and whispered, "My brave little madame!"

43

David woke up to the paling stars, a dying fire, two swaying figures in white kufiyas, hands raised to heaven and then lowered again to the ground.

"Allahu Akbar, Allahu Akbar . . ."

They rose to their feet, Ismaël and Iqbal, with the sand still clinging to their noses and foreheads.

"How is Idris?" whispered David.

"As Allah wills it." Old Ismaël sighed, pouring the morning tea and distributing the last grains of rice. Sylvia rose from her camel rug, looking dark as a bedu.

Idris came up to David now, limping badly, swaying with fever. His face looked flushed and haggard. He was very sick indeed. He slid off his futah, which was soaked in a pale green secretion. The wound had spread hideously, feeding on hunger and exhaustion. A great pearl of pus oozed from the hole in the center. David applied sulfa ointment, which was all he had left. Then he slid two small pills between Idris's lips.

"Will I die, Daïd?" said Idris quite gently.

"Patience, Idris. One week and you'll be strong again."

✿

From the south came the sound of distant unease. Slowly it deepened and darkened into a wavelike clamor. It drew nearer: the real wind. It came with the roar of a stampede. The air grew cocoa-hued with dust—not dark exactly, rather

214

dense with a strange luminescent heaviness. Clothes, body, the air itself, all seemed soaked in molten bronze.

The wind died presently, and they all got ready to move again. The two young camels were terribly thin. One was pitifully knock-kneed. The naga in foal was obviously unwell. A calamity had occurred: one of the goatskins had burst, announced Iqbal. And in this misery and disorientation something odd happened to the men. Their characters were reversed. The gloomy sang, the gay grew hopeless. Yusuf suddenly seemed filled with the milk of human kindness, while Iqbal and the coal-black Ibrahim grew surly and reluctant. Ahmed wandered up to coax them; he promised Iqbal a new camel and Ibrahim a wife on their arrival in Mukalla.

"A wife," complained Ibrahim, with his gold tooth flashing, "is less valuable and more troublesome than a camel!"

They entered a land of sandstone boulders. The rocks looked like a herd of mastodons petrified in the act of flight. It was an inferno of devastated colors and forms, flicked by jetting needles of white-hot air.

Now the south wind grew strong again, gradually parching the water-skins from which their lives and hopes hung suspended.

Each man drew his djellaba tightly about him, trying to keep out the sand. But the sand pierced everything. It spilled from their clothes and drenched their hair and cascaded from their bags. Everything flapped and sang in the sizzling air.

So they halted again and curled up inside the tiny tent, through which the sand kept whipping and whining. One side of the tent shot up with a yelp, tearing the long black pegs with it. They sat without stirring, too weary to care: Idris with his head on David's lap, his fine young face old with poison; Sylvia huddling in her pale djellaba, her eyes shining with fever; Ismaël and Ahmed and Iqbal crouching in a row like three hungering generations; and behind them Ibrahim and Hussein and the beetle-browed Yusuf.

Ibrahim was a pious Senussi who had crossed to Arabia two years ago. He had a deep unshakable faith in the sayyids, and as the wind snarled and squealed he kept murmuring devoutly, "Please! Spirit of the son of Sidi el Mahdi!" Or else—"Influence of Sidi el Mahdi! Protect us, please!"

But Ismaël kept arguing cheerfully. "It is the will of Allah. Let's stop fretting!"

And Ahmed observed in his dignified way, "Allah will unquestionably help us." Or again: "Allah will bring a solution to this difficult problem!"

✿

That afternoon they noticed a panicky look in the pregnant naga's eyes. Her great hide began to twitch as they watched her. She gave an ominous snort and suddenly rose on her hind legs, her front legs dangling like a kangaroo's. She swirled about with a prancing movement, snarling faintly, tassels of foam dripping from her enormous lips, and then she shook off her bags and shot away, making a beeline for the distant hills, moaning like a cow for her calf. Two of the men jumped up and started after her halfheartedly, but soon she was only a loping shadow on the edge of the horizon.

"She's gone mad," said Ismaël stoically, gazing at the broken water-skins.

"One more day we can exist. No more," said Hussein with quiet finality, watching the water seeping into the sand.

The wind grew violent again, and they huddled behind a dune. There was pure hate in this wind, a shrewd and conscious ferocity. Ibrahim's eyes grew desperate. "We cannot wait!" he cried, trying to make his voice heard above the snarl of the khamsin.

Ahmed's voice came back, infinitely remote. "Wait. Be calm. It won't last."

And Ibrahim grew still again, touched by some hidden depth in the older man's serenity.

David had to step outside the tent; his bladder was tingling. The moment he met the wind his eyes grew blinded. He lost his balance and had to crawl on his hands and knees.

The air was filled with a reddish tinge, like a forest fire's. Something struck him—a flying peg from the tent. His cheek began bleeding. Suddenly he felt a shrill, hysterical hatred toward the wind and the whole bleak, merciless world around him.

He crawled back into the tent and fell asleep with his head on Ahmed's lap. He dreamed that he was walking through a foreign city. Cylindrical towers lined the street; tiny white shapes were stirring in the windows. Dusk fell, and the lights began to twinkle. He walked into a black, vaulted room where some men sat at a table, silently waiting. They wore long white jackets, like a surgeon's, and were fondling the knives that lay in neat rows on the table. Sawdust covered the floor; fluorescent lamps hung from the ceiling. Great chunks of meat and empty bottles lay scattered on the floor. David reached down for a slab of meat, irresistibly compelled. A man rose from the table, with close-cropped hair and scar-lined cheeks. He loomed in the darkness, growing taller and taller. Suddenly he leaned forward, seized David's arms, and stabbed him in the heart.

✿

The wind had died again an hour before sunset. The camels were ravenous, searching everywhere for grass. David looked at the shattered faces, suddenly appalled. Their skins were brittle with dryness; lips cracked, eyeballs crimson, hidden deep in their sockets. And, above all, poor Idris. He had changed incredibly. All his strength and intensity had fled into his eyes. His teeth kept chattering; his face was glowing like a furnace.

Sunset came. The dust sank from the air, and finally the view grew clear and distant.

Now it was clear that they were all considering the imminence of death. Ismaël recited an old bloodthirsty ballad in the afterglow. Ibrahim and Iqbal grew subdued, and a distant sadness clung to Ahmed. A haze of mist fell, shrouding everything; a curious lethargy crept over them. Then the mist rose again, and a crazy hope filled them as the landscape emerged, unfamiliar and dappled.

But once more it sank into the same amber monotony.

✿

They were waiting in silence for Idris to die. He lay in the dusk, staring at the sky, sweating and shivering. His clothes were glued to his wasted body like plaster. Now and then it seemed as though he were recovering a little, drawing a brief new strength from a hidden source. He was contemptuous of death, even now. He lived on the sheer intensity of his pride.

He beckoned to David and took David's hand in his own. His dark eyes looked up imploringly. "You won't leave me, Daïd?"

"Idris, Idris," said David softly.

The festering in his thigh had crossed the groin and spread to his knee. A foul stench hung about him. His lips shook with pain.

"You love me, Daïd?"

"We all love you, Idris."

They kept waiting. The sky was gradually darkening.

Suddenly Idris cried out, "Help me, Daïd! Help me!"

Then he closed his eyes, gave a gurgling sigh, and leaned back his head. Two large tears crept through his lashes. But pain left him, terror left him. He smiled gently at David and whispered, "Now I am dead, Daïd."

The men sat quietly and lowered their heads, and three minutes later Idris died.

44

Iqbal stepped past the water-bags and crouched in the shade of the tent. Down by the fire the men were praying, Ahmed and Hussein and Yusuf and Ismaël, sending Idris off on his last, lonely voyage.

He slid his knife from under his sash and ran his fingertip along the blade. "Allah be praised," he whispered.

Then he lay on his back and looked at the stars. A current of feeling welled through him, dark, unidentifiable; not quite hate, not quite fear, neither grief nor anger. All those things he had felt but now he felt them no longer. He repeated the names of Allah, one by one, to calm his nerves. Then he rose and made his way over the empty dunes.

The camels were sleeping. Sacks and skins lay scattered about them. Iqbal ran his hands along the neck of his favorite camel, which twitched its big eyelids in recognition. He picked up a stone and hurled it toward the moon in a fit of exultation. His thirst, his weariness evaporated. The sand slid under his feet, and he leaped over the edge of the dune, inhaling the rich black air in great gusts.

"It must be done," he whispered solemnly, plucking at his sash.

A voice came out of the dunes. "Is that you, Iqbal?"

It was Ismaël.

"Yes. It is Iqbal."

"What are you doing, Iqbal?"

"Nothing. Praying."

"You pray alone?"

"I am weary, Ismaël. My bones are aching."

"Shall I sit beside you?"

Iqbal didn't answer. He felt the hostility in his own silence and said quickly, "Is Ahmed angry at me?"

"Ahmed is too sad to be angry tonight," said Ismaël, glancing suspiciously at the young man, whose eyes were shining with excitement.

"What disturbs you now, Iqbal?"

"Nothing."

Ismaël snorted angrily. "You are up to mischief!"

Iqbal spoke tensely, with a bitter pride. "Ismaël, listen to me! We are close to ruin. There is water for one more day. The rice and the dates are gone. We are doomed if we go on like this. These Christians, these Nazarenes, have brought disaster with them. Why should we die for the Nazarenes? Why should we give our last drops of water to the Nazarenes? They have brought evil with their disbelief. Look! Broken water-skins! Ailing camels! Angry tribesmen, mistaken paths! And now Idris dead. It is the fault of the Nazarenes."

"Continue, please," said Ismaël stonily.

"I hate the Nazarenes!" said Iqbal with violence. "Let them roast in hell. The Messenger of God will gather the true Believers. But the Unbelievers will grovel in filth, devoured by beetles!"

"Yes. Go on." Ismaël grunted.

Iqbal was silent, but his eyes were blazing. It was a loathing darker than mere individual hatred or vengefulness, a loathing deepened with centuries of inculcation and spiced with the natural zealotry of the desert. He turned on his heel and stole past the camels toward the hollow beneath the tent. He saw the shape of David, the Unbeliever, fast asleep in his long white garments, which were the garments of a true Moslem. His heart tightened with indignation.

He heard his name called softly. Ahmed rose out of the dunes and paused beside him.

"Is everything well, Ahmed?"

Ahmed nodded. "Everything. As you can see."

"Shall I sit beside you, Ahmed?"

"I need no comfort," said Ahmed coldly.

Iqbal felt overcome by a wave of guilt, of humiliation. "Why do you look at me like that, Ahmed?"

"I am trying to see into your heart."

"My heart is peaceful and silent, Ahmed."

"No," said Ahmed. "It is full of trouble."

Iqbal smiled furtively. "Why do you hate me, Ahmed?"

"I don't hate you. I hate no one."

"You are too soft," snarled Iqbal, "to be a good Believer. Have you no vengeance in your blood, Ahmed?"

"Don't talk nonsense," said Ahmed quietly.

"You hate me," cried Iqbal, beside himself with confusion and shame. "You hate me because Idris smiled at me, don't you? You are jealous! You hate me because I am young and well-shaped and much desired. Go back to your Nazarenes! Your heart has decayed! You defend the Unbelievers!"

Ahmed towered over Iqbal and took hold of his djellaba and held him tight. "Go to sleep," he growled. "Get rid of your visions, Iqbal. You talk too much. You are a fool. This is a difficult night, and we need peace. We have no use for your fantasies. Go to sleep and stop talking." And he walked heavily over the sand toward the crumbling fire, where the rest of the men were already curled up in a circle, snoring.

✿

Iqbal sat alone in the sand, searching his soul for guidance. Finally he rose and crept down to the little tent. He saw the girl's shape inside and paused for a moment. He could hear her breathing heavily—the breath of deep fever. His instinct called for pity, but his will fought against pity, and he walked three more steps and knelt cautiously in the dark beside David, whose face was shaded from the moon but whose body lay stretched in the pallid light.

All strength faded from his blood. He felt like a man enchanted. He stared at the sleeping face of the Nazarene—the sad, cold lips, the curling hair, the lonely lines in the forehead. There was something strange in this man: lying so still he looked almost like a saint—burning with some dark inner wound, it seemed to Iqbal.

For ten minutes Iqbal knelt motionless beside the Unbeliever, lost in meditation.

Then he drew the knife from his sash and pressed it to his cheek. He felt soothed, fortified by the cooling touch of the metal. He leaned over David's head, peering at the eyes with curiosity. Had they stirred? Was he awake? He listened to David breathing; it was the breath of a dreamless sleeper. Very lightly he drew his hand over David's kaftan, drawing it up and aside, so that the chest lay bared. He raised his knife and held it poised four inches over the left nipple. A strange calm fell over him; he remained motionless for ten seconds, his knife shining in midair, his blood leaping into his fingertips. One quick stroke. Straight to the heart. And the curse would be ended. The Unbelievers would be punished. The Believers would finish their journey in safety. What right had he, Iqbal, not to conform to the preferences of Allah?

One stroke! Still he hesitated. There was something too casual in this killing. The meaning was incomplete. The triumph was too easy. He leaned over and whispered hoarsely, "Sir! Wake up!" David lay without stirring. Iqbal touched his throat and muttered, "Wake up, Nazarene!" Still David refused to stir. His face lay closed and expressionless. To kill a sleeping Nazarene? Adequate, but not noble.

He tugged at David's arm. "Nazarene! You are going to die!"

But still the nasrani slept. He looked curiously innocent, untroubled. His chest rose and fell gently, peacefully, just like a Believer's.

A sting of doubt passed through Iqbal. The flush of fanaticism was passing. The knife felt slippery in his hand; sweat was streaming down his temples.

Something crackled behind him—a lizard, perhaps? He glanced around.

He felt a powerful grip seize his neck from behind and hurl him backward. The knife shot through his fingers. His head came crashing to the earth. He felt his arms pinned to his side and an ugly weight thrust on his abdomen. He writhed with pain and shrieked, "Ayah!" David planted his knees on Iqbal's thighs and lowered his head till his face was almost touching Iqbal's.

"You little fool," growled David.

Iqbal squirmed helplessly.

"You wanted to kill me, didn't you?"

Iqbal gasped for breath. David dug with his elbow into the boy's solar plexus. Iqbal saw comets shooting through the night; he twisted his head and vomited.

When he looked up again, limp and wretched, he saw David squatting beside him with the knife upraised.

Iqbal closed his eyes and waited mutely for the blade to strike.

"Come. Sit up," said David and held Iqbal under the armpits while the boy retched uncontrollably. Finally Iqbal sank back, chin sagging, eyes watering.

"What have I done to you, Iqbal? Why did you want to kill me?" said David gently.

Iqbal stared at the nasrani, numb with surprise.

"Do you hate me?" said David.

Iqbal shook his head miserably.

"Are you afraid of me?"

Iqbal lowered his eyes and began to sob.

"Here. Take your knife," said David, tossing the knife in Iqbal's lap. "We are friends. We must be calm. Tomorrow will be a hard day." He raised Iqbal to his feet and led him over the dune toward the fire.

"Sleep well. You need strength," said the nasrani and placed his hand on Iqbal's shoulder. "All is forgotten. Peace be with you." He started to move away.

Iqbal snatched at David's kaftan. "Sir!"

David paused and looked at him thoughtfully.

"Sir! I am yours. I will die for you!" Iqbal's lips shook as they sought for words.

"Go to sleep now," said David and strode quietly behind the dunes.

Iqbal lay awake for a long time without stirring. His mind was weighted with a thought too great, too radiant for him to grasp. The air grew cold; he started shivering. He snuggled up against Ahmed, feeling the older man's peacefulness against his body. The night paled. Morning was near. The dome of the sky grew limpid, pearly. He fell asleep, lost in the darkness of a strange new devotion.

45

The desert grew flat and white, unbroken by ridges or dunes. In this blinding whiteness everything seemed to shrivel. The men and the camels looked wispy, insubstantial, to Sylvia; everything looked fried to a crisp on this sizzling griddle of sand.

The men had reached the limits of human endurance. They were going on pure nerve—on their third wind, as it were, that almost trancelike strength which exuded from the desert. The camels were obviously incapable of going on much longer; they were limping and panting. David looked wrinkled and bony, with his eyes sunk deep in their sockets. Ismaël looked more than ever like an old salamander. Even the powerful dark Ibrahim looked weak and hollow. As for poor Yusuf Qamish, he looked like a wax doll left in the sun. His features had dissolved; only a blur of misery remained on his face.

Sylvia kept her eyes completely hooded, but the pain in her head was steadily sharpening. She felt a new, needling weariness; her bones felt fragile as glass. Each movement of the camel brought a shattering pang, as though her vertebrae were being splintered.

She tried for a long time to keep a grip on reality, to see and feel in a way that was still recognizable. But finally she let herself go; she floated emptily along, caught on that white-hot thread that dangled out of the sky, skimming over the hollow nothingness of the world. As her fever rose, time and space seemed to fuse, she felt herself moving in concentric circles which steadily narrowed toward the pivot on which everything would finally burst into vapor.

✿

Then the miracle occurred. Dark mounds rose in the distance. The plateau gradually descended, and nests of camelthorn peeped through the stones—dry and leafless, but enough to give heart to the camels. It was a great crescent-shaped valley they were entering, dotted with tiny brown shrubs and tufted with porcupines of grass. They passed a group of pilgrims who hailed them merrily—tall African types with palm staves and rosaries.

One of the men rode up and spoke to them—a stout, effusive little Yemenite. He introduced himself as Sidi Abdul el Mahdi, and made them a present of a kidskin of dates from Suqa. He asked for gossip. How was it in Bir Ali? Any trouble with the Ruqudas?

Yusuf Qamish replied with a harrowing tale of woe. It was the worst voyage he had made in thirty-nine years of voyaging. Calamity had stalked them like a shadow. It was a miracle that he was here to tell the tale. He too asked for news. How far was it to the oasis of Suqa? Had anyone by chance come across a caravan from Raïda? Or heard rumors about a scholarly Ingliz who was trying to reach Mukalla?

No, said Sidi Abdul el Mahdi, there was no report of a caravan from Raïda. As for the Ingliz, yes, there were rumors; an important Ingliz had recently come to Mukalla from Ash Shihr. A scholar, asked Yusuf? Oh, a scholar, most definitely. Small and spectacled? Sidi Abdul nodded emphatically. As for the oasis of Suqa, he concluded, it was only a stone's throw away. Their tribulations were about to come to an end.

"Salaam aleikum!" he said pleasantly, and rode off again.

They paused at noon. A fire was lit, and Ibrahim sang a song of anticipation. Soon, he chanted, there would be sapphire pools, palms shadier than those in Shibwa, delicious banquets and orgies rivaling those of Oman.

✿

That night was their last in the open desert.

"Tomorrow, thank God, we'll be in Suqa," said David.

"What is Suqa? A town?" said Sylvia.

"An oasis, it seems. A day's trip from Mukalla."

"What will we do in Suqa?"

"We'll be quite comfortable in Suqa, says Ahmed. Beds and food. Even a bath, says Ahmed. There may even be a car to drive us to Mukalla."

They sat in silence for several minutes. The scent of the camels, fresh as thyme, joined the warm rich smell of the beduin, who sat in a crescent around the fire, listening to Ismaël reciting a ballad. The firelight flickered on their sly, thick lips, their hungry cheeks, their tangled beards.

"And in Mukalla?"

"Everything will be over."

She looked at him emptily. "Will it really be over?"

He placed his palm on her cheek. "Sylvia, are you in pain?"

"No, not really."

"You look troubled!"

"I was only thinking . . ."

He lifted her in his arms and folded the goat's-hair shawl around her. Then he carried her into the darkness of the tent.

One of the Arabs beside the fire had started playing the rababa. Sylvia listened, feeling her nerves caught up in the web of sound. There was something lost, inconsolable in that frail nomad sound. It wove through the night, a flake of humanity piercing the mineral stillness.

"David!"

He took her hand gently.

"David. Will you do something for me?"

"Of course I will, Sylvia."

"You promise?"

"Of course I promise."

Her voice burned in the darkness. "Make love to me, David."

He sat without moving.

"Please, David. Just once."

"You're very weak, Sylvia."

"David! You promised!"

He lowered his head and kissed her lips. Then he drew his hand over her throat and raised the folds of her djellaba.

46

Women were squatting under the palms of Suqa, veiled in their white *m'lafahs*. A handful of soldiers stood by the gate, sweat pouring like tears from their brainless eyes. The camels strode haughtily along the banks of the tiny lake, their morale fortified, their dignity salvaged.

The village lay at the water's edge, a scattering of long blind walls, windows bolted, hushed as a cemetery. They were expecting a war, said Yusuf Qamish, who had consulted with the local authorities about the possibility of sending a motor-car up from Mukalla. They were led to the guest-house of the *ksourien,* the big landlord of Suqa—a charming cottage, cool and modern as a villa in Mallorca, with mosquito-nets over the beds and pillowcases patterned with forget-me-nots. Water, led in conduits from the wadi, was trickling in the pink-tiled bathroom. Mats of palm leaf lay scattered on the floor; a bowl of water-lilies stood in the hallway. A knock-kneed boy named Ahmar was sent up the palm tree for dates, and a tiny woman in mauve placed a pot of mint tea in the shade of the trellises.

A little later there was a knock on Sylvia's door. It was Ahmar, bearing a bowl of incense in one hand and in the other a sea-blue barracan.

"With the ksourien's most anxious regards," murmured Ahmar.

In the coolness of the evening the ksourien paid them a call. He was sorry to hear the young lady was ill. There were no doctors of consequence in Suqa, unfortunately, he added.

There was, however, a fine, wise doctor in Mukalla—a cousin of his, Hamida ben Lahssen ben Abdelkader by name. Yes, a motor-car would be sent forthwith from Mukalla, he hastened to assure them. He had already sent his man Abdul down by horseback. It could be arranged "inexpensively." His eyes shone meaningly. The car, he said cheerfully, would be in Suqa tomorrow—certainly no later than a week from tomorrow. He wore a heavily embroidered jacket and a striped silk jerd. Coffee was passed; candles were lit; compliments were exchanged in French and Arabic.

Finally he excused himself, promising Sylvia a pair of earrings, and a brand-new servant-boy to David. "More beautiful than Ahmar," he said hospitably. "With a gold-rimmed skullcap and a silver talisman!"

✿

That evening Sylvia lay in her bed, savoring the coolness of the air. She could hear the water trickling into the garden pool—a pleading, insubstantial little sound in the great hot stillness. She was very sick indeed now. But it hardly seemed to matter. Weakness had stripped her of pain. All she wanted was to lie and listen.

She could hear the little wavelets lapping away like cats' tongues; the palm leaves rustling, crisp and lazy; a nightbird calling beyond the palms. The air was sweet and clear, tinged with the musk of jasmine. A wave of hope rippled through her, subduing the pain and fever.

A voice murmured, "Little madame!"

Ahmed was standing in the loggia, silhouetted against the starlit walls of the guest-house.

"Dear madame! Are you awake?"

"Yes, Ahmed. Come in."

He slid barefooted over the tiles and knelt at the edge of the bed. For a minute or two he looked at her silently, his eyes shining into the darkness.

Then he reached over and dropped a chain of agate beads into her lap.

"Little madame," he whispered, "these will guide you through your voyage!"

He kissed her fingertips and tiptoed out again and melted into the darkness of the trellis.

47

The following afternoon, through some miracle of Arabian efficiency, the car arrived. They could see it three miles away, fluttering its cape of white dust. Slowly it crawled through the maze of dunes that flanked the oasis. Finally it lumbered triumphantly into the outskirts of Suqa, coated with flour like a pastry-cook—an old English model with battered fenders and broken hubcaps, radiator steaming, motor hammering, but somehow superb as it lurched to a halt under the ksourien's palms. The chauffeur sprang out, a horse-faced individual with sloping eyes and a weak sly mouth. He wore a coat of green muslin with tarnished silver buttons, and on his head a disorderly oyster-gray turban. He looked like the emissary from some impoverished, anxious caliphate.

The bargaining began. Seventy thalers, suggested the chauffeur, tapping the radiator-cap knowingly. Thirty, said Ahmed; thirty-five at the most. He wouldn't dream of doing it for less than sixty, snapped the chauffeur. To pay more than forty would be sheer robbery, retorted Ahmed.

Finally, after a few crisp repartees, they compromised on fifty.

"You are very greedy." Ahmed sighed, glancing reproachfully at the muslin jacket.

"Ah." The chauffeur smiled. "Perhaps. But my car is a frail, distinguished car. And I want to buy some gold teeth when I get to Aden next month." He glanced at Ahmed uneasily. "You must pay me now," he said quickly.

"We have no thalers," declared Ahmed.

The chauffeur flew into a tantrum. He had come all the

way from Mukalla! A most hazardous journey! Very hard
on the car! Very exhausting to the nerves! He had not come
to be greeted with jeers and insults!

"Who has insulted you?" said Ahmed.

"I am a poor man," quavered the chauffeur. "My car is an
old, illustrious car. I did not come to be given nebulous prom-
ises!"

David showed him a pearl. "What is this worth in Aden?"

The chauffeur sneered. "Four thalers. Not a penny more,
if you please."

David drew off twelve pearls from the chain. There were
only two left now.

"Here," he said. "When we get to Mukalla you can have
your thalers, if you wish."

They started off two hours before sunset.

Hussein and Yusuf were left behind with old Ismaël and
black Ibrahim. Only Iqbal was allowed to accompany Ahmed
and the two faranchis. He sat perched in the back, holding a
blue umbrella over the sun-cracked cushions. Tins of water
were tucked under the seat. The promised gifts, the earrings and the servant-boy, had failed to materialize, but a
basket of dates was tied enthusiastically to the door-handle.
The ksourien's servants stood in a row, bowing sedately.
Hussein muttered his blessings; Ismaël wept; Ibrahim covered his face bashfully. The ksourien waved his sky-blue
handkerchief, and the car started off, with little Ahmar racing after them, ringing a donkey-bell.

✿

For ten miles they plowed their way through the level
sand, which gushed behind them like a geyser. Then the land
rose gradually toward the final ridge guarding the coast. The
car wove stutteringly through a chain of high, rocky teeth.
On their left loomed the first real mountain they had met:
a vast dome, iron-gray, nestling in a labyrinth of cliffs. The
air cooled as they climbed. The sun moved toward the dis-

tant jol. Iqbal's umbrella flapped noisily as a gust of wind rose from the invisible gulf. Plumes of steam began to shoot from the radiator. The chauffeur halted the car to cool off the motor, and the passengers dipped into the basket of dates for refreshment.

The scenery grew dramatic. Great spirals of rock hid the peak—orange-studded cathedrals fantastically carved, with flying buttresses cast airily from pillar to pillar and vaulted grottoes, dark as onyx, reaching into the heart of the mountain. In less than an hour, said the chauffeur, they would cross the pass and catch sight of the sea. Two more hours, and they would coast into the alleys of Mukalla.

✧

The road took a hairpin turn, and a little man in a black headdress shot out from a rock, waving his arms.

"A bandit?" mused Iqbal.

But the man looked quite pitiful, a bony creature with mouselike, agitated eyes. "Stop!" he wailed. "Please, please!" The driver stepped on the brake. The man rushed up, wringing his arms. He was a leather-merchant from Raïda, he explained. Two nights ago a group of bandits had stopped his caravan and robbed him of everything he had—three donkeys, three nephews, five sacks of goat's hide, a bag of hashish. Could they drive him to Mukalla? There he would demand an audience with the authorities, he stated bitterly, and insist on immediate police action. This sort of thing had grown altogether too frequent in the hills. He pointed up toward the pass. A disreputable group of men, he said, had gathered there and had been spasmodically plundering the passing caravans in the old manner of the bandits. No incidents had occurred for the past two months. Perhaps they had run out of ammunition. He had decided to take the risk. And then this thing had happened. Scandalous! Inexcusable!

"A pity," said the chauffeur, coughing faintly. There was no room in the car, he added.

He could cling to the running-board, pleaded the merchant.

No, impossible, said the chauffeur. He glanced carefully at David and started the motor. They would send help on their arrival in Mukalla, he said politely, and took off the brake. That was all they could do. It was most regrettable. They drove on. "A scoundrel," said the chauffeur. "He lies. There are no bandits."

✿

The sun set as they entered the final climb to the pass. The last crown of light hung on the great volcanic cupola. They passed a donkey caravan heading toward Mukalla, and once two elderly men on horseback. The car went rocking over the ruts; sprays of gravel crashed on the fenders, and the chassis started to whine like a tomcat. The road grew steeper. Presently the driver turned on the headlights. The battery was low; only a thin dull glow played over the rocks.

The pass was very close now. The air was thin, nervous, chilly. The road twisted crazily as it wormed its way up the slope, dodging the boulders, edging its way toward the brink of the precipice. Ahmed called, "Look!" Two dark figures were scuttling across the slope, waving their arms. *"Hayah! Hayah!"* The driver frowned and stepped on the gas. The road twisted sharply around the edge of a ravine. The two men ran up, crying, "Hayah! Adaryayan!" But the driver swung at the wheel, and the car entered the defile.

Here it was dark as midnight. Great stone walls hid the range. The road went straight for several minutes, then opened out on top of the pass.

Suddenly the car swung to the left. There was a long, nasty hiss. The chauffeur cried with annoyance as he pulled at the handbrake.

"Broken tire!" he moaned, gazing ineffectually at Ahmed.

"Turn out the headlights," snapped Ahmed.

The driver ran, wailing, behind the car, while David sprang

out to look at the damage. Ahmed knelt and struck a match. The tire was absolutely flat. A blowout? Hardly. The tread was still stalwart—the newest of the tires, as it happened. A gash cut by a flint, possibly? Ahmed was opening the tool-kit, while the driver looked anxiously down the road. The moon was climbing over the summit, and a clear white light poured over the chasms. David groped for the tools and laid them carefully on a rock. There was a flashlight, but the bulb was broken; they had to work by matchlight and moonlight. The jack was placed, the car was raised, the bolts were finally loosened.

David was fingering the inner tube when a voice rose out of the defile. "Hayah!"

The men came up, two wolf-faced desperadoes. They scratched their armpits and leered appraisingly at the car.

"A bit of trouble?" said one.

Ahmed grunted laconically.

"You wish help?" said the other.

Ahmed kept growling as he glued the patch to the rubber tube. Iqbal lifted the little pump and started pumping half-heartedly. The chauffeur was running his hands rather wistfully over the tire. Sylvia sat motionless in her sea-blue barracan, gazing mournfully at the strangers. The strangers squatted beside the road and folded their arms around their knees. One of them took out a knife and whittled thoughtfully at his cane. The other rose and tapped David on the shoulder.

"You are a faranchi?"

"We are respectable travelers," said Ahmed curtly, raising his head. "On our way to Mukalla."

The man peered rapidly at Miss Todd's old medicine kit, which lay on the seat beside Sylvia.

"Do you bring anything precious to Mukalla?"

"Nothing. A basket of dates," growled Ahmed.

Iqbal kept pumping. The strangers watched while the tube was slipped into the tire. The chauffeur had discovered a nail. A mystery, he declared. What was a nail doing here,

on the mountain road to Suqa? Nonsense, said Ahmed; it was
a nail from a horseshoe. The chauffeur looked dubious. There
was something very odd, he insisted darkly, about that nail.

The tire was placed on the rim. A flicker of hope passed
through David. Perhaps these men were perfectly harmless.
They would reach Mukalla quite safely.

One of the men stroked his beard and strode pensively toward Ahmed. He thrust his cane in the dust and rested
his elbow on the knob. He looked like an Old Testament
prophet, with his flashing eyes and calamitous nose.

"There are bandits in these hills," he muttered, glancing
at the pass.

Yes, they had heard as much, said Ahmed casually. But
they were heavily armed; the boy was carrying two English
rifles under his barracan.

The man looked at Sylvia with a puzzled air. "Boy?"

"Of course," said Ahmed. "Don't you see? Does a woman
have eyes like that? Or a mouth like that?"

"Why is he wearing a woman's barracan?"

Ahmed looked subtle. "Because it pleases him!"

The man plucked at his beard in an ominous way. "The
bandits will seize him and violate him! If he wears a barracan they won't care whether he is a boy or a woman."

"We are prepared for the bandits." Ahmed grinned. "Let
them come!"

"They are very ruthless in these parts," observed the stranger.

"We killed five bandits," said Ahmed amiably, "on the way
from Kumra."

The stranger's eyes grew meditative. "Look," he said, pointing over the pass. "Do you see those gullies down there?
Where the road winds into the foothills?"

"I see them," said Ahmed.

"Be careful," said the stranger, running his thumb along
the end of his cane. "Those gullies are bad. The murdering
bandits hide in the caves. Take us along, and we'll fight for
you. We have guns. We'll protect you."

Ahmed gazed at him with an acid suavity. The tire was on the wheel now. Iqbal had gathered the tools and was stowing them in the back compartment. The driver fingered his wheel with a haunted look.

"There is a caravan," said Ahmed, "two miles behind us. Six donkeys laden with silk. Two donkeys laden with silver. Two more donkeys laden with food. They are unarmed. They need your protection!"

He leaped into the car and they crawled over the pass.

✿

The road wound into the moonlit foothills. The chaotic sweep of the summits faded. The great dome of the Jebel Samar was left behind. The cliffs parted, and they saw below them, like a silver whale, the Gulf of Aden. Iqbal bleated with joy. The slopes grew more gradual. The wind died, and the smell of sheep rose up from the valleys.

48

One by one the lamps of Mukalla appeared on the edge of the sea, ten miles away. The sea itself slowly spread, widening as the last of the foothills opened and only the rock of Mukalla still loomed in front of them, shaped like a lion's head. Sylvia leaned back and closed her eyes. The misery in her body was so complete, so stupefying, that it no longer took courage to keep from crying. She sat silently while the jolt of the car shook her bones, feeding the fire that was gnawing away at her membranes.

The road entered a decline and wound its way through the bed of a torrent. They went writhing through the naked boulders; the wheels went spinning in the powdery dust. Once they were stuck; Iqbal and Ahmed leaned down to tug, while David tossed chips of rock and finally laid a strip of matting under the wheels. The motor snarled, the clutch chattered, the wheels kept churning. Finally, with a frantic lurch, the men flung the car free of the rut and they staggered on through the gravel, limp and disheveled.

But the effort was too much. The motor died in a flourish of steam. The car stood frozen at a bend in the road; nothing would budge it. They waited fifteen minutes for the motor to cool down. The driver stepped on the starter; the battery was dead. They tried pushing the car toward the slope, where they could coast. But it clung to the gravel as though welded. The disconsolate chauffeur spread his jacket on the sand and lay down with a little moan. David consulted with Ahmed. Finally Iqbal was appointed to go on foot to Mukalla for help. It would take him three hours, or four at the most. There was nothing to do but wait and submit to the whims of Allah.

✿

She lay awake, merely aware of the clouds floating toward Africa. They traveled in cold majestic forms, like a wandering Himalayan range, peaks alive with a snowy glitter as they glowed under the moon, then gradually changing from a dazzling white to a billowing green in the southern distance, as though winter were swiftly passing and the snows were already melting on the slopes.

There was an encampment nearby, on a crest of rock just below them. She could see the glow of a dying fire and hear the monotonous chant of the beduin.

"Tomorrow it will be over," said David tenderly, lifting her head on his lap.

"Yes," said Sylvia. She was dizzy with fever. "Talk to me, David."

"What shall I tell you? A ghost story?"

"No, no. Something real, please."

"I'll talk about you. You're very real."

"No, we'll talk about places. Think of a place."

"What kind of place?"

"A place that you love."

"Good. I am thinking of a place."

"Now put me in it. What do you see

"I see you leaning over a fountain, drinking the water from a dolphin's snout."

"How lovely! Look again, dear."

"I see you lying in a hammock under a peepul tree, fast asleep."

"Yes? What else?"

"I see you sitting in a rowboat, paddling through the water-lilies—a big straw hat on your head; a tennis racket in your lap."

"Where is it?"

"I have no idea."

"Am I alone in the boat?"

"There's someone with you."

"A man or a woman?"

"Someone you love, I think."

She reached for his hand and held it over her eyes. "Then it must be you, darling."

The moon sank, the shadows spread as they waited for news from Iqbal. One by one the lights of Mukalla died and the brightness faded from the Gulf of Aden.

49

Sylvia stared at the clouds. The whole horizon was swallowed in clouds, great finger-shaped clouds, slowly spreading toward the sea. The tiny cobweb that held her poised over the world was beginning to sway. One more gust and it would go. She lay still, almost breathless, trying to keep the thread from breaking and her body from melting into that terrifying herd of vapors.

"Look! Do you see them?" David was saying.

"No. There's no one." It was Ahmed.

"Down by the bend. Look. Something is moving."

"It's too soon. Wait. Be patient."

From far away she heard the sound of hoofs hurrying across the sands—very faint, very far, no more than a throbbing in her eardrums. *No, no,* she said to herself, forming the words in her mind with a curious effort, as though she were articulating some strange, primitive language.

"Look! Down there! Is it Iqbal?"

"Yes. It's Iqbal. They are coming now."

"When will we get there, Ahmed?"

"Not until sunrise, I think."

The sound of hoofs sharpened into a fine metrical purr, like the pendulum of a clock. Ahmed and the chauffeur were talking excitedly. David leaned over and whispered to her. But the words were lost in the stealthy tick-tock of the pendulum inside her. The clouds were racing over the sea; she could see their enormous manes streaming, and a moment later she heard their hoofs galloping over the bay from Maqdaha.

✿

"They say the road is steep and ugly. They want to be paid before we start."

"How long will it take?"

"Two hours, they say."

"Two pearls. That's all we have left."

"That will do. Here. Hold the rope, Iqbal."

David leaned down and lifted Sylvia cautiously in his arms.

"Careful, now. Lift her gently."

"Is she sleeping, Ahmed?"

"Yes. She is very weak."

"There. Now. Tell them to go carefully."

She heard the pebbles clattering under the donkeys' hoofs. Someone shouted. Ahmed replied. But the sound of his voice was lost in the rush of winds from the gulf.

"Be careful," Ahmed was saying. "The road bends sharply. It is very steep."

"Hold her, Ahmed."

"I am holding her."

"Is she still asleep?"

"Fast asleep."

The thread was trembling, finer than air, as they wound their way into the gorge. One more jolt and it would break. The stars were gone, the sky was lost in a great cascading cloud. The pendulum in her heart was ticking ever so faintly.

The light was graying. Goatherds called over the gullies to the donkey-men.

"Allah be praised!" cried Iqbal as they entered the steep white alleys of Mukalla.

50

A bridal procession was passing through the arcades. The bride was invisible, but the bridegroom shone in his splendor, wearing a sequined turban with a gold-fringed band flung down to his shoulder. His coat of rose-colored taffeta shone in the rich, watery light. He walked languidly through the arches, swaying his slender hips. Two little boys pranced behind him, fanning him with long azure feathers. The musicians followed: three sad-eyed youngsters, beating away at their drums, and a tall, cadaverous man playing a silver flute. Then came the elders of Mukalla, all garmented in white, wearing a flamboyant variety of headdresses—encrusted turbans, shawls, tarbushes, braided skullcaps, and gold-embroidered kufiyas. And then the servants, bearing rice. And finally a bevy of veiled ladies in a tight, animated group, a mass of red and black gowns from which a monotonous chant exuded, faint as an aroma.

The procession wove through the soukh and vanished behind the mosque. David walked past the curio shops toward the aisle of offices along the harbor. The Resident Adviser sat in a hot, low-ceilinged room festooned with flypaper—an elderly mustachioed gentleman with a deprecating slant to his eyes.

David explained. The Resident Adviser looked enigmatic.

"We were informed of the wreck," he murmured, pressing his fingers into the shape of a turtle. "We were also informed of the death of Miss Todd. Beyond that we had no authenticated reports, I regret to say. There is very little, in circumstances like these, that we can hope to accomplish."

"Has there been any news of Professor Moss?"

"None," said the Resident Adviser rather caustically. He ran his thumb over a heap of documents with an air of distaste.

"Is there any way of communicating with Kumra?"

"Not in a profitable manner, I am afraid. In any event"— the Resident Adviser coughed suggestively—"I think we can assume that Professor Moss is no longer in Kumra."

There was silence for a minute of two. The flypapers swayed lazily. The sound of high rasping voices along the quay seeped through the window.

"If the young lady, Miss Howard, is physically able, I strongly recommend," said the Resident Adviser, "that you continue to Aden without delay. The medical resources in Mukalla are of a limited nature unfortunately."

"There is a boat sailing for Aden?"

"Tomorrow morning, as it happens."

"What kind of boat, may I ask?"

"Rather primitive, as you might imagine. Still, consider yourself fortunate. Two passages will be arranged. I dare say you have certain financial resources?"

"We spent our last penny on the way, I'm very much afraid," said David.

The Resident Adviser looked fatigued. "The sum required will not, I suppose, be considerable." His gaze grew pointed. "Have you any personal belongings that you might dispose of?"

"One small item, perhaps," said David absently. "A diamond brooch."

"Ah." The Resident Adviser looked indulgent. He scribbled a name on a small blue card. "Here. You might have a chat with this gentleman. The little red door just beyond the coffee shop. One flight up. You may mention my name. It's always useful, you know, to have a bit of cash about you in Arabia."

✿

After he had sold the brooch and made his arrangements at the shipping office, David went for a stroll along the waterfront. Stripes of sunlight were filtering into the sheds. A sweet, heavy spice hung over the burlap sacks, where women sat in the shafts of dust, heads and shoulders hidden with veils, sorting with birdlike fingers the beads of luminous gum from the incense trees, and casting them into long green baskets. The old mariners had gathered in a tavern behind the sheds. An ivory-haired patriarch sat on an upturned basket, dipping his hand in a dish of radishes. He was haranguing the men in a shaggy, monotonous voice which melted into the drone of the surf outside the harbor.

David was walking very slowly, measuring his footsteps on the lava flagstones. The heat of the day was beginning to ooze out of the east, from Ash Shihr. The sound of the surf grew more languid; the dhows swayed more lazily. Flies were swarming over the heaps of corrugated iron outside the sheds.

A tiny figure emerged from the shade of the customs shed and walked cautiously toward David.

"Sir Daïd!"

It was a moment before David recognized him. It was Iqbal; he was wearing Idris's old djellaba, which was much too large for him. His burning eyes looked pleadingly at David.

"Do you forgive me, Sir Daïd?"

"I forgave you long ago, Iqbal."

Iqbal's lips began to tremble. There was something he was trying to say. But he could not find the great, shining words to say it.

He held out his hand toward David. An amulet shone in his wet brown palm, a fish of gold no larger than an almond, with every scale infinitesimally carved. It was Iqbal's most precious possession. David had once remarked on it admiringly.

"Yours," he whispered and pressed it into David's hand. His face was filled with a quivering joy. "For you! Always!" he said softly and turned his head quickly.

"Iqbal! Wait a moment—"

But Iqbal couldn't wait. He slipped back into the shade of the customs shed and vanished from sight.

✿

Down on the sand the young fishermen were laying out their fish. The fish flashed in their hands like flexible knives, gasping and writhing before death; then they were laid out in blue satin rows on the carmine sand. Boys came wading through the shallow waves with nets bulging on their shoulders. They seemed to be wading forth from some immemorial deep, dark and smiling, ruthless and agile; an incarnation of Arabia. A flock of cranes stood on their delicate gray stilts among the rushes. At the end of the beach the shells were rolled about by the breakers, churned and polished and tossed on the paws of foam.

Ahmed came running down the quay, threading his way through the dusty bales.

"Come quickly, Daïd!"

They hurried back through the soukh to the hotel. Sylvia lay in the darkened room, wild-eyed with fever. Ahmed ran up to the bed and fell on his knees. "He is here, beloved madame!" He pressed his lips to her bony wrist.

Then he shot a quick, hot look at David and tiptoed silently out of the room.

David sat for a long time on the edge of the bed. Once he said, "Sylvia!" But there was no answer. The light shifted slowly. It fell on a wicker table, a thin blue glass, a towel tossed over a jug of water. It was so still that he could hear the ticking of his wristwatch, clear and tense. The water gleamed in the lily-shaped glass like mercury. Sylvia opened her eyes, and they fell on David without seeming to see him. There was a deep brown stillness in her eyes, an animal stillness and amazement; the power of wonder, for another moment or two, was still alive in her. But a little later he realized that something within her had changed. He was aware of a casual, almost imperceptible cessation, like that of a wheel that has stopped revolving. Her eyelids tightened ever so slightly; her fingers sank on the wrinkled coverlet.

The glow from the window shifted lazily. He rose and kissed her on the forehead. Then he climbed down the steps and walked back to the harbor.

✿

The wandering fishing boats had returned. A cool light covered the sea—that pearly brightness before nightfall, when all lies steeped in indifference. The dhows showed their riggings and sterns against the smoke-tinted sky, and the Abyssinians lay fast asleep among the bales by the customs shed, their limbs black and shining among the shadows.

Ahmed stood at the end of the wharf, waiting for David.

"Now I leave you," he said quietly.

For several minutes they stood side by side, watching the sea. There was something noble and exultant and yet infinitely sad about this sea, which brought men so close together and then drew them apart again so far. David felt an accumulated weakness rise up in his body; the exhaustion of the many days' journey was closing in on him. But under the weakness a keen, arrowy heartache was stirring. The grief of loss was finally gripping him: the loss of friends whom he had loved in his own evasive, troubled way; the loss of a land which had brought him so much cruelty and strangeness.

Down on the beach two naked youths were trotting across the sand with bundles on their shoulders. A gray-haired man limped after them, dragging a net. Up by the stairs two other men were waiting, hatchet-faced men in crimson loincloths, and they lifted the bundles from the shoulders of the youths and poured fish into their flat green baskets. A group of tiny twittering boys came scrambling down from the soukh and gathered around the baskets, craning their necks to look at the fish. Then the Arab fishermen—the naked youths and the men with baskets and the limping gray-haired man—sat down on the stairs to rest. David could hear the gentle buzz of their chatter.

Ahmed tightened his kaftan about him. Tears sprang to his hard bright eyes. "After much love and friendship we must say good-by now, Sir Daïd."

"Good-by, Ahmed," said David, motionless.

"Into the hands of God," said Ahmed quickly.

Then he turned on his heel and left David forever.

David watched his figure growing smaller and smaller as it circled the harbor and climbed the broad white steps toward the soukh, where the other beduin were waiting for him. Torches were lit at the end of the pier; the fishermen were gathering for the auction. A bell rang. The men bowed, spreading their arms in prayer. Somewhere a cageful of African parakeets was screaming. A breeze ruffled the sea; the great sails stirred uneasily. The air seemed filled with a muted lamentation. Then all was still; the birds grew silent; the sails sagged; the waves died. Night fell, reaching out over the sea from Tamridah, and the donkey-bells tinkled as they started on their way to the mountains.